SAND IN MY SUITCASE

A Stella Kirk Mystery #3

L. P. Suzanne Atkinson

lpsabooks
http://lpsabooks.wix.com/lpsabooks#

Cover Design by Majeau Designs
Editing by Tim Covell

ISBN
978-0-9958-6968-4 (Paperback)
978-0-9958-6969-1 (eBook)

1. Fiction, Mystery/Detective-Cozy/General
2. Fiction, Mystery/Detective-Amateur Sleuth
3. Fiction, Mystery/Detective-Female Sleuths

Distributed to the trade by the Ingram Book Company

Table of Contents

Old habits die hard, and if you're not careful, the person you used to be can overtake the person you're trying to become.
—Lecrae

They always say time changes things, but you actually have to change them yourself.
—Andy Warhol

Other works by L. P. Suzanne Atkinson

~Creative Non-Fiction~
Emily's Will Be Done

~Fiction~
Ties That Bind
Station Secrets: Regarding Hayworth Book I
Hexagon Dilemma: Regarding Hayworth Book II
Segue House Connection: Regarding Hayworth Book III
Diner Revelations: Regarding Hayworth Book IV
No Visible Means: A Stella Kirk Mystery #1
Didn't Stand a Chance: A Stella Kirk Mystery #2

For David, always

Thank you to Wyneth, Kat, Barb, Harriet, and Beverley
for all your help, and a special thanks to my editor Tim, because he's as fond
of cars and RVs as I am.

Recurring Characters:

Stella Kirk	Owner of Shale Cliffs RV Park; amateur sleuth
Aiden North	RCMP Detective
Rosemary North	Aiden's wife
Nick Cochran	Park Manager; Stella's love interest; 10% owner
Alice & Paul Morgan	Park Employees; brother & sister
Eve Trembly	Park Employee; Del Trembly's granddaughter
Duke (John) Powell	Park Security
Kiki	Duke's Pomeranian
Trixie Kirk	Stella's sister
Brigitte & Mia Kirk	Trixie's daughter & granddaughter
Norbert Kirk	Stella & Trixie's father
RV Park residents	Mildred Fox, Buddy McGarvey, Curtis Walsh & Elroy Brown, Louise & Bob Stone, Sally & Rob Black, Ted Metcalfe
Jewel & Ken Winslow	Former fish plant workers, now caretakers at Painter Farm
Hester, Cavelle, Jacob Painter	Siblings
Farley & Meredith Tompkins	Owners of Grey Cottage Realty
Paulina McAdams	Owner of Yellow House
Lorraine Young	Murder victim May 1980
Lucy Painter	Murder victim November 1980

CHAPTER 1

Can You Tell Me Any Other Details?

Stella didn't see the blood at first. Her brain identified Paulina, leaning back in her over-stuffed red velvet club chair—the one with the wood carvings down the front and around the feet. Her black negligee set had lace straps and a bottom fringe. The robe drooped off one shoulder and the satin tie was loose. In the part of her mind where death was not yet registered, Stella felt a pang of hope for her future self. Paulina looked sexy for her fifty-six years.

Yesterday was Friday, May 1, and she had been invited to Paulina McAdams' home for lunch. Together, they decided that day was their last opportunity for a visit before the 1981 summer tourist season in Shale Harbour began to ramp up. Yellow House, Paulina's residence and business, would open for the season this weekend, and afterward the bookstore and lending library would keep Paulina busy.

When they confirmed their plans, Paulina revealed she wanted to discuss a recent unpleasant experience. Stella uneasily anticipated any discourse opportunities with her friend.

Her bouquet of Mayflowers, picked less than an hour earlier in a clearing behind her home at the Shale Cliffs RV Park, and held in an ever-tightening grip, wilted in her grasp. "One Fine Day" floated in the background and broke the unsettling silence.

Heavy quiet moved in and out through the strains of music. Stella saw the blood soaked into the velvet, then the small hole in Paulina's forehead. One dark congealed rivulet ran through her matted makeup. Stella stood at the door of Paulina's reading room, situated to the left of the entry. Her fingers sensed the wet paper towel wrapped around the flowers' stems.

Paulina. What happened? Her vision blurred. She felt tears. *Call Aiden. Call him now.*

She managed to move her feet along the hall and into the kitchen. It took her a moment to locate the telephone because the avocado shade of green blended with cannisters and appliances on the countertop. Coloured phones are the latest rage. Stella's are black—practical and easy to see. Sergeant Moyer answered and she calmed. "Let me talk to Aiden. He needs to come to Yellow House right now."

"Stella, Aiden's in Port Ephron, but I'm on my way. What's wrong? Should I send an ambulance?"

"You can, but Paulina's dead. Call Aiden." She expected Sergeant Moyer to do as she asked because of their experience at the bank a year ago. He was reluctant to cooperate at the time, but now he knew she wouldn't ask for his help if the situation wasn't urgent.

Waiting on the front steps, she forced her thoughts away from the horror she couldn't yet grasp. Last night was weird, erratic. She had invited Trixie and her boyfriend, Russ, to supper. He cancelled. Trixie was in a snit and said she didn't want to come alone, which was unlike her. Then she arrived unannounced. Apparently, she first tried to convince her friend Cavelle Painter to skip a staff meeting at Grey Cottage Realty and go to dinner. Trixie then decided Stella and Nick were better company than yet another evening at home with her daughter and granddaughter. Although devoted to Brigitte and Mia, Stella's flighty sister can be a mystery of contradictions when in the throes of a new relationship.

She rolled up the sleeves of her cotton blouse and felt the warmth of the spring sun. An overwhelming desire to hear Nick's voice clouded her thoughts, but she didn't want to go inside the house again to use Paulina's phone. Parlour Antiques, across the street, wasn't open, and if she were to ask to use the phone at Cocoa and Café, she might create a stir. Their lunch trade this time of the year consists mostly of people from off the isthmus who come into town for work.

"What's happened, Stella?" Sergeant Moyer climbed out of the big Caprice and talked as he strutted across the lawn. He's a heavy-set man, which made it challenging to successfully accomplish a strut.

"Paulina's in the room to the left. She was shot. She's dead." The second the words left her mouth, she began to shake. She stood.

"Are you okay?"

"No." She sat again.

"How did you get in? What did you touch?" Moyer's anxiety bubbled.

"The front door was ajar. I pushed it open. I used the phone in the kitchen. I opened the door from the inside to come out here and wait for you." She struggled to prevent her tears from spilling over.

"I'll go in and assess the scene. Detective North is on his way. Are you sure she's dead, Stella? I called for an ambulance. How do you know?"

"She has a hole in her forehead and blood has oozed into the chair." Her voice shook, despite her internal struggle for control. "She's dead."

"Wait here." Sergeant Moyer hesitated, but donned a pair of plastic gloves and entered the house. He seemed to be gone a long time, but he was inside for barely five minutes, when she checked her watch. "I'll call forensics and the coroner, Stella. Stay put for now."

"Can I find a phone and contact Nick?"

"Not yet. The fewer people who know, the better. Wait, okay?"

She obeyed. Her mind explored what little she knew of her mysterious friend from the United States; the woman who chose to make Shale Harbour her home; the woman who dated Leon Painter twenty-five years ago and befriended his unusual daughter, Hester; the woman who opened her house to the public and helped parents expose their children to the joys of reading; the woman who always kept her private life private, including a current clandestine affair with a married man. Surely Paulina wasn't killed because her lover is married. People in Shale Harbour don't live in fear—despite Lorraine Young's disappearance and murder a year ago, and despite the Painter family tragedy last fall. Is there a killer on the loose? Her shocked mind wandered the rooms of her experiences.

When Aiden arrived, he ordered her back to Shale Cliffs. He said Moyer could drive her once forensics showed up, but she protested and ultimately drove herself. He said he'd come out to the park to take her statement the next day.

Her trip home was a blur. "One Fine Day" tumbled out of the radio. She twisted the knob until she could no longer hear the music. She knew in her heart she should have accepted the lift from Moyer. Solace was her reward. She found Nick sitting on the veranda with a cup of tea when she arrived.

"Want a cup? The water's still hot. How was your lunch?"

"No lunch—murder."

His face turned the colour of paste. "Stella, who? Where? Not Paulina?"

"Yes." She gulped and took a deep breath while she hauled her suddenly exhausted body up the veranda stairs. "I found her in the reading room, slumped in her chair with a bullet hole in her head. She was dressed in a black nightgown and robe. She must have been waiting for her secret boyfriend last evening."

He crossed the decking and wrapped her in plaid arms. She cried for a very long time.

****

Car tires crunch on the gravel of her parking lot as his gas-guzzling sedan swings into a spot. Stella has been expecting Aiden. Thoughts of yesterday have tumbled around inside her head since she got home. She's confident the shock will fade, but the act of discovering Paulina has played like a movie in her mind ever since. Focusing on the present is a challenge.

Her memory of last evening is hazy. Nick, her park manager, partner, and lover, cooked her a meal. She appreciated the effort, but her brain was muddled. He agreed, without question, to be by her side when Aiden took her statement. Despite his objections, she left him in front of a *Perry Mason* rerun when she crawled into bed. He's patient.

"Aiden has pulled in. Will you make us coffee, please?"

Nick's lanky frame appears around the door casing, tea towel in hand. "Done, my love. Trust Aiden to arrive in time for Saturday morning coffee."

His impish grins usually melt her heart. Today, she turns her lips up with effort before he returns to the kitchen.

"Come in. I hoped you'd be here earlier."

"Thanks. Lots of paperwork." The police detective's head remains tilted in a perpetual expression of curiosity, making her want to answer a question he hasn't yet asked. "I wasn't worried about your memory." His hand rests on her arm. "I'm sorry you were the person to find her. Have you talked to Nick?"

"Not in detail. He knows I found her. I asked him to sit with me while I make the statement for you." She pulls a sheet of paper from the pocket of her trousers. "I documented the details in point form." She snatches a quick look. "Since I eliminated any feelings, the list isn't long."

Nick enters their big living room, expertly balancing a tray with mugs, cream, and sugar. He turns on his heel and disappears, returning with the coffee pot. The room remains silent.

They sit—Stella and Nick on one of the leather couches; Aiden in an armchair he hauls closer to the coffee table. "Okay, Stella. Point form, if you prefer, but tell me step by step." He lifts his pad. "I will still take notes, even though you've put your findings in writing. I'll stop you if a detail isn't clear."

She inhales and lets the expelled air drift away from her body. *Relax.* Nick leans closer. "Paulina invited me to lunch. We expected it to be the last time we could do a daytime date because the season will pick up soon. She also mentioned she had an unpleasantness of some sort she wanted to discuss. I arrived at noon." She examines her hands resting in her lap. "I took her Mayflowers I found in the field yesterday. They're still in the Jeep." Her eyes drift toward the veranda. "The front door was ajar. Paulina's tape player must have been on auto-repeat because Carole King was singing. I shouted, but there was no answer. I assumed the music drowned out my voice, so I went in." She stops for a sip of coffee and meets Nick's gaze. "Thanks."

He nods but doesn't interrupt.

"I started to go straight back to the kitchen when I noticed her sitting in a chair in the reading room—to the left of the entry. I thought she was asleep." Stella makes eye contact with both men. "My brain eventually came to terms with what I saw. She was dressed in a very revealing peignoir. Blood had seeped into the velvet of her chair." A tear trickles. "I saw a hole in her forehead. The colour was gone from her face. The music stopped and then started again. I can't get the damned song out of my head."

"What did you do? Did you touch her in any way?"

"No. I knew she was dead. I ran straight to the kitchen, found the phone, and contacted the detachment. Moyer answered."

"My God! Whoever killed her might have still been in the house!" Nick has blanched. The whites of his eyes are red. His mouth hangs open while he stares at her.

Her voice is quiet. "The possibility of someone inside never crossed my mind. I talked to Moyer and waited outside until he showed up." She faces Nick and tries to explain. "I must have felt she had been gone for a long time."

"Can you tell me any other details?"

"I expect she had a date with her secret lover the evening before." She frowns at Aiden. "Don't ask. I have no personal information except he's married. As a result, they kept their relationship very private." Stella's mind makes a sudden leap. "Could she have been waiting for her boyfriend who arrived and killed her?"

"Any options are possible, as you know. We'll dig into her past because we have no idea why she lived here and why she immigrated so long ago. The bank gave us the name of the lawyer who handled her mortgage, which is paid up. The law firm has no will or other records. Apparently, she appeared here out of nowhere." He repositions his pen. "Are you able to enlighten me in any way regarding her history?"

"Before she dated Leon Painter, more than twenty years ago, she travelled south when the weather turned cold. She described the one winter she spent in New York City right after Leon died. I'm not sure she's returned to the States since."

"When did Leon die?"

"October 1959, if my memory serves me."

"Then it's been twenty or twenty-one years since she last took a trip stateside," adds Nick, no doubt reminded of the length of time he avoided his home country before his pardon kicked in.

"Serious research will be needed to dig into her background."

"May I help in any way?"

"I don't know yet. I'll keep you informed. Since you found the body, it might make circumstances complicated. Let's see what forensics and the coroner report. Then we'll try to wrangle a clearance for you."

****

Her staff start their summer jobs today. It's Monday, May 11. Duke Powell, and Kiki, are the first to turn up at the back door. "A cup of coffee for security?" Kiki barks and struggles to be put on the floor. "A murder in town at the start of the season can't be good." He places the squirming Pomeranian, bedecked in a pink tank top, gently on the hardwood. Her nails search for traction before she scrambles toward the reception office at the front of the house.

"Alice isn't here yet, Kiki. You're outta luck." Stella turns to Duke. "Let's not blather about Paulina, okay?"

He nods.

"Have you moved out to your trailer now, or will you sleep in town until the weekend?"

"Once the water's on and I get my rig hooked up and cleaned, I'll stay.

Depends on how much help Nick needs. Is Paul comin' back?"

"Have a coffee. Yeah, Paul and Alice are both hired—and Eve, too. Where did Kiki go?"

Duke saunters over to the kitchen counter and reaches for a cup. "Good people. Fond of each one of them, but Alice is the keeper." He leers at Stella.

"Remember our talk about your behaviour. Alice can mind Kiki from time to time, but don't take advantage...and don't torment her."

His expression is sheepish. Stella's confident she'll have no problems with Duke, at least not where her staff are concerned. Duke has learned how even harmless remarks to young women might lead to assumptions about motive.

"She's here!"

Alice enters the kitchen as Kiki rounds the corner. It's unclear if Duke meant Alice or Kiki. "I'm excited to be back, Stella." She peruses the freshly painted kitchen. "You two were busy over the winter."

"This room is nothin'. Take a gander at reception because Nick painted there, too. I bet Stella will give you a big tour of the upstairs." He hitches his pale blue polyester pants. "I helped."

Paul, Alice's younger brother and Nick's helper, has lingered behind. He and Nick are deep in conversation on the veranda. Stella hears Eve's Honda 50. Eve turned nineteen recently and starts her second year of accountancy in the fall. Her strengths at the park run to mowers and the gardens, although Stella has promised her ledger work as an alternative on rainy days. She piles her mountains of dark hair, revealed when she removes her helmet, high in a knot and ties the unruly bun with an elastic fabrication. Stella brushes her wisps out of her face as she admires Eve's unruly mane.

Everyone gathers for their inaugural set of instructions. Stella nods toward Nick to begin.

"First off, our condolences, Eve. Circumstances were difficult at the Painter farm this winter. How is your grandmother since the dust has settled?"

Eve sits in a ladder-back chair at the big wooden table and nurses a glass of orange juice. "Grandma Del is satisfied she was right from the beginning, but it doesn't help the fact my second cousin Opal is in jail. The family's still shocked."

The tight-knit group is well-aware of the details. They read the stories in the papers. They know Stella's role in uncovering the information surrounding the poisoning deaths of Jacob Painter's wife, Lucy, plus Leon and Velma

Painter years ago. Quiet envelops the space for a moment.

"Anyway, it's over now and no trial, which helped. Where do you want me to begin today, Nick?" Eve takes a sip of her juice and waits for Nick's response.

"Flower beds. Start nearer the park and work your way back to the house. If the weather holds, three days ought to do it. When you're finished, we'll have water to the bathrooms, and then they'll require a serious cleaning." Nick turns to Paul. "You and I will handle the spring checks on the equipment. I want to have services ready by Wednesday."

Alice strokes a contented Kiki as she addresses Stella. "I'll write up contracts for the seasonals and do inventory in the office. We'll need reservation cards and site maps."

Nick turns to Duke. "I want you to take a tour on the golf cart. Report any tree damage near lots. Make me a list. We plan to deliver fire pits and picnic tables by Friday. Regulars will start to move in then.

"Okay, are we set? Who wants a peek upstairs? Might I add how Duke, here, was my assistant for the project and I couldn't have managed without him." Nick gives their security guard a nudge.

The group stands in unison. Nick leads the way to their second-floor suite. Stella hangs back, content to let Nick have his moment.

"Most of you have been up here at one point or another. We tore out the little kitchen and the bathroom, too. Come see the big bath." They shuffle along like herded sheep while exclaiming over the fixtures and the refinished pine floors. Nick natters excitedly about electrical and plumbing.

"I gather the manager's cottage is now a rental?" Alice lingers near the seating area by the balcony door. Her expression is kind, her smile honest.

Stella nods. She watches her staff show a respectful, yet awkward, interest in their bedroom. When she and Nick first became involved, they attempted to hide their affair from the employees. It might have worked for a season, but Alice saw through their ruse and Duke wasn't far behind. She has come to realize that Nick Cochran, nine years her junior, wants permanent involvement in her life. He has invested in the park—five percent from her half and five percent from Trixie's half. He used inheritance money, received from the estate of an aunt, to pay for the renovations. She wants to believe he's serious. At forty-six years of age, she still struggles to accept the idea she might be loved.

CHAPTER 2

There Were Secrets

Since the staff are busy and her paperwork is under control, Stella spends some time with Hester on Wednesday afternoon. She parks her father's ancient but serviceable Jeep by the fence in front of the American Foursquare farmhouse—the centre of their attention less than two months ago. The new bungalow nearby, once planned to be the future home for Jacob Painter and his bride Lucy, nears completion.

Jewel Winslow, whom Stella first met at the fish plant while investigating Lorraine Young's disappearance, responds to her knock. "Great to see you, and who is this sweet creature?" Stella holds out her hand to the baby she estimates to be six or seven months old, balanced on Jewel's hip.

Her appearance has not changed despite the elevation of her circumstances. Jewel remains frail, with mottled skin and greasy hair. The young mother produces a proud smile. "Say hello to Kenny, named after his daddy," she gushes.

Her little boy waves both arms and wriggles with chubby delight.

"Well, aren't you a happy guy?" Stella turns to Jewel. "I came to visit Hester. Is she around?"

"Yes. Up in her room. She ain't been much company since her lady-friend died. Jacob told us you found her, Miss Kirk."

"Call me Stella, please, and yes, I found Paulina. The police investigation is ongoing. I thought Hester might be upset, so I wanted to visit." Stella begins to remove her jacket.

"Throw your coat over the banister. Do you want me and Kenny to go find her?"

"No need."

"Okay. I'll make tea. Jacob and Ken should be in soon."

Stella makes her way to the upstairs foyer. Hester's room is what might be considered the master—the largest and situated in the back.

When she approaches the door, which stands slightly ajar, she hears, "Come in, Stella," before there's an opportunity to make her presence known.

Hester, dressed in a clean wool skirt and multi-coloured cardigan, sits cross-legged on the bedroom floor. She is focused on the reference books scattered around her. Angel, her black cocker spaniel, toddles toward Stella, tiny tail wiggling with the rhythm of her gait.

"I guess Angel's my greeter today. And you? Can you say hello?"

Hester places a pamphlet, with exaggerated care, on a pile of other documents, then lifts her face to meet Stella's. "I said you could come in, which is a sufficient salutation."

There are times when Hester's communication methods are a challenge. This might be one. "I came to see you; to discuss Paulina."

"Paulina's dead. You found her." Her muttered response is soft.

"Yes, I found her. I need to talk to someone who was her friend and liked her as much as I did. I thought of you."

"Oh. Okay. Jacob and Cavelle constantly ask if I'm all right. You're not worried about me. You're worried about you. How can I assist?"

Her expression becomes open and helpful, as if she has somehow summoned a hidden counselor who has waited inside for just such an opportunity. Stella is confused.

"She was our friend, and I thought we could reminisce. You spent many hours with her after Lucy died. I'm ashamed to admit her personal life is a mystery to me."

"Are you aiding Detective North to determine who killed Paulina? You found out Opal poisoned Lucy...and my parents." She brushes her hair from her face. "Although I knew the truth," she adds. Tears have welled in her eyes.

"Correction. You and I helped Detective North. It's my hope we can try to do the same in Paulina's case."

Hester's gaze suggests patience for the uninformed. "Circumstances will be easier for me now. I'm no longer forced to wait for the right questions to be asked, and Paulina's death is obviously murder. You took *so* long to figure out my clues last time."

Due to the dramatic emphasis, Stella giggles despite the macabre context. "Is your remark a criticism of my deduction capabilities, my friend?"

There is no response.

Jewel shouts from below. "Are you two ready for tea?"

"I'm coming." Stella races to the kitchen and returns with mugs of steaming cranberry tea.

"Tell me the topics you and Paulina researched? What did you work on at her place when you visited?"

"We spent most of our time engaged in one of three activities. I explained our tree study." Her voice takes on a professorial quality. "We discovered a number—six—species once common in the area but now disappeared. We wrote a report and then met with government officials to strategize a program by which we could reintroduce them to Shale Harbour."

"Your work sounds fascinating. I hope you'll be able to follow through."

One tear tumbles down her cheek. She doesn't notice. "We also studied cryptography."

"Cryptography? What do you mean?"

"Secret codes. They are a way to communicate. No one without the code can understand. Paulina idolized a family member who was a cryptographer in the war. She was correct when she said coding suited me. I can make up a sequence no one could ever decipher—that's the word you use. The definition means to break the code."

"You have such a good memory, I bet you're able to remember your code without transcribing the key." Stella recalls Hester's list of every meal in the Painter household for two solid weeks, who ate what, and the ingredients for each dish.

"I do. Shall I tell you the third subject we worked on?"

"By all means."

"Paulina encouraged me to keep a journal, like a diary. She said I should document my thoughts and concerns; she said writing about Opal and Lucy would help me to grieve."

"Have you followed her advice?"

"Yes, but I'm unsure if there's been any improvement. My anger with Opal after she killed Dad eventually went away, although I remain mad at her because of Lucy." The heaviness of her sadness wraps around Stella. "Lucy was going to have a baby. Now we have Kenny, but he's not part of our family."

"This has been both a shock and a struggle for you as well as Jacob and Cavelle."

"Yes. The black space of pain has gotten bigger because the darkness made room for Paulina beside Lucy. Mom and Dad don't take up as much of the darkness as they used to when I was younger." She strokes Angel's long curly ears with a steady rhythm. The dog is stretched out on the carpet snuggled against her mistress. "You have a difficult task, Stella."

"Exactly what is my task?"

"To see inside her house. The house will reveal Paulina's secrets to you." Her eyes are round. Her tone is hushed. "There were secrets, although she never told me what they were. She wrote in her own journal. You need to convince Detective North to let you help him and it's imperative you find an opportunity to absorb the ether inside Paulina's house, and to find the hidden door."

Stella disguises her initial shock. "What door?"

Hester's intensity subsides as quickly as it arose. "I think I hear Jacob and Ken. Let's go downstairs now. I have to help Jewel with supper."

****

Friday of the May 24 long weekend is a huge deal at Shale Cliffs RV Park, so Stella keeps Alice company in reception. Today, most of the seasonal campers return to set up their summer accommodations—locals including Ted Metcalfe, Mildred Fox, Buddy McGarvey, the Blacks, and the Norths. There will be folks from as far away as northern Ontario and Alberta. Both women are surprised when Louise and Bob Stone, from Calgary, roll up to the door first. Their four-wheel-drive quad cab blocks the light. Louise is in the driver's seat. She jams the gear shift into park and jumps off the running board with more athleticism than expected if you were aware the classic beauty is over seventy.

"Alice, you sweet child. What a joy to see a familiar face. I can't believe I drove the whole way. I wanted to fly, but despite the circumstances, Bob said we should drive. No need to rent a car for the summer and we can pack the truck with any remaining stuff after we sell." She takes a breath. "I guess he's right. Did Nick find time to open our trailer?" She pauses to hug Alice, then Stella.

"Welcome back. Nick's finished. He said he left the bill on the counter." Alice turns to retrieve the Stones' contract.

"Has Bob improved? You drove," Stella remarks while they wait for Alice.

Bob experienced a significant stroke over the winter. They decided to return to Shale Cliffs, despite his physical weakness. They called Stella in January to request Nick connect their services in the spring. Their plan is to put their unit up for sale. Rarely do big trailers like theirs last long once the For Sale sign goes up. Louise and Bob want to squeeze some of one last summer in before their camping days are over. Sad to see the Stones' lives change so drastically.

Louise brushes a strand of her glorious red hair away from her cheek. "Lots of work. He thinks he can do more than he can. I don't trust him on his own. He's a big man."

Alice offers Louise a pen, and she signs.

Stella's heart twists. *Aging isn't for sissies. Didn't someone say that once?* "If you need any help with him, send a neighbour to the office. Between Duke, Paul, and Nick, someone will always be nearby." She walks around the counter to touch the woman's arm. "We're pleased you came back for a final year and don't worry. We'll find a buyer for your unit."

Before Louise pulls away from the space at the front of the house, Ted Metcalfe's 1960 Oldsmobile 88 lumbers in behind her. Ted must be out to impress because his turquoise two-door coupe with the white leather seats spends endless months in a rental garage in Port Ephron. Ted drives his prized possession in the Dominion Day parade and little more. He claims he's holding on to the vehicle for his grandson. There's a woman in the passenger seat. Since his wife died over a year ago, Stella expected him to be alone, and in his Datsun pickup.

The elderly park resident, as Stella surmises him to be well past eighty, bursts into reception, an unarguable spring in his step.

"Good morning. I have your contract ready. Who's your friend?"

Ted gives Alice an acknowledging wave before he takes the necessary two strides to shake Stella's hand. "Awful nice to be out here at the park again, Stella. I wondered, when I left last season, if I'd come back or sell my rig." He glances toward the Olds. "Then I met Lily."

"Always a treat when friends can visit. Is she impressed with your Olds 88?"

"She's not a visitor, if you get my drift." Ted wiggles fluffy white eyebrows—albino caterpillars twitching. He leans over, Stella assumes to be out of ear shot of Alice and whispers, "We're shacked up."

"You and Lily...?"

"Lily Dunn. She lived at the seniors' in Port Ephron. We met at the Remembrance Day dance last year. Been together ever since." He signs his contract with a flourish. "I'll introduce her to you later, once we're settled."

"Well, you and Lily are invited to the house for tea any time, Ted. Great to have you back." Stella leans over to wave at the car's occupant as Ted lets the office door slam on the way out. Lily Dunn remains focused on the windshield.

Stella turns to Alice and winks. "Wonders never cease."

Alice pretends to pout. "If Ted Metcalfe can find a girlfriend, why can't I land a boyfriend? Life's not fair, Stella." Her laugh is self-deprecating.

Buddy McGarvey enters the park later in the afternoon, dragging his minuscule and bouncing tent trailer. When he jumps out of the truck to come into reception, the biggest bulldog Stella has ever seen stumbles out after him. Buddy turns to render assistance before they enter the office.

"Welcome back. Who's your friend?" Alice repeats for a second time today, as she rushes out from behind the counter to pat the old, wrinkled, and bow-legged specimen.

"Meet Tinkerbell, but I call her Bell. Suits her better." His wide lips stretch across his unshaven face in an unfamiliar expression of affection. "My sister's mother-in-law died and Bell, here, was alone. We're a team, now."

Stella can't contain both her surprise and delight. She never pictured Buddy focused on much besides himself. "Is there room for both of you in your trailer?"

"Yeah, but I might scout around for a bigger place." He leans over to pat the panting Bell. "She's ten, and bulldogs aren't known for livin' to be really old, but I promised my sister I'd take care of her, and I will."

Both women watch him boost Bell back into the truck.

By mid-afternoon, the park hums with activity. Aiden and Rosemary are busy opening their trailer. Duke Powell has transported Mildred Fox and her gear out from Shale Harbour and Nick is helping her move in. Paul is with Sally and Rob Black, connecting their services and flushing their lines. Curtis Walsh and Elroy Brown called long-distance from a village in Quebec to tell Stella not to expect them until Sunday. Their 1965 Winnebago is, on this trip, not as reliable as previous years, and their travels from northern Ontario have been a definite challenge. Stella expects she'll hear every gory detail.

****

Move-ins and registrations have quieted down by holiday Monday. Stella attempts a retreat to her office, but the veranda door opens, and she hears a familiar voice. "Are you here, Stella? Nick told me you were here."

"Back here, Rosemary. Is your set-up finished?" Stella wrangles her chair, pushes out from behind the desk, and enters the main living room. She finds Rosemary, in rainbow coloured pedal-pushers and a white peasant blouse, her hair contained in a red bandanna, standing by the door. Her medication has started to kick in. Rosemary was in the psych ward at the hospital in Port Ephron most of last winter. Since her pills are well-managed, she's reverted to her old self, which is not to suggest her behaviour is normal. She presents as an exaggerated version of Annette Funicello from the 1960s. Rosemary North, Detective Aiden North's wife, has coped with mental illness issues most of her life. Stella relaxes when she sees Rosemary's attire fits within the bounds of normalcy.

"I was bored, and Aiden told me to drop in. I have a question. He said he'd be up later to talk to you because a lady was shot." She claps her hands together like a child at a birthday party. "I am excited I'll be here for the summer, Stella. Oh! Oh! I remember what I need to ask you. Is it true you have a cottage to rent now? Can my sisters Toni and Mary Jo visit with me and rent it? Can they?"

"Absolutely." It's like having a bouquet of balloons waved in your face. Stella attempts a soothing voice and steady communication. "Have one of your sisters call me to make a reservation. We haven't advertised. There's lots of time, although I informed the planning committee, so they could include the cottage in their materials for the writers retreat in September." She tries to calm Rosemary. "Tea? Do you want to sit for a minute?"

"No, not today. Time to race back to our trailer and gather our stuff. I told you he plans to come by, correct?"

Stella nods.

"And my sisters can rent the cottage?"

She nods again.

"Fabulous! I will call Toni when we go home tonight. Aiden said we could move out for the summer, but the weather must be warmer. Today is nice, but the nights are still cold."

The old screen slams. Stella watches her navigate the stairs in her platform sandals.

The afternoon flies. Nick and the crew turn up at three o'clock, on the hunt for tea and snacks.

"Knock, knock." Stella hears tapping just as someone out in the kitchen cranks up the transistor radio. Neil Diamond belts out his latest hit. "Anybody home?" Aiden walks in the back door, as she hears her staff settle themselves at the table.

"Since when did you stand on any ceremony when my house is open? Come in. Tea?"

"No time. We're almost ready to go back to Port Ephron for supper. First weekend of the season under our belt. I wanted to check with you regarding the Paulina McAdams case. Are you able to lend a hand?"

Stella holds her breath for a fraction of a second. Will she obtain permission to go inside Paulina's home? They stand at the door. "Is the scene released? Have I been cleared to help?"

"No. Partially." An exhale accompanies his cumbersome response. "Your assistance is permitted for now. My superiors haven't decided if you can go back to Paulina's, and forensics needs more time. I would appreciate your participation in a few interviews though."

"By all means. I've spoken with Hester. She spent many hours with Paulina once Opal was out of the picture. She told me they worked on codes for their diaries. Did forensics find a diary?"

"I have no report of one. Paulina could have helped Hester because Hester's good with numbers. Maybe the focus was a journal for Hester. Does she have her own diary and code book?"

"I'm sure she does, although I didn't ask to see them. She said she remembers Paulina has a journal stashed away in the house. What about a secret door?"

"A hidden door? Inside? Outside? Damn! Forensics will need to go through the place again. Really? And we need to find her journal. It might reveal her lover's name. He's my focus. Was Hester aware of a boyfriend?"

"She never mentioned anyone, but we can visit with her again."

"A secret door might be her boyfriend's access, which works with my request. Are you acquainted with the Savioli couple across the street from Paulina?"

"Certainly. They've been in town for years. Mercedes and Matteo emigrated from England when they were in their early twenties. Parlour Antiques caters to those who favour Victorian pieces. They were on a buying trip recently. They just got back and opened for the season on Saturday."

"I want to interview them, and I hoped you might accompany me. It's possible they've seen Paulina's beau. Their side deck gives them a perfect view."

"Sure, I'll go with you. When? Tomorrow?" She's breathless with relief because she's been permitted to help. "I imagine mornings are better. Their hours start at eleven."

"I'll call them and ask for an appointment at nine on Wednesday morning and confirm with you." He pushes open the screen. "Must trek back and organize Rosie for the trip home. She wants to stay, but I told her weekends until the first of June. Talk to you soon, and thanks for your help."

Her staff have dispersed, and Stella returns to the kitchen to start work on supper. Trixie and Russ will turn up any time after five, provided Russ doesn't cancel again. Nick has been too busy with campers to lend a hand, except for a casserole he's made to put in the oven anytime. She has a rare undisturbed moment to think.

Chapter 3

Further Public Details are Sparse

"Will anybody pour a glass of wine for a very thirsty sister?" Trixie whines when she strolls through the living room to meet Stella at her kitchen door. They're late, but at least they didn't cancel again.

"You're obviously out to impress. Tarted yourself up for a long-weekend dinner at the park with Nick and me? All this," she makes a circle with her index finger pointed in Trixie's general direction, "must be for Russ' benefit." Stella assesses the skin-tight blue jeans, leopard print short jacket, and revealing T-shirt. Crystal nuggets decorate her ears. "Are you cross because he worked the last time we tried to have dinner?"

"Shush. Yes," she whispers. "I'm still miffed." She swings her hips in a veiled attempt at confidence Stella's convinced she doesn't possess. "I manage my impatience by showing him what he's missed." She winks.

"Where are you two?" Nick bursts into the kitchen. "I came to find Russ a drink. What's the ETA on supper?"

"We're good." She reaches into the fridge and produces two beers. "We have another thirty minutes for the eggplant Parmesan. The salad is chilling, and the garlic bread needs to be heated." She turns to Trixie. "Dessert will be a surprise." She bought a rhubarb crumble from the hotel.

"Welcome, Russ. Our first summer dinner of 1981," she states, while entering the lounge from the kitchen.

Trixie's boyfriend traverses the living room and grips Stella's shoulders with both hands before he brushes a kiss to her cheek. "Sorry for last Thursday. I was 'volunteered' to work."

"No problem. The weekend has been busy, which bodes well for business." She nods to Trixie, who is always concerned Stella won't be able to produce the partner cheque she requires each month to survive. "With the first annual Shale Harbour Writers Retreat in September, I can report we have confirmed reservations straight through to fall—a new record."

She points out the leather furniture which flanks the massive stone fireplace. "Sit everyone. Dinner will be in thirty minutes."

"Russ," Nick begins, "we're happy you weren't called to work tonight. And new wheels?"

Stella knows Nick finds Russ' profession mysterious. He travels most of the time and Trixie often complains when there are sudden cancellations.

"Human Resources Management Consultation can be tricky." Russ sips his beer. "I go to the customer and we brainstorm ideas when an employee needs to be fired or disciplined. Business owners think they need to find a resolution to a problem any time day or night. When I receive a request through my boss, there are no options." He runs a manicured hand over the knee of his khaki slacks. "But tonight, I have an announcement."

His focus is on Trixie, and Stella interprets his expression as both conspiratorial and playful. "I have completed the required paperwork and officially retired. Now I can drive my new sports car whenever I want, instead of parking it in the garage."

Trixie throws her body across the sofa and her arms around Russ' neck. "What? I'll have you totally to myself? There's sand in my suitcase, Russ. Time for us to go away again."

He pats her back, kisses her cheek, and returns his attention to Stella and Nick. "Do you think she's excited? Yes, I've retired from the human resources business. No more consulting."

Nick stands. "Congratulations—to both of you." He shakes Russ' hand. "Another beer? Wine, Trixie? Retirement news calls for a celebration. You can tell us over supper what you plan to do with your time, now." He winks at Stella. "We could always use more help to trim trees and mow lawns. How are your skills with water pumps and sewer tanks?" He picks up their glasses and chuckles as he turns toward the kitchen.

Wrapped around Russ in a position not unlike a pet boa constrictor, Trixie kisses his cheek and mews her satisfaction into his ear.

At the dinner table, discussions begin with Russ, who shares his plans to pursue real estate. The decision is to retire from one occupation and jump into another. His enthusiasm is evident as he reports how Meredith Tompkins, owner of Grey Cottage Realty, agreed to take him on as a new agent. Her husband, Farley, wants to pull back from the sales team and spend more time at home. He's writing a book and preparing for the retreat in the fall.

"Did Cavelle Painter ever mention Farley Tompkins was an author, Trixie?" Cavelle is Hester's older sister and a real estate agent at Grey Cottage Realty. She and Trixie have been close friends since they were in school.

Trixie's blond curls shake. "Not a peep. Must be a new endeavour. I met her for lunch the other day. She told me Meredith is in a snit because Farley doesn't want to work anymore. As far as I can tell from Cavelle, he's never closed many sales." She pats Russ on the hand. "You'll change that, my love, and give Cavelle genuine listings competition."

"Cavelle is a very successful realtor. I hope to learn from her and work with her. I won't compete."

The topic of conversation switches to Paulina's murder. The papers have reported she was killed late Thursday night or early Friday morning, May 1, and the body was discovered by Stella when she arrived to have lunch with the victim. Further public details are sparse, although the police said they considered the community not to be in any danger.

"Are you working with Aiden again?" Her sister has a way of barreling straight to the point. She proved helpful in both previous murders where Stella assisted Aiden with the investigations, although indulgence and cajoling were often required.

"Not exactly. The scene hasn't been released. If his superiors decide I'm to be excluded because I found the body, I may end up outside the house and the case. Right now, I can help with interviews only."

"Are you implicated?" Russ' question pops out of nowhere.

Nick jumps forward in his chair. "She went to Paulina's for lunch and found the poor woman shot," he gasps. "Implicated? Why would you ever suggest she's involved?"

"You didn't mean any offense, did you Russ, honey?"

"Certainly not. Oftentimes the police leap to the wrong conclusion, but your friendship with the detective explains why he assumes you're not a suspect."

Stella is cognizant of the circumstances in which she's been thrust. Anyone who finds a body, under any conditions, no matter how benign, can be considered suspicious. She nibbles on a nail. Russ is practically family now, so she harnesses her impatience. "I've been cleared by forensics. She had been dead for hours before I turned up on the scene. Aiden is sure I'll be able to work with him if he needs my help. We're scheduled to interview a couple on Wednesday."

Nick's annoyance remains palpable.

****

"Tell me a little background on Mercedes and Matteo Savioli."

She's seated across from Aiden at a bistro table in Cocoa and Café. The essence of fresh brewed hazelnut coffee wafts around her face. "They have an interesting, although vague, history not unlike many who settle here from away. They call themselves British-Italians. I think the story involves both fathers as Italian bricklayers who immigrated to Bedford, England, back in the fifties. Mercedes and Matt are at least five years younger than us. They married and came to Canada in their early twenties and turned up here a dozen years ago."

"How do they fit in with the Shale Harbour crowd?"

"They're well respected. Parlour Antiques has a reputation for authenticity—no American glass or china which has become collectible the past few years. They sell only the highest quality Victorian silver, British pottery including Torquay which is surprisingly valuable, stunning furniture, and high-end glass and china. You should see their selection of flow blue dinnerware." Stella samples her coffee. "Not many of my campers come to Shale Cliffs RV Park in search of antiques." She smirks. "On the flip side, customers often make special trips over here to Shale Harbour to visit their shop. They maintain a steady market with clientele from Port Ephron and beyond."

"Are they friends with anyone in particular?"

"Not to my knowledge. They're active on the Board of Trade and are sponsors of many community hall and playhouse projects. Each intervention or contribution adds up to increased village visibility. I'm not aware of any close relationship with Paulina. Their interview could reveal interesting tidbits or no information whatsoever."

Matt and Mercedes Savioli open their locked shop door together. They welcome the detective and Stella into their establishment. "Good morning, Stella. Nice to see you today. I suspect I'll appear crass, but I hope our season won't be ruined because of Miss McAdams' death." Matt acknowledges her before he extends his square and slightly hairy hand toward Aiden. "Detective North, I am Matt Savioli. May I present my wife, Mercedes? We want to help you in any way we can—such a horrible turn of events in our village. I worry for our safety, despite what the papers say. Our home is open to the public all day."

Mercedes frowns at her husband as she leads them through their commercial space, cluttered with mahogany sideboards and velvet slipper chairs, to a small sitting room at the back of the house. "Please, have a seat. We spend most of our time here during business hours." She nods in the direction of a set of stairs. "We live on the second floor." Her long green cotton skirt scuffs the hardwood when she turns. She adjusts her sweater and pushes a loose strand of thick black hair off her cheek. Mercedes is the only woman Stella has ever known who wears chandelier earrings whether dressed in shorts or a ball gown.

Matt stands while they make themselves comfortable. "You mentioned on the phone you wanted to discuss the murder."

Matt possesses charisma; the kind often seen in politicians. His dark hair hangs over one eye. He continually runs a hand through the strands—an absent-minded gesture which projects a fidgety quality construed as nervousness by Stella. He fills the room with his olive complexion and deep brown eyes. His voice is buttery.

"Didn't I hear you found her body?" He stands across from them, fixated on Stella.

Mercedes shivers.

"Yes, she did, Mr. Savioli. Stella and I often work as a team. Although she accompanies me to assist with interviews, Stella will not discuss her personal experience with the case." Aiden sounds anxious to reach the point; to close the door on any assumptions. "You live across the street from the victim and your side deck overlooks her yard. We're interested in your observations of the people you might have seen entering or leaving her premises."

Aiden stops long enough to make eye contact with both Matt and Mercedes. Mercedes purses her lips—a barely detectable movement, but Stella notices.

"Many members of the public availed themselves of Paulina's expertise. She provided library sessions for mothers and their children. Her home was open to the public in the summer, the same as ours. I couldn't list everyone who visited Yellow House, even if I bothered to watch continuously, which I didn't." Matt blushes the colour of port and looks flustered.

Stella interjects in response to his impatient tone. "We don't expect you to be able to report everyone who entered Yellow House during business hours. Our interest is in after-hours visitors—anyone who might have arrived to see Paulina, not her library and bookstore."

Matt glances toward Mercedes. They exchange one of those knowing looks couples use to communicate without words. "Tell them."

Mercedes pats her tangled bun ensnared in a tortoise shell clip. "I don't want you to consider me a nosy neighbour, and I have never observed anyone suspicious around her house, but I imagine there were secret arrangements."

"What makes you suspect she was meeting someone, Mrs. Savioli?"

"Last season, she often placed the Closed sign in the window even though she never left. Her car remained parked in her overgrown and weedy driveway."

"She locked up her business in the middle of the day? Did you see who entered after she closed her shop?"

"No. I'm embarrassed to tell you, though, that I made a point to watch because closure at that time appeared strange. Many people came and went, Detective North, but she never admitted a customer after her sign was in the window. People will knock regardless. Shoppers can be rude when they expect you to be open. They forget you might be sick, or even in the bathroom for a few minutes. Matt and I have a paper clock we hang on the door. If we need a break to make tea or use the washroom, we set the time on the little clock. Then people are aware. Paulina never placed a notice on her door to tell clientele when she would be open again."

✳✳✳✳

"Well, what do you think?" They are back in Aiden's car, on the return trip to Shale Cliffs.

"The Saviolis are more than a little afraid, and I don't blame them. In addition, we know Paulina had a boyfriend—her 'affaire du coeur', as she labeled it—and she refused further details except to emphasize it was hush-hush because he was married. We assume he found a way into the house in the middle of the day without detection. Matt and Mercedes suspect someone came around because the place was closed at odd hours. The front door is open to the street and the back door is visible to the neighbours from the property behind her. Maybe Hester was correct when she mentioned a hidden door. We need to inspect Paulina's house."

"Surely to God the forensics team can find a secret door...not to mention her diary." Frustration seeps into his tone.

When they reach the park, he refuses to stay for lunch, saying he prefers to rush back to the station and issue detailed instructions to the forensics team. "I'll telephone the minute you're given access. Thanks for today."

****

"Are we done? Let's lock the doors and take our tea upstairs." Nick, sporting his best end-of-the-day scruffy and contented demeanour, stands in the office doorway.

"Good idea. I don't expect any more rigs tonight. I'm exhausted." He follows her into reception, where she hangs the sign inviting any late-day travellers who arrive in the park before the gate is closed to choose a spot and check with the office in the morning. "Everyone's been busy. I've missed your company."

"The park finally quieted down after the long weekend. Paul and I found enough time to condition most of the machinery. We're ready for the season. Eve worked steady. I never thought I'd say this, but I miss those snowy winter days when the park's empty." He wraps an arm around her waist, and they trudge into the kitchen.

With black currant tea steeped and poured, they make their way to the second floor and the part of the house they've come to refer to as their oasis. They settle into the chintz-covered wingbacks arranged to face the veranda door and the distant ocean views of white-capped waves. Tonight, they are graced with the sounds instead. Darkness has begun to fall, and the antique shades of the table lamps cast yellowed shadows. Nick, in an effort to convince her of his commitment, spent an enormous sum of money on the renovation project. Stella kept the old chairs and lamps. He said she should buy new, but she couldn't justify the additional expense. They kept the wide antique pine floors, too. Although he needed to match the wood and patch spots where walls used to be, Nick's skills created a seamless effect. The resulting master suite provides the peace and security she feels when his arms wrap around her after a hard day. She's safe.

"Paulina fills my mind. I'm not obsessed," she adds, as she checks his face for arguments, "although absorbed, and I need a sounding board. Aiden is focused on Paulina's affair. There's more to Miss Paulina McAdams than we understand to this point. A married boyfriend may be just the beginning."

Their hands touch while they relax side by side. Nick's left hand holds his tea while his right covers Stella's left. The screen door rattles in the wind and the breeze is strong enough to caress their faces. "Pick any topic you want. I've been concerned ever since you found Paulina's body. Shock can take a while to set in. Talking is good."

She turns to face her love. Nick is thirty-seven years old, tall, trim, and fit. His faded tan has begun to return. Her breath still catches each time she studies him. He is kind, understanding, and thoughtful. He loves her. Regularly, she wonders why. "I'm sure I'll improve once we can explore Yellow House. Hester says Paulina kept a diary, maybe in code, and she often mentioned a secret door. Hester's recollection may not be accurate, but if Paulina's lover visited her at home, as I'm sure he did, both the front and back entrances are visible. Hester is rarely wrong, so I guess a more thorough inspection will be needed to find another entry point."

"How are Matt and Mercedes coping with a murder across the street?"

Fingers stroke her palm. He sips his tea and watches her. She tries to focus. "They're both worried about the season, which makes sense. They tried to help as best as they could. They claim they've not seen anyone who might be considered out of the ordinary, but Mercedes said Paulina often closed the house to the public at odd times during the day. People arrived, expecting to visit the library or the book shop, and the Closed sign was in the window. Mercedes concluded Paulina was involved in a clandestine affair. The two of them glanced at one another, like they knew what the other was thinking."

"Couples exchange thoughts without words." His fingers wrap around hers. "We do."

Her spine tingles. "Yes." She attempts to sound serious, but her voice catches.

"Do you and Aiden have a plan?"

"I'm not sure. I'm frustrated. Forensics will go through the place again, for both a journal and a hidden door. The lawyers haven't found any family. Their one interaction with Paulina was when she bought Yellow House." She clears her throat and tries again to focus. "The court will assign the firm to liquidate her estate if they come up empty in their search. The police will tell the law firm when the house is released. Then the lawyers are in a position to give me permission to enter the premises if Aiden's boss agrees."

"Aiden's boss should put you on the payroll. Paulina's murder is your third case with Aiden. You could be their cost-saving measure." He sniffs his annoyance. "They'll never hire an investigative partner at this rate."

Stella knows Nick supports any work she carries out with Aiden. Despite their romantic history from high school, Nick understands she and Aiden interact as friends and colleagues only.

"Not to change the subject, but I was pissed when Russ wondered if you were implicated in the murder. Why would he assume, even for a second, you were involved?"

"Pissed? I guess. You were royally miffed," she teases. "I imagine, as with you, he watches too many *Perry Mason* reruns. To be serious, it was necessary to clear me, and a formal written statement was required by protocol. His question was fair."

"Do you think Trixie and Russ will take the next step and move in together?"

"Trixie certainly wants to live at his place. Not sure if Russ is on the same wavelength. He irritates you, doesn't he?"

"He's okay. Too much like a politician to suit me. I always wonder if he has an angle I can't figure out."

Nick releases her hand. The loss is unexplainable.

"Let me take our cups downstairs and then we can turn in."

"Leave them." Nearness to Nick is important right now. It might have been the handholding. She wants him beside her. *Poor Paulina. Was she killed by her lover? How terrifying to reach the point where you discover you're in fear of the one you love the most.*

CHAPTER 4

Our Partnership Will be Official

Stella rests her butt against the trunk of Paulina's white 1966 Buick Electra. She noticed grass sprouted around the tires when she arrived. While she waits for Aiden, she examines her immediate surroundings. The car hasn't moved for weeks. Most local residents shop on foot for their basics from the grocery and drug stores, so the situation wouldn't be interpreted as unusual. Mercedes was correct when she mentioned Paulina's overgrown driveway. Dead leaves have blown up against the sedan's wheels. Between the narrow passage and the huge Forsythia ready to bloom, she imagines access to the inside of Paulina's vehicle was difficult for forensics. Who knows? Perhaps there's a door to the house underneath this damned bush.

Aiden called last night to tell her Yellow House was released by the police and the law firm has provided ongoing permission until they decide what to do with the estate. Stephens and Stephens are on the search for relatives.

This is the north side. The light is subdued at best. A monstrous elm marks the lot line between Paulina and her neighbour. Once the leaves are mature, the car will be partially obscured from the street.

"Good morning!" Stella hears Aiden before she sees him appear around the corner. "Been here long?"

"Nope. Musing. Did the identification team go over Paulina's Buick? The ground is hardly disturbed."

"The report states the prints inside and out were hers. See the smudges? They saw no need to drag her car back to the police barn."

"Well, the way her vehicle's parked, coupled with this big old plant behind me," she casts a thumb over her shoulder, "a guy might easily sneak into the yard from this side. Can we have a snoop around?"

"Be my guest. You start toward the back and I'll wander across the front."

"I want to find a secret door."

His response is unexpected. "A hidden access would certainly simplify our job. Forensics should have found one, if it exists," he grumbles.

Stella, while struggling to protect herself from branches, makes her way past the passenger side of the car to examine the north border of the house before she follows the addition to the rear corner. The dwelling is covered in canary yellow wood siding and the trim is creamy white. The original structure boasts two downstairs windows which match two of equal size on the second floor. The windows are old with storms over original three-light single-panes. Paulina never bothered to have them removed in the spring. They appear painted shut.

She rounds the corner and sees Aiden on the small but comfortable back deck. The windows are newer, as is the structure. The air has a chill, typical for near the end of May, and she wraps her cranberry sweater around her torso to break the wind.

"No surprises. She has an outside tap virtually covered by her overgrown Forsythia. She must have washed her car where she parked." Stella climbs the steps.

"Strange. She has a spigot right here, with a hose attached. What would she need with two?"

"Maybe the side tap existed when she bought the house, and she added this one for convenience."

"Let's go back around and examine the one you saw."

They both return to the vicinity of the Forsythia. Aiden peers at the tap, installed higher than expected for a hose attachment. "Who installs their outdoor faucet at this height?" He turns to Stella. "The water line must run from the main floor and not the basement."

"Paulina obviously did serious renovations years ago, Aiden. The horizontal siding's cut on one side for sure." She points out the vertical seam as if a tradesman ran a saw through the siding. The tap is about a foot away. *Curious.*

Aiden dons a glove and reaches up to the spigot. He attempts a turn and a rattle. "Seized up. Maybe she needed to have the siding cut out and replaced because of water damage. Any theories?"

Stella considers. "A door? Her mystery man waited until the coast was clear and cruised in the side. Can we arrange for this area to be checked for fingerprints again?"

"Consider it done. Once we access the inside, we'll have a better idea regarding connections. We might have the process backwards. Maybe she disconnected the pipes before replacing the siding because of water damage. Afterward, the plumber ran a new tap closer to the rear entry." He wiggles the knob again. "Frozen."

They tramp around to the rear and sit on rusting metal chairs near the kitchen window. Stella leans back and closes her eyes. Despite the cool breeze, the spring sun flashes pink, red, and magenta through her lids. The deck, which faces east, has begun to warm up. Stella imagines Paulina sitting out here on many mornings with her coffee, before she opened her home to the public for the day.

She studies the back yard. Due to an abundance of foliage, the space is surprisingly secluded. In the resulting gloom, it's possible for a person to sneak past the Buick, access the deck, and enter the house with relative anonymity. Matt and Mercedes Savioli never saw a figure hanging around, but a skilled sneak, one who has a wife from whom to hide, would find a way. "Have you talked to the people who live over there?" She points at the ranch-style bungalow on the lot behind Yellow House.

"At the time of the murder, they were interviewed and said they have never seen anyone around except for Paulina, most often in the early morning when the weather's nice."

"If you parked your car a few businesses away and kept to the shadows, it's possible to sidle past the Buick and up to Paulina's back door unnoticed. Without lights on, detection would be difficult, although my theory doesn't account for Paulina's midday closures. Let's go inside."

****

The air is heavy and smells old—old books, old furniture, and old plaster walls. The familiar musty aroma is now mixed with the sickly-sweet scent of Paulina's blood, hovering even after three weeks. The red velvet club chair may still be in the front reading room. She rubs her index finger under her nose.

"Does the smell bother you? Brace yourself, because her chair hasn't been moved. Except for forensics, no one has been inside. The law firm still has inventory to complete, according to their communication with us."

"I'm fine," she lies. "I want to search the drawers. Her journal is likely hidden in plain sight."

"Surely she didn't leave her diary where customers had access to her personal property, though. Take the kitchen and I'll start up front. No need for you to return to the room where you found her."

His attempt at protection isn't necessary despite the troubled loss which overwhelms her right now. She plans to stand beside the chair where Paulina died; to listen; to let the space absorb her; to feel.

In the kitchen, she dons plastic gloves while surveying the cabinets. They were built on site, unlike the fancier prefab ones she saw at the lumberyard when they shopped for products during their renovation. This addition was completed over twenty years ago. There was nowhere to purchase cupboards in the 1960s. Leon no doubt found a carpenter able to build them. She opens the first door. Dishes. Lots of dishes, piled high and with precision. Paulina liked to entertain, and she owned the accessories as proof.

Although she pokes in every cabinet and pulls open each drawer, nothing presents itself beyond the expected. A few of the drawers are shallow, and two of the cabinets aren't as deep as hers at home. The counter tops are covered in kitchen paraphernalia.

She wanders out to the porch where the door leads to the deck. Paulina's washer and dryer, a pantry resembling the kitchen units, and a small freezer occupy the space. She opens the appliances. They remain plugged in and contain the obvious. The freezer is half full of frozen berries, rhubarb sauce, a chicken, and various packages of other meat. She sees a metal tin. Stella takes the lid off and finds chocolate chip cookies. Paulina liked to bake. When she opens the top door of the thirty-inch pantry, she discovers a stack of metal tins and sheets. Most are square or rectangular. A few are odd shaped. The bottom of the cabinet is empty, with no shelves—a coat closet but without hooks or hangers. She observes mud on the floor, and a knob on the back. "Aiden!"

"What? Where are you?"

"Out here in the porch. What do you make of this?" She points out the unusual pantry cupboard. She suspects they've solved the mystery of the non-functional outdoor tap but wants Aiden to be the one to determine the answer.

He races from the front of the house. "A doorknob...inside a cabinet? Did you touch it?"

"No, but I can see the knob pushes to lock. It's locked."

"Right." He reaches a gloved hand past her and unlocks the mechanism. "Stay where you are." He dashes outside. Stella hears a muffled click and Aiden is suddenly visible in the driveway. "This is how her boyfriend came in undetected." He climbs through the pantry into the porch. "Now, the door is locked." He pushes the knob back to the previous position and closes the unit. "And the neighbours are none the wiser. Dammit, I'll call forensics again, and tell Stephens and Stephens to stand down for the time being. We missed a damned doorknob and Hester Painter was right. Paulina had her secrets."

"There's no sign of a journal or a code book, Aiden. I've searched inside each cabinet and opened every drawer." She sits in the kitchen and stares at the tin "P" and "M" hanging on the wall. While pointing toward them, she adds, "Paulina told me Leon bought those for her when they dated. She said they're valuable collectibles, and she never managed to find any more except for two tins shaped like numbers. I assume they're with the stack of baking sheets in the top portion of the pantry. There are other expensive pieces in the house—rare books, too. I hope Stephens and Stephens hire an expert to sift through this stuff before throwing her lovely possessions into an auction."

"If they can't find any family, and I gather the chances are slim, the tax man will end up with most of the proceeds. Might as well let a few auction hunters grab a treasure." He stands. "Ready to go upstairs? We'll cover every room before we send for forensics again." He adds, "we won't rummage through the books today. I'm sure she didn't store a personal journal where there's customer access. If she has one, it'll be in her private space."

"She has one. Hester observed her writing but never saw where she stashed it." She scowls at the letters. "I'll be up in a few minutes."

Stella returns to the reading room, stands in the gloom, and focuses on the red velvet club chair. Now tolerant of the smell, she allows her thoughts to collide at random. Paulina was dressed to suggest she was waiting for her lover. She expected him to enter through the back, but the inside knob of the secret door was locked. Did he come through the front? The front door was ajar. Did she let him in and return to her chair? Was the person an acquaintance but not her lover? Had she forgotten to unlock the secret door? Logical answers refuse to reveal themselves.

She trudges up the stairs. They explore three bedrooms and an obvious fourth converted to a bathroom years ago. Each room is decorated with

Victorian elegance, thanks to Parlour Antiques, no doubt. The master bedroom is furnished with Eastlake pieces, designed to be ornate and simple at the same time. They are made of cherry. The other rooms are decorated with iron bedsteads and turn-of-the-century oak washstands. The pine floors are protected by worn oriental carpets. A possible journal is elusive. This visit to her dead friend's home has unsettled her more than she expected.

****

Back at the park, and after lunch, Stella spends time with Alice and Kiki while Eve, Paul, Duke, and Nick return to work. Reservations for the first annual writers retreat have started. Alice asked Stella to help her sort out visitors' needs. They are reviewing the site map to allocate spots when the phone rings.

Kiki has earned a place on Alice's lap while they sit at the kitchen table. "I'll answer. Stay where you are." Stella leans around the corner of Alice's chair to reach for the wall phone. "Shale Cliffs RV Park."

"It's me. Can we talk for a minute?"

"Sure. Let me move to my office. Alice, will you hang up once I connect with Aiden?"

She nods and stands, Kiki under her arm.

Once settled, Stella picks up the receiver. "Thanks, Alice." The extension clunks. "Okay, I'm alone. Did you hear from forensics?"

"No."

"What's the matter? Is Rosemary all right?"

"Rosemary's fine. We're on our way out to the park later tonight. This is work related. I guess I bugged my superiors too many times for your clearance to assist with the McAdams file."

"Oh." Her heart thumps. The bile of disappointment rises in her throat. "They won't let me help, eh?"

"The exact opposite. They want to offer you a contract as a consultant on a case-by-case basis. No big money, but authority to be at a scene with me, liability insurance," his pause fills her ear, "and my undying gratitude. Well?"

Her silence lasts long enough he asks if she's still there. "I'm here."

"Are you pleased? Our partnership will be official. Even if they hire another major crimes detective, your contribution won't change."

"It sounds great. Can we meet tomorrow morning? I have a lunch date at

Cocoa and Café with Trixie and Cavelle."

"Eleven o'clock?"

"I'll be there, Aiden. Don't misunderstand. I'm flattered that the RCMP consider me an asset of sorts, but our visit to Paulina's today set me on edge. Let's discuss tomorrow."

"No problem. See you at eleven."

After the staff leave for home, Stella covers reception, as usual, until eight in the evening. They settle in the office, tea in hand. "There's something we need to talk about, Nick." She's put off telling him about Aiden's offer because he seems ill at ease already. Might as well find out now if there's a problem.

"Aiden called and said the RCMP have offered me a consulting contract and I want your opinion."

Relief spreads like sunshine across Nick's face. The muscles in his neck relax. He strides across the room and hugs her to him.

"Listen, mister, I'm the insecure half of our relationship, not you. What's the matter?"

"When you asked me if we could talk, I wasn't sure if we had a problem." He hugs her again. "Have you seen the contract?"

"No. Aiden invited me to the detachment tomorrow before I go to lunch. I expect there'll be the standard stuff related to confidentiality, liability, hours, money—not complicated or earth-shattering." She's behind the desk and he has taken a seat on the other side. She jumps up and joins him in the wooden chair nearby. "Tell you what. I won't sign, and we can discuss with the lawyer if the wording makes me uncomfortable. Better?" She wants him to relax. He understands Aiden isn't a threat. "Are you okay?"

"No, but it has nothing to do with your contract. I have felt, all along, the RCMP need to formalize your role with Aiden." He places his tea on the desk, clasps his hands and lets them hang between his knees. He resembles a disciplined schoolboy.

Stella hasn't seen overt anxiety in Nick for a very long time—not since Aiden first came into the picture. "For heaven's sake, Nick. What the hell's on your mind?" She softens her tone. "If you don't have a beef with me working with Aiden, then tell me the problem."

He lifts his eyes to meet hers. "I talked to my parents earlier today. They weren't happy I didn't go visit them in Florida for the holidays. Dad is riled up

I spent money here in the park. The conversation was not pleasant."

She touches his knee. "You are a grown man who has now morphed into the Cochrans' little boy. They can't tell you what to do."

"You have never met Tobias and Yona, Stella. My father still calls me a traitor because I left the military. I can cope with the negative media crap in the States, but when my own father joins in, I go to pieces—my Achilles heel, I guess." He frowns. "Don't be surprised if they turn up on our doorstep."

"Both of us can't be insecure at the same time." She stands, holds his face, and kisses him. "As long as we synchronize who is insecure and who is supportive, we'll be fine. We're a team. Agreed?"

He nods but his expression suggests he's unconvinced.

"Besides, my father likes you and assumes you own the park. He can't remember me most of the time, but in your case—you always have Norbert to fall back on." She tries to be flippant; to ease his tension so he knows he can depend on her. She understands. Parental alienation disguises itself in many forms. In her case, her father's drift into dementia has resulted in his loss of recognition of her as his daughter. Oddly, and as the disease manifests, he remembers Nick. Now she's identified as Nick's wife, for the sole purpose of enabling Norbert's recollection of her name. In Nick's case, he left the United States because of the Vietnam War. He was gone for years before he received a pardon in January 1977. His parents refuse to recognize the life he's built here, with her. The idea they might turn up at Shale Cliffs has never been a possibility before today.

CHAPTER 5

Don't Interfere

Cocoa and Café is their go-to spot for coffee or lunch. Fast-food franchises aren't permitted in Shale Harbour and the hotel is too stuffy and dark. Stella admires the pine floors of the converted carriage factory. She's surprised Trixie didn't insist on occupying a table on the deck, but keeps her thoughts hidden. A quiet murmur of conversation surrounds them. The tiny bistro does a respectable, although lighter, trade on weekdays this early in the season.

Stella sits across from Trixie and Cavelle, who appear to be sisters rather than friends. They're near the same age and possess a similar aesthetic—short skirts, lots of leather in purses and boots, skillfully tussled hair, and pounds of chunky jewellery. Stella considers herself to be void of any style whatsoever. She sports linen drawstring pants, a droopy T-shirt, and a green scarf knotted at her neck. The scarf is her homage to the attire she knew would confront her in the café today.

"Russ will be great in the office, Trixie. He'll answer phones and greet prospective clients. We'll go out on showings and listing calls together. Orientation takes patience."

"But he wants to write for his license right away." Trixie huffs when she talks. "What's Meredith's plan? Keep him under her thumb? Make him do the grunt work for her? I assumed office detail was Farley's job."

The weekend was busy—more than normal for post Victoria Day. Poor Alice was run off her feet. Nobody slowed down for the duration. Stella purred around on the golf cart, welcomed new campers, and touched base with her seasonals. The house was chaotic. Their master retreat proved invaluable—an occasional solace from the din.

Stella makes a vague attempt to pay attention. Trixie sounds incensed.

She's taken Russ' new career at Grey Cottage Realty too seriously—or personally. Meredith and Farley Tompkins have owned and operated their successful real estate operation in town for years. They employ Cavelle Painter as their other agent. Russ must learn the trade. Stella supposes her sister imagines him selling a million-dollar house on his first day.

They prattle on while waiting for their chowder. She silently reviews her trip to the RCMP detachment earlier. The contract was straight-forward. The organization will pay for her to work with Aiden at the rate of fifteen dollars an hour. The sum is significant, but compensation doesn't include extra for gas or travel. Finance will deduct her taxes. She signed the deal.

Later in their meeting, she and Aiden called Hester. The conversation was a challenge because Hester evades the telephone at every opportunity. She mentioned the device should have pictures of the other person, like the television.

"Hester, Aiden and I need your assistance and expertise in Paulina's investigation. Will you visit Yellow House with us and help search for her journal? I can collect you on Thursday. We'll go to lunch."

"I am happy to be of service in any way possible. Detective North has been kind to my family, and you are my friend. I do not know the location of her journal, Stella, but she owned one with a leather cover. She wrapped the book with a ribbon. I, conversely, used a scribbler." She sounded annoyed as she recalled her choice.

"We need to wander through her home before her possessions are removed. You always remember every little detail. I'm sure you'll recall what she did with her journal. May I pick you up at ten on Thursday?"

"Yes, you may. I will be on the front step at ten o'clock on the morning of Thursday, May 28. Please do not be late." The phone clunked, and Stella was rewarded for her communication efforts with a dial tone.

She turned to Aiden. "At least she's accepted our invitation. Life is always an adventure when Hester's in the picture."

Aiden nodded. "I'll stay in the background. She trusts you. I hope she'll be able to recall Paulina's movements around the house and we'll discover where the poor woman secured her journal." White hair fell across his perpetually tilted forehead. "I'm certain her diary will help us. I can only hope she revealed her lover, and possibly, her killer."

"I'm not as convinced as you are. The secret door was locked from the inside. If she expected him, their rendezvous was later in the evening and she hadn't unlocked the access yet."

"Paulina forgot to unlock the door, so he entered through the front and then killed her."

They discussed scenarios back and forth until she left to meet Trixie and Cavelle.

Focus on the conversation at hand.

"Meredith hired Russ because Farley is useless in the business. At one time, he enjoyed engaging with new clients. He was our welcoming committee. Now he stays home and works on his 'so-called' manuscript."

"Russ wants to sell; to be out in the field." Trixie directs a red lipstick pout toward her friend.

"Everybody has to learn. Try to understand. Besides, Meredith and I reviewed the situation in detail. She has resisted hiring a receptionist because the first contact with a client when they approach the business is the most important. An agent needs to be that contact." She leans over her chowder to focus on Trixie. "We plan to rotate office days, once Russ is comfortable. We'll all pitch in, you'll see."

Cavelle rummages inside a huge turquoise leather satchel and retrieves her wallet. "I'll pay my bill at the counter and run. I have three showings this afternoon while Russ and Meredith stay in the office." She bends to give Trixie a quick peck on the cheek and waves at Stella. "Later, you two."

Stella pats her sister's hand before she digs for her own money. "Grey Cottage Realty needs time. Don't interfere. Russ is pleased to be retired from his work and finished with travelling. He'll be fine."

Trixie closes her eyes for a moment. "If I'm honest, I wish he had stopped work, period. I told him again I've got sand in my suitcase. I want to go away and now he's tangled up with another job."

"You work, too." Trixie's position at the fish plant isn't great, but she manages. Money is scarce. Stella knows she depends on the one thousand dollars a month the park is obliged to pay her for her share of the business.

She opens her eyes and stage whispers, "My goal is to move into Russ' stunningly renovated Craftsman cottage with him and become a kept woman." Her nose points to the ceiling and she leers for effect. "If he didn't work, we could travel. Do you see my vision?"

"Well, if what you want is for him to quit, you'd be wise to support the status quo for now. He might sit in the office for a few days and be bored as hell. There's a better chance he won't stick around if he doesn't have fun." She leaves Trixie with her mouth open when she stands to walk over to the cash to settle her bill.

****

Rosemary's arrival is unexpected. She stomps into Stella's living room from the back veranda unannounced. Alice attempts an interception, but Aiden's wife will not be stopped. She materializes in Stella's office doorway breathless and red-faced. She pushes a strand of hair, dislodged from her French roll, off her brow. Then she adjusts the poodle clips which hold the open cardigan of her canary yellow sweater set in place. "Stella, I insist we talk right now."

Cognizant of Rosemary's mental health ups and downs, Stella has judged by various other experiences that there is no emotional upheaval at present. She wonders what triggered the poor woman. She stands and indicates for Rosemary to have a seat. Alice hovers at the door, which Rosemary grabs and slams in the poor girl's face.

"I didn't expect you. Do you have an issue with your trailer, Rosemary?" With experience in the de-escalation of difficult interactions, she maintains a level tone and makes an inquiry she is convinced is not remotely related to the outrage emitting from her guest. Stella hoped working with Aiden wouldn't cause repeated difficulties with Rosemary after they bought Lorraine Young's unit near the end of the season last year. Nick and Stella took extra pains to clarify they were a couple and illustrated clearly that Rosemary's initial jealousy was unfounded.

"Any issues are with you, girlie. I hear you and Aiden now have a formal contract, so you can gallivant around the countryside all the time. I told him I want you to stop."

Apparently, their serious talk with her when she was in hospital had little or no effect. Aiden must have revealed the arrangement and their conversation triggered an episode.

When Stella realized Aiden was back in the area for good, they put their past behind them and embraced a renewed bond. First loves never fully vacate your heart. Rosemary, and even Nick initially, did not comprehend the lasting friendship which endures.

Rosemary's mental health issues are a challenge. When she's over-medicated, her affect is flat, her eyes dull. The balance is delicate, and Stella is never sure which condition is worse—no personality, or one that's over-the-top.

"Rosemary, the RCMP have contracted with me to be their consultant. It's a working relationship with the whole department," she emphasizes. "We've discussed the idea numerous times."

"I've decided you people at the big house will be seeing more of me." She points a red lacquered index fingernail at Stella. "I refuse to permit my husband to spend all of his time up here with you." She turns in her platform sandals, which do not support decisive spins, and marches out the way she came.

Standing behind her desk, Stella watches the empty doorway until Alice returns. "She was miffed at you!"

"No kidding. I'll call Aiden and tell him we've managed to precipitate another event. I hope he'll be able to figure out what to do."

The call is transferred immediately.

"Is Rosemary in a downward spiral again, Aiden?"

His sigh fills the space of his momentary silence. "I worried when I described the contract. She was huffy with me regarding—as she coined the term—the formalization of our relationship."

"Maybe I shouldn't consult if the idea sends Rosemary over the edge. Has she stopped taking her medication?"

"Have no idea, but I'm not with her every minute of the day, either. Any chance I can rent the cottage for her sisters? Toni and Mary Jo both said they'd come out if I needed help."

"Over the long weekend, I told Rosemary the cottage is available and to have one of her sisters call the park. Alice can make those arrangements for you anytime. As for tomorrow, don't stop here for me. I'll go over to the Painter farm, pick up Hester, and meet you at Yellow House."

"She can't see your place from our trailer."

"Understood, but she said she expected to hang around up here more often, so there's no need to add fuel to her fire."

"Okay, whatever you say. I'll talk to her later today and try to iron this mess out."

When the staff turn up for lunch, Stella fills Nick in on the visit. "We need to keep an eye on Rosemary. The whole idea of her here at the park for the summer might not have been wise."

"If she turns up in our neck of the woods, one of us will engage her. We'll encourage her to use the main reception door when she wants to access the house. Everyone will keep track of her whereabouts."

Relief and doubt compete.

****

"I'll get it." Stella flies off the couch and races to the office to pick up the phone. They had been stretched out end for end on one of the leather sofas in the living room, trying to read and relax. She must consider another telephone extension. The office, reception, and kitchen aren't adequate since she and Nick make use of the downstairs space as their main quarters. "Good evening. Shale Cliffs RV Park. How can I help you?"

"Let me talk to Nick Cochran. Be snappy, miss, I'm callin' long-distance."

Stella, shocked by the echoed boom, and confident she knows the caller's identity, engages her perfect operator voice. "One moment, please." She presses the hold button.

Nick stands in the doorway. Even though the line is on hold, she whispers, "I suspect it's your father."

"What?"

"He told me to make it snappy because the call is long-distance. You'd better answer." She produces a playful smile which he doesn't seem to appreciate.

"Nick Cochran here. How can I help you?"

She starts to leave the office, but he motions her to stay.

"Hi, Dad. I didn't expect to hear from you. Where are you?" Nick's face is flushed. His eyes widen.

"I know you live in Florida, Dad." He sounds exhausted before the conversation gets started. "What can I do for you?"

He listens and nods. "We have power. Water, too."

"No. No sewer. The honey wagon provides the service."

Slumping into her chair, he runs his fingers through his hair and closes his eyes.

Stella takes a position near the door and watches various emotions make their way across Nick's troubled tanned face.

"When do you expect to be here?" Nick squints at Stella. "Dad, the park is busy in the summer. You can't just say later when the weather's warmer."

His exasperation is revealed in his tone. "Okay, the latter half of June. What will you be driving?"

"What? You plan to borrow a brand-new Class A and drive from Orlando to Shale Harbour? Dad, fly in and rent a car. We have a cottage where you can stay."

"Okay. We'll find a place for your rig when you arrive." Nick meets Stella's gaze and widens his eyes.

"You two will love Shale Cliffs, Dad. Most beautiful spot in the world. Yeah, calls to Canada are expensive. See you next month, I guess. Bye for now." He drops the phone into the cradle. His neck is blotched with anxiety.

Stella remains seated on the wooden side chair positioned near the door. She waits, albeit with a measure of uncertainty, while Nick takes a breath.

"My parents are driving up here from Orlando in a thirty-foot rig. They'll arrive the middle of June."

"I gather." She refuses to show her anxiety. He has enough trepidation of his own.

"They haven't made up their mind how long to stay—depends on the success of the trip, he says. My father expects me to return to the States."

"And?"

He circles the desk, rests his hands on her shoulders, and bends to meet her gaze. "Never! My life is here with you."

She remains unsettled, but for now, his response is what she needs and wants to hear. "Okay, let's make a plan to handle Tobias and Yona Cochran. Tell me whatever information I'll need, and we'll present a united front."

They opt for tea. The scent of her favourite, black currant, fills the space while Nick describes his parents. "Dad is a caricature of the Texas oilman everybody imagines when they're reminded of loud-mouth Americans."

"What does he look like?"

"My old man is handsome, like me," Nick smirks. "Dad's a charmer—tall, barrel chested, bald, and with a perpetual tan."

"And your mother?"

"Mom is the exact opposite. She's a mousy little creature. She always wears black or grey clothes, hates Florida, and wants to move back to Texas where her relatives live. Her single homage to vanity is her dyed hair. The black makes her skin seem white and pasty."

"Your parents are well off." This is a statement, not a question. She knows the Cochran family made a fortune in the oil business. Tobias' sister left Nick lots of money. Her bequest gives him the freedom to work at the park for a pittance, allowed him to buy a ten percent share when the pumps needed an upgrade, and paid for the upstairs renovation.

"Very. Dad plays the market now. He sees himself as a big shot, in no uncertain terms."

"Tell me more about Yona."

"My mother is the definition of a shrinking violet. I remember times when I was a kid, I told her to stand up to Dad; to make her feelings known. She stared at me as if I was a crazy person. I often wondered if she would have been different if there were other kids. I still panic because I'm an only child. I got the equivalent attention of a whole houseful of brats. Lots of pressure." He pats her hand.

She decides to be the strong one. "We'll have fun with Tobias and Yona, my dear. I'll plan a big dinner party. We'll invite Trixie and Russ, along with Brigitte and Mia—and Aiden and Rosemary. And don't forget my father. Your folks won't see what's coming." She wraps her arms around his neck. "We've got this. Let's lock up for the night." *Once they meet my family, they'll want him to go home for sure. Might as well show them the works.* For now, the confidence she portrays is no more than an act of support.

CHAPTER 6

The Morning Should Prove Interesting

Rain sweeps across her windshield. The Jeep's relic wipers slap an uneven rhythm as she makes her way around the point and along the lane to the Painter farm. At five minutes to ten, Stella has made a valiant, and now successful, attempt to be on time.

She left staff management in Nick's capable hands. Wet days elicit different chores. Eve and Alice will work inside. They clean the reception rooms and catch up on filing. Eve always attends to the public bathrooms and their laundry facility. Paul and Nick spend time on machinery maintenance in the shed.

When Duke showed up with Kiki, they sported coordinated rain gear. He sat at the kitchen table and drank cup after cup of coffee. Duke, whose real name is John, starts his day by opening the gate. He makes a few rounds on the golf cart, keeps a check on campfires and visitors, and locks up near ten o'clock in the evening. He suffers through fewer site excursions in inclement weather, preferring the company of Alice and Eve in the main house. Since last season, he has tempered his sexual innuendos. He experienced an epiphany after Lorraine Young's death, when he was momentarily a suspect, and Stella made her position clear. His leers and comments weren't appreciated. She told him to respect her crew and assist instead of pestering, or she would find someone else to handle his job.

She pulls up to the wire and wood fence which separates the lawn and walkway from the parking area. As expected, Hester stands rigid in the sun porch, waiting. Stella interprets impatience. Hester retrieves her huge flour sack-style cloth bag from a chair, opens the door with care, closes it behind her, and gingerly navigates the stairs. Rain pelts. She bends to protect her face, even though she's attired in a bright yellow slicker which stretches almost to her ankles, and an over-sized sou'wester. She holds the brim against her cheek.

Stella leans across the seat to open the door. "Good morning, my friend. Not the nicest day to be out, eh?"

"Good morning, Stella." She climbs in, sitting rigid and square, with both feet planted together on the floor. She clutches her bag in her lap. Rain drips off the edges of her hat. Her coat emits a smell reminding Stella of tires at the garage. "I hope you are a cautious driver because I do not appreciate cars."

"Don't worry, Hester. I'm careful. What's in the satchel?"

"I have brought the tools necessary to do a complete search of Paulina's home." Hester examines her lap. "Are you not prepared?"

"Aiden always has gloves. What else do we need?"

Hester's mutter and expression of annoyance encourage Stella to pay closer attention to the road.

"I have my own gloves. I have a flashlight." She scowls at Stella once more. "The house will be dark because of the rain. I have plastic bags for evidence. I have my notebook to document what I see and find. I am very thorough, Stella. Was my compulsivity not the reason you asked for my help? Did my evidence collected over the years regarding the deaths of my parents not prove pivotal?"

"To be sure. On both counts." In truth, she wanted Hester to accompany her to Paulina's in the hope Hester's mind might be jogged as to where Paulina hid her journal. A forensic investigation was not the goal. "Aiden and I need to find Paulina's journal. We assume, once we're inside, you'll remember her hiding place. You have an excellent memory." Her attempt at flattery may be unnecessary.

Hester pauses for a moment. "I do, but a person cannot recall an occurrence they did not experience. I did not see Paulina hide her diary. Do not expect I did."

Slightly deflated and firmly put in her place, Stella navigates the Jeep toward Yellow House on Main Street. Aiden's sedan is parked out front. She pulls into the yard behind Paulina's Buick.

Her passenger climbs down as soon as they're stopped, and takes a position beside the vehicle, standing rigid like a guard at Buckingham Palace.

"Good morning, Detective North. The weather is unpleasant, but I expect our inspection will prove fruitful."

Stella purses her lips at Hester's formality. She makes eye contact with Aiden behind Hester's back. The morning should prove interesting.

The three of them climb the steps to the rear deck and enter through the porch, thanks to Aiden's key. After removing their raincoats, they proceed as a group to the kitchen. Aiden turns on lights as they crowd into the main portion of the addition. "Let's talk before we go any further, shall we?"

He offers Hester gloves which she declines while she hauls a pair of her own out of the flour sack. Stella struggles into hers. Surgical issue fingerprint concealers are uncomfortable for her longer fingers and what she considers her ham-sized hands.

"I'll start with the library shelves downstairs. I don't expect to find her diary, but I want to open every book in the house this time through." He turns to Hester. "You said she returned the journal to a spot upstairs, but you never saw where."

Hester nods. Her face is devoid of any expression.

"You two go upstairs and search every closet, drawer, and container you can find. Call me if you discover something or if you need my help."

"We'll work together since I've been through much of the furniture and closets before."

"Fine." He raises his eyebrows, "but go over the same spots. Forensics came up empty—again—so today is our very last opportunity before the house is released to the lawyers for good. They weren't too happy when I requested an extension." He turns toward the reading room at the front; the place where Paulina was killed. "Let's find her journal today."

Hester and Stella start with the built-in linen cupboard in the upstairs foyer.

"We must take each piece out, Stella. She may have wrapped her book in a towel."

"Good idea. I sort of rifled through the towels and sheets, but I didn't remove every item. I doubt forensics did either."

They methodically extract two dozen towels and six sets of sheets. They unfold and refold. There are extra bottles of shampoo, packages of toilet paper, and cleaning supplies. After the cupboard has been emptied, they replace the contents as they found them. There is no hidden book of any description.

"The furniture is almost all Eastlake and original." They stand on the oriental carpet at the foot of Paulina's bed.

She turns toward the younger woman. "Yes, it is. I didn't know you were interested in antiques."

Hester provides Stella with an indulgent smile. She scrapes a strand of long hair behind her ear. "I am studying period furniture because we have many pieces in our house. They might be valuable. Aunt Del says they came from her parents; my grandparents."

"Well, let's do a search of Paulina's personal items. Closet?" She opens the hinged door to reveal a generous space where Paulina's stylish clothes are hung with care. There are two hat boxes on the shelf above the hangers, and shoes on the floor. "I opened the boxes before and all I found were hats, Hester."

"Hat boxes were often made with false bottoms which enabled an owner to hide their jewellery. We should check them again."

"Another valuable piece of trivia." She pats her friend on the shoulder. "You are an absolute mine of information, which is precisely why I wanted your help."

Hester makes an almost imperceptible move to withdraw from Stella's touch.

The hat boxes prove to be merely hat boxes. Stella smothers her disappointment with a search of the dresser. They pull open each drawer, set it on the bed, sift through the contents, and check both inside and out for hidden spots. Again, they come up empty-handed. Nightstands flank the bed. Each is walnut with a single drawer and splayed legs which frame the shelf below. The lower tier is decorated with a fence-like spool design. The result resembles an upturned basket. They are very ornate and, she expects, rare.

Hester pulls open the drawer of the table closest to the side where they suspect Paulina slept. The telephone extension is on top. Despite her sophisticated and eclectic selections in the store and library downstairs, Stella can make out a copy of *Scruples* by Judith Krantz inside. Paulina liked to read best sellers the same as everybody else. She places the drawer gently on the bed and removes the other contents including hand cream and lubricant, before she examines the bottom. In the end, neither this drawer nor the one on the other side yield their owner's secrets.

Conflicted, Stella sits in the tub-shaped armchair positioned between the two corner windows. "We've examined every inch of this room." She isn't sure if she is discouraged or relieved after this breach of Paulina's privacy.

"I will check the pockets of her clothes."

"You saw her journal." A distinct lack of enthusiasm colours Stella's voice. "You already know a book won't fit in any of her pockets."

"To be sure, but we can report to Aiden we explored everywhere. We'll search the other rooms, too."

Stella sits in the uncomfortable chair and watches Hester dig into each coat, pair of trousers, and dress where pockets exist. The longer she sits, the more frustrated she becomes. In exasperation, she stands and turns to stare at the green brocade piece of furniture. She's annoyed. First, its more modern style doesn't fit in the bedroom, and second, the construction is poor. A pile of bricks might be more comfortable.

"Hester. Look."

"What?"

"Please come help me with the chair cushion."

The girl scuttles over while Stella pulls the cushion out and places the flat side down; the curved side with the zipper facing the top. She holds the slider with her thumb and index finger. The sound of their breathing and the grinding of the zipper's teeth fill the space between them as she exposes the stuffing. Her arm senses the prickliness of the fibers when she reaches inside. The leather spine is soft. With one tug, Paulina's journal is exposed.

Without a word, she opens the book to its middle. Every line is composed of random numbers.

"Aiden!"

"On my way." He clomps up the stairs. "Where are you?"

"In here." He appears at the entrance to the master bedroom. She keeps turning the pages of the diary.

Hester takes a step back. "We should have found her secret place sooner." Her voice is flat.

Stella turns toward her. "Did you and Paulina write in code?"

"Yes. She taught me cryptography." Hester throws her hands up in the air. "I've given you that information before. I told you not to be surprised if her journal was encrypted because a family member in the war was a cryptographer and she liked secrets."

Stella passes her find to Hester. "Did she share her code?"

"Absolutely not. No one gives their code away. We will need to decipher it."

"May I see?" Aiden reaches for the leather-bound volume.

A faded blue ribbon, used to wrap it closed, has fallen to the floor. Hester bends to retrieve it.

He holds the book with one hand and digs for a plastic bag in his suit jacket pocket with the other. He ignores Hester's offer, preferring a police issue evidence bag to one he likely assumes was recently used for frozen vegetables.

"I'll take her diary to the lab in Port Ephron. They'll decipher or decode or whatever. I saw code books downstairs in her library. I suspect she used one of them."

"I'm sure Paulina's code is not founded on the idea of another cryptographer, Detective North. To decipher her code, one must be familiar with her on a personal level. Stella and I could try."

"The diary can't stay here or go with either of you. Stella, do you want to transcribe a paragraph or two before we leave? You and Hester can try and see what you can do. We'll attempt to complete the deciphering at the office, but you can take a stab at it yourselves."

Stella doesn't argue.

They return to the kitchen where Stella sits at the table to write the first page of Paulina's musings into Hester's lined scribbler.

26.9 20.20 14.30.26.7.8 4.1.29, 34 27.30.32.34.3 9.33.34.8 35.4.10.7.3.26.1 26.8 26 12.4.2.26.3 12.33.4 3.30.11.30.7 27.30.1.34.30.11.30.29 8.33.30 28.4.10.1.29 31.34.3.29 1.4.11.30 26.32.26.34.3

33.30 12.34.1.1 27.30 2.14 1.26.8.9 1.4.11.30.7

26.1.9.33.4.10.32.33 33.30 34.8 2.26.7.7.34.30.29, 34 28.26.3.3.4.9 26.27.34.29.30 9.33.30 9.33.4.10.32.33.9 4.31 1.34.31.30 12.34.9.33.4.10.9 33.34.2

29.30.8.5.34.9.30 9.33.30 3.30.28.30.8.8.26.7.14 30.3.32.26.32.30.2.30.3.9 4.31 2.14 30.8.28.26.5.30 29.4.4.7, 33.30 34.8 2.14 33.26.5.5.34.3.30.8.8

4.10.7 8.30.28.7.30.9 34.8 2.14 1.34.32.33.9

****

Hester chomps away on her salad. They are settled at Cocoa and Café for the promised lunch. She makes little rabbit sounds while she munches on crisp lettuce. "Paulina likely used a substitution code. We need to figure out her key."

"You mean 1 is A and 2 is B?"

She dabs her lips with a napkin. "The ordered substitution you have described is too simple. Besides, I read over your shoulder and 1 is definitely not A." She crunches for another moment. "Although 26 or 34 might work."

"Don't tell me you have Paulina's code figured out."

"No." Her expression is puzzled. "She employed a substitution, but I hope the code is orderly and not random. In a random substitution cipher, the discovery of the answer to one letter doesn't mean the others follow in a logical order."

Stella smothers a moan, daunted by the process. "Forensics will figure out the code before we do."

"E is the most used letter in the alphabet. We could find the number which recurs most often, and it might be E. Will we have dessert?"

"The menu board says brown sugar cake with hot maple sauce. Are you up for dessert?"

They order and wait in companionable silence. "I hope Paulina used numbers but without folds."

"Folds?"

"Yes. Paulina could have written her diary entry on a piece of paper folded like a fan and opened the fan to create a whole different message. If she transcribed her writing back to a flat piece of paper, it will be extremely hard to find out what the actual message is."

Stella sighs. The complexity of the task overwhelms her. "We'll work with what we have. You mentioned her key?"

"A key is the code to decipher the message. She may have assigned each letter of the alphabet a different number. If such is the case, we will need a twenty-six-part key. If she has assigned one specific letter to be a number which has some significance to her, and the other ones follow in order, we're home free once we figure out the one number and letter reference—her personal key. I sincerely hope she followed an order. Paulina was not given to randomness." She drops her spoon into the empty bowl with a flourish. "Are you any good with anagrams? Some codes use anagrams."

"My God, Hester." Stella is exhausted and confused by the options. "We may never learn Paulina's secrets."

"Oh, we'll figure them out. Maybe you can come to my house after the weekend and we can work together. I'd very much appreciate a drive home now. The morning has been long."

After she pays the bill, Stella delivers Hester back to the farm. The rain has stopped. Jewel must have heard the Jeep because she's waiting in the porch with Kenny on her hip.

Stella doesn't stay.

****

"I'm back." She struggles out of her raincoat. Alice appears from reception with Kiki under her arm. "Did lunch go okay? Everybody find a bite to eat while I was gone?"

"The egg salad you made was great. There's been more check-ins than I expected—three groups with no reservations. One bunch with three trailers, another with two motor homes, and a couple with a pop-up."

Stella's eyes narrow as she tries to remember the reservation list.

"Don't worry. We made room. Duke took off around the park to see if everyone's settled in—the reason I have the pest with me." She gives Kiki a squeeze.

"This is new. Duke used to be the pest," she teases Alice, as she trudges toward the kitchen in search of tea.

"Duke has changed. I can't put my finger on why, but he's more respectful. Maybe the visit to see his mother made a difference."

"I've seen a change as well. He was considered a suspect in Lorraine's murder because of his smart mouth and disrespectful attitude toward women. The experience affected him."

Despite Kiki's objections, Alice places the dog on the floor and reaches for the kettle. "I'll make tea. You look beat."

"My brain hurts. I've been with Aiden and Hester the whole morning." She avoids additional details of the active investigation.

Alice smirks. "No explanation needed."

CHAPTER 7

Obsessing and Ruminating

"Are you okay? When you're quiet, I worry."

A warm breeze makes the cotton curtains dance and fresh air fans the room—a moment of indulgence on this bright June morning. Nick often sleeps with the sheet pulled up to his chin, cocooned. She wraps one arm across the bedclothes and rests her hand on his shoulder. "I'm fine. Obsessing and ruminating, I suppose." She snuggles closer. "Although there's no rule book, Aiden suggests recovery is complicated after a person finds a friend dead by a gunshot wound." Her tone is facetious. She refuses to accept she's traumatized. It's a month today.

"We can talk whenever you want." His voice is soft. He's made his point.

"We were busy over the weekend." Deflection. "I expect Hester's figured out the cipher by now."

"Any ideas on the purpose of the secret door you and Aiden discovered? I wonder if Paulina was involved in the installation."

"It was part of the addition Leon helped her build. Not sure if it was her idea, or his. She told me once, when we had lunch together, how he encouraged the renovation. She wanted to create a sitting room for her private use upstairs, but he was nervous when he imagined the number of trips she would make to the main floor during the season. Maybe he wanted a convenient way in and out to avoid gossip. I wonder who the contractor was."

"Their affair wasn't clandestine. The sisters were aware of their father and Paulina. In the end, their relationship was the reason Leon died." He pauses to meet her eyes. "Opal couldn't tolerate the time Hester spent with Paulina."

"I understand, but none of those facts explain the door." Stella sits.

"Give Borden Fisher a call. He might know who built the addition. It wouldn't hurt to ask." His eyes twinkle.

Voices rumble below them. "Alice and Paul are here early." She leans across his body to kiss a stubbled cheek. "Sometimes, devoted staff are a nuisance—always at work ahead of schedule. I could stay here in our warm, gushy bed with you for the entire morning."

He wraps both tanned arms around her waist. "They'll wait," he mumbles into her neck.

As she makes her way into the kitchen, late and flushed, she wonders if Alice will notice.

"Nice to see someone enjoyed a wee romp." Duke has made himself at home. He sips his coffee and munches on toast smothered in Painter farm homemade strawberry jam, as she examines the contents of the near-empty carafe. Kiki, in a pink T-shirt which says "Girly-Girl" in sparkles, waits for crust tidbits.

Stella tries to hide her burning face with a sudden focus on the cupboards.

"Good morning! I expected you were on your way." Alice's neon orange camp shirt clashes unmercifully with her red curls, tied in a ponytail.

"Hi. Nick and I were delayed. We discussed Paulina and lost track of the time." Not entirely false. "Quiet?"

"The same as every Monday in June. Once school's over for the year, they won't be eager to check out on Sunday."

Although the bottom of the pot, Alice's brew tastes good. Stella makes fresh for Nick. "Where's Paul?"

"He decided to mow. Eve is over in the bathrooms. Paul said Nick has a few items on his work list, but he wanted to wait for instructions."

"Paul said he could wait?" Nick rounds the corner, fresh and pink from his shower.

She senses a flutter. Happens every time. She assumed she was past the heart flips. Guess not. "Coffee's almost ready, and no, you missed the part where Paul is attending to the grass. He said he'd wait for you before he tackled any of the other chores."

Nick nods and makes a beeline for the caffeine.

Duke stands. "I'll take a tour around and survey the vacated campsites. We found no problems yesterday, but I'll do a run to be sure. Alice, do you mind?" He waves Kiki in the air like a sacrificial lamb. Her shirt sparkles in a beam of sunshine poking through the kitchen window.

"No problem, Duke." She reaches for the Pomeranian, whose tiny feet spin in vain for traction.

Once Duke takes off, Stella sits with Alice and Nick. They eat breakfast and discuss the day. "I have the writers retreat meeting at the community hall. Alice, will you prepare a list of reservations we already have and what's still available? The organizers want to make sure anyone who travels here from away understands how tough the search for accommodations can be on short notice."

Alice, always efficient and often one step ahead, jumps up from the kitchen chair while Kiki remains pinned under her arm. "I made a list. The conference, or retreat or whatever, is September 24 to 27. We aren't busy in late September. There'll be plenty of room. Someone named Frances Ellis booked the cottage. Give me a sec."

After she leaves, Nick leans over to kiss Stella full on the lips. "Although I've had a grand start to my day, I need to go to work now," he whispers. His chair scrapes across the Lino when he stands.

Returning to the kitchen, Kiki and her list in hand, Alice mouths in Stella's ear, "He doesn't need to whisper on my account," as Nick disappears around the door frame.

****

The Shale Harbour Community Hall and Playhouse sits with stately pride halfway along Main Street. Once a Presbyterian Church, the building was converted and renovated from top-to-bottom years ago. The town is supportive, with fundraisers and entertainment. Visitors travel long distances to attend a play or concert. They avail themselves of Shale Harbour's quaint amenities. Local businesses sponsor events—part of their collaborative effort for the benefit of the village.

Despite the positives, and the deep cranberry-red painted cement floor, Stella's walk along the basement corridor is eerie. The wall sconces are dim as she passes the public bathrooms, a storage room, and two offices. Four workshop rooms, each smaller than the space they are booked to use today, make up the remainder of the square footage on the lower level. Voices drift up the hallway. She's not the first to arrive. The conference room door is open and yellow light creates a triangular glow at the end of the span.

The space is crowded because the furniture consists of a long table and over-sized office chairs. A few years ago, Stephens and Stephens donated their board room furniture to the hall. Although the room is overwhelmed with the size of the pieces, no gift is ever refused. Stella sidles along the wall and settles on a chair at the end where she has an unobstructed view of the other participants. She acknowledges her fellow residents with a nod. Every one of them looks expectant, as if she's about to give them information about Paulina's murder.

Russ stands to lean over and pat her hand. "Glad you could come, Stella. Trixie told me you'd be here."

"Hi, Russ." His realtor training must encourage increased familiarity. "I imagined Meredith and Farley would be here to represent Grey Cottage Realty, since Farley is one of the instigators of this event."

"Oh, they'll be here. Cavelle said she'd mind the office." He swivels toward the door. "Here they come now." He purses his lips at Stella. "Better behave. The boss is here."

She finds his behaviour annoying. Charm spread peanut butter thick.

Meredith Tompkins floats into the room. She's dressed in a rich burgundy business suit. Her long dark hair is pulled back into what Stella considers a severe knot. Her neck and wrists are hung with heavy gold linked chains. Farley, by contrast, enters rumpled and distracted. He's in an expensive sports jacket, but the buttons are in the wrong holes. One side hangs lower than the other. He makes a desperate attempt to support a sheaf of papers as he wiggles behind the occupied seats on the other side of the table.

"Could you people move along two chairs, please? I need to sit nearer the head of the table. My role is pivotal in the organization of our event and I must be visible to everyone." Meredith exerts her perceived authority. "Farley will sit beside me."

Obedient as sheep, they lift bums and bump chairs to move as requested. Stella watches and waits for introductions. There are a couple of unfamiliar people seated at the table.

"Let's begin." Meredith taps her nails on the imitation wood grain. The group falls silent, and each attendee turns in her direction. "I imagine I'm the one person here who knows everyone. We'll go around our little circle and introduce ourselves, shall we? Russ, since you are with our company, you may start."

"Good afternoon. I'm Russ Harrison. I started to work for Grey Cottage

Realty a short time ago and will assist Meredith on the committee."

"Hi. I'm Andrew Blair." He taps the woman beside him on the arm. "And my wife, Tiffany. We own Cocoa and Café." He turns toward Meredith. "We created special menus and prices for the event. We hope to cater your lunches, if you decide on a more in-house arrangement."

Meredith glares. "We'll discuss contributions after introductions, Andrew."

Stella nods at them. They've crossed paths at the café often. She senses their embarrassment. No one needs to be humbled over enthusiasm.

"Most of you see me at the Harbour Hotel. I'm Pepper Ferguson and I work as a waitress, but the owner has asked me to represent her."

"You know my husband, Farley Tompkins. He and I imagined a retreat for writers in the first place." Meredith pats his hand.

Stella is struck by Farley's reticence. He didn't pull away from his wife, but her touch seemed unwanted.

"I'm Frances Ellis and this is my better half, Edward Thomas." She tilts her nose toward Edward. "We're writers from Port Ephron. We'll assist Meredith and Farley with the cultural side of the event, whereas they will use their expertise to manage logistics. Along with our talented son, Owen, we will avail ourselves of the hospitality at Shale Cliffs RV Park and stay in their rental cottage." She acknowledges Stella with a polite, yet indifferent, nod.

"And I'm Stella Kirk, owner of Shale Cliffs RV Park. We're happy to be a sponsor of what promises to be the first of many retreats."

Matt represents Parlour Antiques and introduces both himself and Mercedes.

Meredith taps her nails for a second time. "Now, Frances spoke of logistics. Let's go over the details. The retreat is scheduled for Thursday, September 24 to Sunday, September 27. Registration will be here in the hall from ten o'clock in the morning through until four in the afternoon on the first day. Volunteers are lined up to manage participants. They are very excited." Meredith turns to Frances. "Workshop leaders and writers will gather for a discussion panel in the evening. Correct?"

"We are excited, too. In addition to Edward and me, five additional authors will present classes, as well as take part in the panel." She gushes. "I'm thrilled these renowned writers consented to participate, since the event is in such a remote village."

"We are not without our conveniences, Frances." Meredith provides the writer with an expression of pure disdain. "Let's move along," she addresses the group. "Tell us your ideas, Andrew."

Andrew, obviously miffed because he was shut out earlier, turns to Tiffany. "Please share our plans, Tiff."

"Sure." Tiffany wiggles in her chair to sit closer to the table and opens her portfolio. "Special menus are already designed. The same offers will be available to the public. Our biggest question is if you want us to cater lunches on location. Prepared noon meals are easier. We can set up tables, charge a basic price, and people stay put." She pats her notes. "Any thoughts?"

Pepper steps in. "I expect participants would appreciate breaks. Given an opportunity to stroll around, they might prefer the hotel or a walk to the bar and grill on the wharf. We should encourage people to choose their own option."

The girl has spunk!

"I agree with Pepper. The best idea is to allow enough time for meals when we print the schedule of events. People can wander our cute little community as they see fit, perhaps leaving some cash behind in the process. Now," Meredith straightens in her chair, "accommodations. Russ, you have prepared a report for us?"

Russ stands for the second time. "Grey Cottage Reality manages twelve cottages nearby. Half are booked for the time of the retreat. Our listings will be in the mailer which goes out to registrants in early August, in case people need additional information. You may forward your available spots to me by the end of the month to allow time for the printer."

"Pepper?" Meredith resumes.

"The hotel is occupied. Participants appreciate a location within walking distance. The weekend bus tour from the city has filled our facility to capacity for the three nights. Can you imagine a bus load of writers!" She covers perfect teeth with her hand when she laughs.

Farley glances at Frances and Edward, in an apparent show of camaraderie. "I can't imagine what you mean." Dust particles float in silence for a moment.

Stella pipes in. "As Frances mentioned, our cottage is taken. My staff reported several participants scheduled for the retreat weekend. They arrive on the Wednesday. We know they're attendees because Alice always asks. Registrants receive a special rate. People are delighted." She turns to Russ.

"Please add Shale Cliffs to the mailer, as we always have room for one more."

"Great! Now, what's the sponsorship status? We need money for tea and coffee, both morning and afternoon, as well as gift bag donations."

Meredith runs a tight meeting.

"I've arranged for the publisher of each of our latest books to provide copies for the gift bags." Frances claps her hands. "The other facilitators plan to contribute as well."

"I spoke to the manager at the Savings and Loan. Notebooks and pens will come from them." Russ' expression is smug.

Andrew will provide gift certificates for a dessert at the café.

Pepper glares before she offers tickets for a free beer in the hotel bar.

Matt Savioli reminds the group he and Mercedes are the people responsible for organization and management of the volunteers. They are overwhelmed with the response, given there's still almost four months to go.

The meeting lasts another fifteen minutes while they establish goals for the first week in July. Matt will use his position as volunteer coordinator to check in on everyone at that time. Happy to be done, Stella imagines tea at home.

Mercedes stops her in the corridor near the steep red cement stairs. Stella's fingers grip the handrail. "Any news about Paulina? Matt and I have been very impatient to talk with you. The police seem to be taking their time."

"I can't discuss an active investigation." She smiles to soften what she assumes will be a perceived rejection and begins her ascent.

"We saw you over at the house on Thursday with the Painter girl—the strange one."

"Hester isn't strange." Mercedes may have seen more of the activity at Yellow House than she's willing to admit.

"Oh, I'm sure she's fine. I wasn't aware you two investigated murders."

"She doesn't." Although not wanting to appear rude, Stella refuses to reveal details related to her own arrangement with the RCMP and Aiden in particular. The minute she reaches the upper foyer, she attempts to make her escape. "See you later. I'm off to the park. We seem to be busy for early in the season."

"Stella! Time for a quick word?"

"Russ, aren't you needed at the office?"

"Can I talk to you for a minute? Grey Cottage received a request today."

"How does a request relate to me?"

"The cops gave Stephens and Stephens the keys to Paulina McAdams' house. They came to us and asked if we could recommend somebody who might be interested in management and oversight. They don't want to liquidate until they've exhausted all options related to family." He leans closer than Stella finds comfortable. "Since no will was found, the Public Trustee is involved now. They want a caretaker to live in and manage the business. The person can run the bookstore to make a few bucks and open the library to children and parents if there's a need. The focus is occupation of the premises."

Stella is surprised and afraid of the answer he will provide if she asks the obvious. "Did you recommend Trixie?"

"Good God, no! Trixie has no interest in books."

She ponders her sister's response to Russ' assessment.

"I thought about Brigette. She needs to do more than mind Mia...and live off Trixie," he adds, creating a conspiratorial effect with his posture.

Her tone is flat. "Do you plan to share your idea with the women in your life?"

"Tonight, at supper. Trixie invited me over after work. Brigitte will be home, too. I wanted to run my thoughts past you first. The lawyers said they wouldn't approach anyone else until I get back to them."

Stella ponders Russ' idea. The opportunity might be exciting for Brigitte if there's no chance they would sell the place out from under her. Trixie, nevertheless, has waited without a great deal of patience for Russ to ask her to move in with him. Perhaps he wants to see Brigitte squared away before he suggests a change. He's no doubt reluctant to share his house with a young mother and her little girl underfoot.

"Russ, talk to Trixie and Brigitte." This might be a leg up for her niece to gain more independence. Trixie always wanted to make sure her daughter was given every opportunity possible to stay home and care for her child. Her sister's goal would be fulfilled without the need for financial support, if the idea was accepted. She keeps her thoughts to herself. "Brigitte may have qualms about living alone in a house with her little girl after Paulina was shot in the front room. I can't imagine her response."

Trixie's boyfriend shuffles along beside her. "I'll catch up," he hollers across the street toward Meredith who is halfway back to her office. Farley stayed behind to visit with Frances and Edward. "I plan to talk to them tonight."

She opens the door of the Jeep. "Good luck. Gotta go."

On her drive home, her mind drifts to Trixie and Russ. He didn't indicate he's ready for the next step. Trixie has had her "next step" boots on for months. She hopes her sister doesn't burst into flames when she realizes Russ supports the idea that Brigitte should move out and take over Paulina's business, but makes no mention of Trixie's immediate move to his place. She will no doubt assume her days at the rundown rental are numbered and Stella expects she's dead wrong.

CHAPTER 8

Not My Story to Tell

Her first chore of the day is to telephone Borden Fisher. He may know who built Paulina's addition. The origins of Paulina's secret door might turn into a tidbit of information, important to Brigitte if she takes up residency.

The phone rings before she picks up the receiver to dial. "May we talk a minute?"

Trixie's voice is breathless.

"Yes, but today will be busy, Trixie. I wanted to spend the afternoon with Hester, but I'm forced to wait until tomorrow because Alice needs to leave early this afternoon." The staff work seven-day weeks all summer. She feels obliged to grant time off if it's requested.

"Can you meet me for lunch? I'm off and in dire need of a second opinion."

"Since when was I ever your second opinion?" Stella chortles at her own joke, but the truth lies underneath. They have never been close. "What's the problem?"

"No surprise." Her voice is harsh and tinged with accusation—the real Trixie. "Russ said last night he told you Stephens and Stephens need a resident manager for Yellow House, and he wants to recommend Brigitte."

Stella attempts to pacify. "Has he talked to your daughter? What does she say?"

"Brigitte is thrilled. What did you expect? Why didn't you tell me?"

"Not my story to tell. Listen, early lunch at Cocoa and Café—my treat?" She qualifies her invitation since her sister is a notorious late arrival. "I have to get back to cover my front office."

Trixie's sigh withers into Stella's ear. "Okay, I guess. We can meet at eleven. Brigitte expects to go to the law office after Russ talks to them, so

65

I'll be babysitting Mia anyway."

"Cocoa and Café it is. Now, I need to run—calls to make and people to see."

After the conversation with her sister, Stella is sure she was correct in her assumption that Russ will not ask Trixie to move in with him. Her sister is scared she'll be alone at the rental. A sudden flash of insight skitters across her mind. *Could Russ be interested in Brigitte, and her move will serve as his opportunity to separate them for his own convenience? Stop, Stella. You imagine the worst in people.*

"Fisher's Contracting. How may I help you?"

She hopes to catch Borden before he's left for a job site. She makes her voice sound as upbeat as possible. "Hi, Mrs. Fisher. Stella Kirk here. Has Borden gone off yet, or is he still at home?"

"Oh yes. He's in his office on the other line. Hold on."

"Borden Fisher here." If a voice can be gruff but kind simultaneously, this is Borden Fisher.

"Hi, Borden. This is Stella Kirk." She attempts to maintain her cheerful tone. "You and my park manager, Nick Cochran, are acquainted."

"We are. Good mornin' to ya, Stella. What can I do ya for today? I don't expect you want to be addin' on to your big old monster house out at Shale Cliffs." His chuckle rumbles.

"No, but I need some information and want to ask an historical question. Are you able to tell me who built the addition on Yellow House?"

"Why yes, as a matter of fact. My father, and me as his helper at the time, worked with Leon Painter on the place. The renderings were complicated, and he decided my old man was the fella for the job."

Stella's breath comes in short gasps. She may discover answers sooner than she imagined possible. "Are you aware of the secret door in the pantry, Borden?"

"You betcha."

He stops. Stella isn't clear if he expects her to ask another question. She hears him cough.

"I don't imagine confidentiality matters anymore. Jesus, Paulina's dead, Leon's dead, and Opal's in jail. What a mess, eh?"

"Yes, a mess for sure. What about the door?"

Borden clears his throat again. "Most people were never aware, but Leon

Painter was paranoid. In the end, he had good reason, but at the time he seemed crazy, at least to my father and me."

Stella tries to curb her impatience. "Was the purpose of the door for him to gain entrance without neighbours observing?"

The contractor emits a startling guffaw. "No, Stella. The door was for Paulina to escape. He said that if a person came into the house when she was open for business, and she was uncomfortable with the cut of their jib, she had the option to run around the corner, disappear into the pantry, and gain access to the outside. Paulina never argued. We built what he asked. He hired us."

Are there other details Borden is protecting? "When you said Leon had good reason to be paranoid, did you suspect the secret door was to protect Paulina from Opal?"

"Excellent question. I couldn't say for sure. Most of the people comin' into the Yellow House were, and are, mothers and toddlers, or customers searchin' for a book, for God's sake. Possibly he was jealous of another guy who kept showin' up and botherin' her. She never mentioned nuthin', though. I wonder now, what with the other murders, if he suspected Opal killed Velma. Maybe he worried for Paulina's safety if Opal came in unannounced."

Stella shudders as she recalls her own experience last winter when Opal appeared in her front room without warning. A secret door of her own might have been a welcome add-on.

"Dad or I never asked, as I recall. Leon said he wanted a quick escape for her, and we created one. The pantry idea was slick, especially with the fake outside tap. That was my idea, in case she ever needed access from the driveway."

He's still proud of the job. "Thank you for your help, Borden. Don't be surprised if Detective North wants to ask you the same questions, okay?"

"No problem. I gather Paulina didn't run to her secret door the night she died. I wonder why. Bye, now."

"Because she was familiar with her murderer and wasn't afraid," Stella mumbles into her cooled coffee before she prepares for a sojourn into town.

****

"I'll be back close to one o'clock," she assures Alice. "You'll find enough food in the fridge to make lunches for everyone if Nick can't come up from the machine shed early. I'll tell him where I'll be. Any errands I can do?"

"I need cash." She returns to the office.

"Don't we all," Stella replies to her back.

Alice presents Stella with a stack of twenty-dollar bills. "We need fives and tens, if you manage to spare a minute to run into the bank."

"No problem. See you later. Don't worry, you'll be clear of here in time to make your appointment." As a back-up, she adds, "Call Eve to come up if I'm delayed, and by the way, we'll plan to deliver Paul home at the end of his shift, so you don't have to come back."

She drives the Jeep as far as the machine shed. Nick told her the chain saw needed to be fixed before he could finish the tree trimming. The old Ford pickup is parked nearby. "Are you here?"

"If *you* means *me*, then yes." He emerges from the building's gloom, and wipes his hands on a raggedy tea towel, turned black many repair jobs ago.

"Don't poke fun at me, mister. I came to tell you I'm off to town for lunch with my sister and to do a bank errand for Alice. I'll be back in time for her to leave for her appointment."

"I'll go up to the house beforehand and help her in the kitchen, in case the front office is busy. What's the problem with Trixie?"

"She's in a dither because she expects Brigitte wants to accept the offer to take over and run Yellow House. Russ has engineered the position, but never added a suggestion that the time would be ideal for Trixie to move in with him. No doubt she's upset with the status quo. Same old story. I'll be back soon." She knows her diatribe makes the situation sound mundane, but Trixie's history with men is all too familiar.

She sticks her face out the window long enough to give him a quick smooch on proffered lips before she slips the Jeep into drive. "Oh, by the way, wait until I tell you what Borden Fisher said. I was shocked. Must be off. See you for tea." She pulls the vehicle around and toward the camp road. In the rear-view mirror, she doesn't miss Nick's quizzical expression.

❉❉❉❉

Stella spots Trixie seated at a bistro table in the back corner of the café. She normally prefers the front, where she can observe the patrons. Her eyes will dart around as she assesses various interactions and examines faces for recognition, as if she's trolling for men. Today, she holds her coffee cup and studies the brew inside.

Trixie is her opposite. Unlike Stella, she dresses to impress, even on an off day. Although attired in blue jeans and a white blouse, she is minus the chunky jewellery which always sets her apart from Stella, and almost everyone else. Basic flip flops adorn her feet. Stella can't remember a time when Trixie was in public without her high fashion boots, platforms, or stilettos, often paired with tight denims. The situation may be worse than she expected.

She sits as Trixie drags her eyes away from the cup long enough to look at her. "Why the sour face, old girl? I already said I'd buy you lunch." Her attempt at generosity falls flat.

Trixie produces a pained expression but doesn't acknowledge Stella's offer.

"You asked me to meet you, but you won't talk? What the hell, Trixie?"

"I spoke to Tiffany when I arrived and ordered chowder for both of us. She'll be over to find out what you want to drink in a minute." Her voice is monotone.

"Okay. Thanks, I guess." Stella studies Trixie's face for a sign of the issue. "You're not very animated today. Tell me the problem."

"Russ baffles me." She stares at the bottom of her now-empty cup. "He suggests Brigitte should run Yellow House. She's excited and scheduled to meet with Stephens and Stephens around three. Russ did not so much as mention he wants me to move to his place at the beach." Now, her voice trembles. "He must expect me to be happy alone in my dump of a rental house after Brigitte moves out. Did he want to impress Meredith Tompkins because he was the one who made the recommendation to the lawyers?" She leans over the table and whispers, "What about me, Stella? What about me?"

Stella is unsure what to say. Soups and coffee are delivered. She does what she often does. She asks another question. "Did you discuss your concerns with Cavelle? Can she shed any light?"

"Cavelle is under the impression Russ is not enamoured by children." Her bottom lip trembles. "Besides, she's positive Meredith has the hots for him."

"I'm doubtful Meredith is the problem, but it's fair he might not want to start a live-in relationship while a daughter and granddaughter are underfoot. That said, he appeared to want to recommend Brigitte for the job because he assessed her to be a good fit."

"Okay, okay, but Meredith calls him at least once every evening. Nevertheless, do you think his preference is to take our current arrangement to the next level after Brigitte is out of the picture? And this opportunity for Brigitte is convenient for him?"

"No idea, but what would be the consequences if you moved out to Russ' and left Brigitte in town without this Yellow House opportunity? Would you give her your vehicle? Would she stay at the rental and you pay? How do you think she'd manage, Trixie?"

"I guess I assumed she and Mia would be with me, regardless," she mumbles.

Stella tries to be the voice of reason. "This new set-up is ideal for your daughter. She earns free housing in exchange for management of the place. She'll generate her own income through the current resources, if what Russ explained is correct. Once she's settled, you and Russ can discuss your future." She pats Trixie's hand. She can't remember the need to console before. "And I am positive Meredith is not a threat." She wiggles her index finger toward Tiffany for the bill. "After a quick bank visit, I need to hurry home to cover off Alice's shift. Let me know what happens."

Trixie's expression suggests she's unconvinced.

****

Back at the park, despite working reception, Stella decides to call Aiden.

"Port Ephron RCMP Detachment."

"Hi. Stella Kirk calling for Detective North.

"One moment."

She waits. The line crackles. "Hi, Stella. What's up? I wanted to talk to you today, anyway, because the autopsy report was released."

"What autopsy report? The cause of death is no secret."

"True, but there's the matter of protocol. First off, she was killed by a nine-millimetre handgun, not a weapon the normal guy next door would own. A curious detail was uncovered. Did Paulina ever mention a pregnancy or a child?"

"A child? No! Did she have a baby? Are they sure?" She tries not to sound flustered, but she is.

Aiden's voice is calm and contained. "The report says she has a Caesarean scar and further examination revealed what they determined to be a full-term birth, years ago."

"Stephens and Stephens claim they can't find any relatives, Aiden. Did she put her child up for adoption?"

"No information. She didn't give birth anywhere near here. The surgery wasn't a hack-job. Forensics report the Caesarean was professional. We gave any details ascertained to the lawyers. Although minimal, this is now the basis in their search for relations. Perhaps Stephens and Stephens will turn up more leads."

"Paulina keeps surprising me."

"Was there a specific reason you called?"

"Oh, yes. I spoke with Borden Fisher earlier. The call was to find out who built Paulina's addition. The contractor was his father with him as a helper. They created the secret door, but our concept was backwards."

"Backwards? What do you mean?"

"Leon wanted Paulina to have a secret way out of the house in case someone came in to harm her. Borden said Leon was paranoid. Since the information regarding Opal is now public, he wondered out loud if Leon suspected Opal in Velma's death and sought ways to protect Paulina."

"I understand the idea of an escape door, instead of chancing a run out the back only to be caught on the deck, but the rest of Borden's idea is pure speculation. Besides, the door didn't help her the night she died.

"She recognized her attacker and admitted the person into her home. There's no other possibility."

"You're probably right. She was prepared for a personal visitor, and the secret door was locked. Whoever killed her gained access by simply arriving at the front."

"Agreed, but where do we go from here?"

"Have you worked with Hester on the journal code yet?"

"Tomorrow. We'll start with the portion I wrote out by hand. If we need more, I'll ask. I'll not be surprised if she's cracked the cipher by now."

"We can hope. Good luck. My people are no further ahead."

She hangs up the phone as Nick arrives. "Quiet here today. Are you ready for tea?"

"Yes. As usual, the minute I hold a cup in my hand, a camper will turn up, but let's visit while the place is quiet. Where are Paul and Eve?"

"I left them in the women's showers, painting." He translates her expression. "Don't worry. We put a sign up. They'll be done in another hour and the paint will be dry by tomorrow. We'll lock the door and leave the sign."

They wander from the office to the kitchen. Trixie worries her, and the slow progression of Paulina's murder investigation is troubling. "May I ask a question?"

"Anything."

"From a male perspective, would Russ support an opportunity for Brigitte to move to a place of her own because he wants Trixie to live with him at his cottage, but he doesn't want her family along?"

"Yes and no."

"You're helpful."

"Tell me the details."

Stella relays her conversation with Russ from the day before.

He nods. "Russ *may* observe potential in Brigitte that Trixie doesn't. He might want her out of the picture, true, but a gig at Yellow House is not guaranteed to be permanent. Paulina's estate can't support her little business forever, even if Brigitte manages the place and makes her expenses. If they don't find any relatives, the property will be sold and the residual from the estate will go to the Public Trustee."

"And everyone appreciates the goal of lawyers is to send money to the government." Her sarcastic tone is drippy. "Russ might want to purchase Yellow House or be assigned the listing when the house eventually goes up for sale. The circumstances confuse me. And besides, related to the murder— and this is confidential—the autopsy shows evidence Paulina gave birth to a baby once upon a time."

He places steaming mugs of orange tea on the table. "She used to go to the States every winter. Maybe she had the child then."

"Possible. She's been involved with various men over the years, but Leon was a true love. I want to study her journal. I can sense the answers hidden inside."

"How has Hester done with the piece you transcribed?"

"She hasn't called. She hates the phone, but I'm sure I would receive a call from either Jewel or herself if she unraveled any encryption. We're scheduled to spend the better part of the day together tomorrow." She drains her tea. "They're going to feed me, too."

"What? On our own again?"

"Don't worry. The freezer is full of muffins and cinnamon buns from the café." She turns toward his chair. "Now give me a hug. I promised Alice I'd organize the reservations for the rest of the week. In turn, she and Paul will be in late tomorrow. Alice said she would pick up our groceries."

"Sometimes we need the whole village to run this park. Seriously Stella, with no end in sight regarding the investigation, I expect you'll be gone as much as you're here this summer."

"Couldn't manage without you." She meets his eyes. "Am I dumping?"

"No way, but I'm worried you're so busy you're off in all directions."

"I'm okay." She attempts to sound cavalier, but Paulina's death has affected her in more ways than she can count. "As for the length of the investigation, it's still hard to say. Progress is slow. The lawyers are completing most of the background work right now. We have a journal entry. Hester and I will tackle the puzzle tomorrow."

"Anybody got a Coke and a bag of chips? We're starving." Paul rounds the corner seconds after his question, Eve at his heels.

"No problem, you two. Check the fridge and the lower cupboard on the right. Eve, did you lock the door and put a sign up?"

"Yes, ma'am." She salutes. "Finished and pretty snappy if I do say so myself."

"If *we* say so *ourselves*. Don't pretend to Stella you're the only painter." He hands her a Coke and gives her shoulder a gentle punch.

CHAPTER 9

20.20 Cannot be a Word

"The English language has no two-letter words where both letters are the same." Hester expresses Stella's frustration. She arrived at the Painter farm at eight-thirty this morning. She and Hester have been sitting on Hester's bedroom floor ever since. Scrap paper and code possibilities surround them.

"20.20 cannot be a word." She slaps her cheek in annoyance.

Stella listens to Hester emit little growls as her aggravation escalates in the face of their dilemma. She tries to keep calm, afraid Hester will lose interest and refuse to help. The girl thrives on both success and control. "Let's review what we've determined already, Hester. The letter A could be 26 or 34. The letter I will be the other one. The alphabet has twenty-six letters, but the numbers go up to thirty-five. And no, 20.20 can't be a word."

"Paulina was very smart. She could have created a code within a code."

"Explain, please." Stella leans forward against her leg, now tingling and numb. "I hope this doesn't make our task more complicated."

"If Paulina dropped the last letter of one word and added it to the front of the next word, she created a code within a code." Hester smirks. "The numbers are letters as well. *The brown dog* becomes *th ebrow ndo,* after which the creator of the code can transpose the letters to numbers."

"Are you serious? Why bother with a more complicated cipher?"

Hester's eyes remain fixed on the transcribed sheet Stella first copied from the journal. "I told you Paulina liked codes."

A soft tap distracts them. Jewel has gently pushed the door ajar. "Coffee, Stella? Hester, do you want a cup of tea?"

"Thank you, no. We are very busy."

"Don't be rude, Hester." Jewel hitches Kenny into a more secure position on her hip despite his constant wriggling. Kenny's chubby little arms reach for Angel, asleep on the floor beside Hester. "Stella might enjoy a hot drink."

The woman's patience is admiration-worthy. She and her husband, Ken, appear to have settled in to both the Painter farm and the routine. They moved into the bungalow originally meant for Jacob and Lucy. Ken helps Jacob as a farmhand and Jewel keeps both homes running smoothly. It helps to have someone with Hester. "I'd love coffee, Jewel. Hester, I have pins and needles in my legs. Can we please take our work downstairs to the dining room table? I prefer to sit on a chair and drink my coffee."

"If necessary. Do you require more exercise to manage occurrences of leg stiffness?"

Jewel grins at Stella. "She says what's on her mind."

"I know. She sounds like a brochure." Stella addresses Hester. "Exercise isn't what I need. I need a solution to Paulina's code. Come on, let's move." She plucks papers off the floor.

"Your coffee will be on the big table in a minute."

Stella runs her hand along Angel's silky back. The black cocker spaniel is one in a million; a beautiful and well-behaved dog, devoted to Hester. Angel never leaves her side.

They run down the stairs. Hester plunks herself on the seat in the bow window and fixates on the little house where Jewel, Ken, and Kenny now reside; where Lucy died when construction was at the basement stage.

After placing their minimal research on the dining room table, Stella picks up her coffee. The bitter smell is a welcome relief. She shuts her eyes for a moment to absorb the caffeine and try to increase her energy. "Come sit beside me, Hester. Let's go through the possible standalone As, or Is. There are three occasions—one 26 and two 34s. An additional sixteen 26s and nineteen 34s are inside other words. Am I correct?"

"Yes. I counted them yesterday," she mumbles into her knees, pulled up to her chest while she's curled into the window.

"Come on, Hester. Help me."

"I can't crack the code, Stella," she whines. "I can solve ciphers. I'm good at numbers and puzzles, but Paulina's journal is too hard."

Stick to the facts. Encourage her. "The difficult stuff is certainly more of a challenge." Stella picks up the sheet with the coded message. "I bet you remember every number in the transcription. I can't, but I'm ready to work on the mystery by myself if you won't help." She starts to write. One word contains two 26s and one 34. The word is 26.32.26.34.3. "I found a word which might turn into a clue. You look."

Hester climbs out of her corner and peers over Stella's shoulder. "Make the 26s into Is and the 34 into an A," she commands, taking charge.

Stella writes I.32.I.A.3.

"Try the opposite."

A.32.A.I.3

"Okay, now we'll review the alphabet. Start with IBIA, then ICIA, then IDIA, IEIA, IFIA, IGIA." They write and rhyme off every possible letter, but no word emerges.

"Shall we work on the other possibility?"

She drags a chair closer and sits.

"We begin with ABAI, ACAI, ADAI, AEAI, AFAI, AGAI, AHAI..."

Hester whispers her idea. "AGAIN is a word. AWAIT is also a word."

"What? If you're correct, then 32 is G or W and 3 is N or T. Let's reprint the message and fill in what we know." They decide in favour of the former letters because the word AWAIT at the end of a sentence doesn't ring true, whereas AGAIN could be appropriate.

"The valuations can be changed if we run into a wall—the second set is our back-up if this choice doesn't work."

Hester almost smiles.

Jewel calls them to the kitchen. Hester objects but Stella coaxes her to take a break and join her family. Jewel has assembled sandwiches made from left over baked ham, homemade bread and butter pickles, sharp cheddar cheese, and apple tarts. The scent of her baking has wafted around them since mid-morning.

"After lunch, we'll work on the word that contains an N, G, A, and another G."

"Okay, but if you want to leave to have your tea with Nick, we'll need to hurry."

Angel accompanies Hester out to the back yard. Ken and Jacob join them while Stella watches through the window. She's struck by the normalcy surrounding her. Despite the horrific history of loss and murder, they have chosen to move forward. She admires Jacob, in particular.

While she munches on her sandwich, Stella listens to the two men discuss the condition of the fields and seeding the remainder of the crops. Ken holds his son, so Jewel can grab a bite to eat. Although there's a playpen in the corner of the kitchen, Kenny is constantly on someone's knee or in their arms, unless he's asleep. When Ken rises from the table, he turns Kenny over to Hester. The little boy snuggles into her lap, gurgles contentment, and shuts his eyes.

Jewel whispers, "Let's hope he'll have a nap while I clean up. Lay him in his playpen when you go back to your figures."

Hester nods while she rubs Kenny's clenched fist with her thumb.

They struggle to progress in their search for a clear key to Paulina's code. "The answer has to be related to the word coded as 20.20," Stella hypothesizes. She has tried to view the transcript as a complete work; to examine each group of numbers holistically.

"A word with GAG in it is ENGAGE." Hester mumbles at her worksheet.

"ENGAGE? Paulina's word has ten letters, Hester. Do the Es work in the right spots?" She leans over to check the cipher for herself.

"Plus another 30."

"What are the variations of ENGAGE?" She wonders aloud. "Engaged, engaging, engagement. Ten letters! Does ENGAGEMENT work?" Stella can't contain her excitement.

"Yes." Hester turns to Stella. "Was Paulina engaged? I would be very surprised."

Stella prefers not to discuss speculative theories with Hester, so sticks to the facts. "What can we put together with Es as 30s, Ms as 2s, and Ts as 9s? We'll have a few words we can work with until I come back on Friday. You take 2.26.7.7.34.30.29 and I'll take 29.30.8.5.34.9.30. The word 20.20 is still our problem. Once we determine the meaning of 20.20, I bet we'll be able to read the complete journal." She glances at her watch.

"I know you want to go home. Angel and I will walk you to your car." Hester stands, straightens her wool skirt, which is much too heavy for the weather today, and pats her leg for the dog to extricate herself from beneath the table.

"Let me run out to the kitchen to say goodbye to Jewel."

Hester remains by the front door with her hands in her pockets.

As Stella returns along the hall, she is struck by the expression on her friend's face. Without a direct inquiry, she remarks, "Don't be disappointed. I'm convinced the code will emerge. We'll need a couple more days."

"An unknown person shot Paulina. Our work is not fast enough to find out who the murderer is. Detective North has lost interest. I, for one, still care for Paulina. He should be worried about a murderer on the loose."

Her impatience with the progress is palpable, and not unreasonable in Stella's opinion.

They've reached the Jeep. Stella leans against the door. "Everyone has concerns regarding the investigation. I know you're frustrated. I am, too. Paulina was very secretive. We can't determine what happened until we reveal those secrets." She reaches for the handle. "We'll figure out the puzzle. You work on your word. I told Jewel I'll be here on Friday, but not for lunch. Fridays are busy in the park." She touches Hester's shoulder. "If you break the code between now and then, call me."

Hester averts her face toward the sky.

"Fight your anxieties around the phone. You call...or have Jewel call."

"Okay." Her voice is soft, and the syllables scatter with the breeze.

****

The park is humming with activity as she rolls in the drive. It's three o'clock. Two cars pulling trailers and a motor home idle near reception. Alice is swamped. She hears the mowers. Eve and Paul are hard at work. The Ford is parked in the same spot as when she left. Nick must be in the vicinity. The golf cart is gone, which means Duke, and maybe Kiki, are out for a spin.

She enters the living room via the back veranda and makes her way straight to reception. The phone rings. She races to her office to answer. "Shale Cliffs RV Park. May I help you?"

"No, probably not, but can I cry on your shoulder for a minute?"

"What's up, Trixie?"

"Brigitte did the deal with Stephens and Stephens. She's scheduled to move into Yellow House tomorrow. Other than clothes and Mia's paraphernalia, she doesn't even need a spatula. One trip over to Port Ephron to pick up a big-girl bed for Mia and she's gone."

"Within walking distance, Trixie. She will live within walking distance." Stella is not accustomed to a needy sister. "Come for supper. I'm sure we can whip up chicken on the barbecue. Invite Russ."

"Russ is scheduled to show a house with Madame Meredith tonight." Her snide delivery does not go unnoticed.

"Don't be jealous, Trixie. You wanted him to stop travelling and be around. Now he is."

"I didn't know a job in real estate meant he'd spend both his days and his evenings with Meredith Tompkins."

"Might your observation be a slight exaggeration?" She doesn't expect an answer. When he materializes at the office door, she motions for Nick to sit.

"No. Three nights out of four, he's with her."

She ignores her sister's heavy sigh. "Come to the park and Nick will cook supper for us."

He raises his eyebrows.

"Shall I bring shrimp?" The quiver has gone from her voice.

"Certainly, you may contribute shrimp. Way better than chicken."

Nick widens his eyes.

"Now we have an enthusiastic response from the cook. See you after work, okay?"

The line clicks. "Management of Trixie Kirk is not my long suit."

He chuckles. "Time for tea?"

"Yes, but I want to check on Alice and make sure she's under control."

"She's fine. I already checked and told her a cup of tea will be delivered to reception. We can handle the phones for a while until the office slows to a dull roar."

As they meander toward the kitchen, she wraps her arm around his waist. "I have a few of your delicious buns in the freezer and we can whip up a salad for tonight."

"I'll make a marinade for the shrimp. Dessert might be an issue."

"Nope. Ice-cream. I'll make butterscotch sauce. Do we have beer?"

"My love, we always have beer."

She hoots her response just as the phone jangles again.

****

Trixie arrives straight from work. Nick relieves her of a generous bucket of shrimp and prepares them for his marinade. Stella pours her a beer and they wander outside. The evening has shaped up to be the perfect time to take advantage of the veranda.

After adjusting her tight denim dress, Trixie settles into a rattan chair.

"I assumed you'd prefer to help Brigitte." It's a statement. Trixie does not respond well to "why" questions. She instantly becomes defensive despite Stella's efforts.

"No need. One of the lawyers loaned her his truck. She'll pack tonight, and he'll help her unload in the morning. She wanted me to invite you for tea tomorrow afternoon."

"I'll make time. I expect to be busy here, though. I want to do a park tour. The seasonals are settled, now, but we have a few spots where campers are in for a week or more, and I should meet them. I'll do my ride-about in the morning and come into town later."

Trixie's voice quivers again. "Tonight will be Brigitte's last night with me."

"Which is why I expected you to be home instead of enjoying beer and shrimp with us."

"She wanted me to leave. Said I blubber too much, and she's right."

"Her move will be temporary, Trixie. If the law firm discovers relatives, Paulina's house will be turned over to them. If they don't locate anyone, the place will be sold, and the money raised will go to the Public Trustee. Either way, unless you can find the funds to buy Yellow House yourself, Brigitte won't be living there forever."

"Lots of circumstances could change, Stella. The lawyer who loaned her his vehicle likes her a lot."

"You want her to have a life of her own, don't you?"

Trixie's eyes glaze. Her makeup shows wear after a day's work. "I always imagined us together. I wanted Mia to grow up under my roof."

"But your goal is to live with Russ."

Trixie sounds conflicted. "A life with Russ shouldn't mean separation from Brigitte." She takes a huge gulp of beer. "And now, with Meredith in the picture, I expect I'll end up alone...again."

"Don't be foolish. She has Farley. Meredith is married, for God's sake."

"When did marriage ever stop anybody? Paulina's an example. She had a secret lover who was married—at least, she hinted he was."

"She never spelled out his marital status. Maybe she tried to make her romance sound intriguing because the reality was boring."

Nick interrupts. "Are you ready for me to cook?"

"I am. Trixie? Lemon garlic shrimp with Nick's homemade rolls, salad, pickles, and ice-cream with butterscotch sauce for dessert?"

"No need to watch my weight anymore. I'll eat whatever you put on the plate." She holds her glass out to Stella. "Any chance of another one of these?"

They visit for an hour. Trixie will not be consoled. She's sure Russ has dumped her but not said so yet. She fears Brigitte and Mia are lost to her forever. Her drama is theatrical. The conversation is exhausting.

Nick attempts a subject change. "Very busy at the plant?"

Trixie's response is puzzled, as if Nick has posed a question with an obvious answer. "Yes, we're always busy, except for a few months in the winter." She turns to Stella and ignores him in her abruptness. "Which reminds me, I wonder if Jewel and Ken Winslow want to stay at the Painters'? We need experienced workers. H.R. could do a callback."

"Human Resources better start to make inquiries elsewhere. Those two are as happy as clams at the Painter farm. I was over today. Stayed for lunch. They lucked out with their arrangement, thanks to you. Didn't you introduce them to Cavelle in the first place?"

"Yeah." She doesn't sound proud of herself.

When the phone bleats, Stella takes the opportunity to jump and run. She graces Nick with a wordless apology on the way to her office. "Shale Cliffs RV Park. How may I help you?"

"I think the nights are warm enough for Rosemary and me to move out. What do you think?" Aiden starts the conversation with no preamble.

"Hi, Aiden. Yes, the nights aren't cooling off too much. Tenters are returning and that's a good sign. Will you be here on the weekend?"

"Thought we might. Is the cottage rented?"

"Hold on while I go into reception and check the reservation book." She runs around her desk and into the front area where Alice works. She flips a page. "The first confirmed booking isn't until the second week of August. Do your sisters-in-law want to come out, too?"

"Yes. Rosemary's on the edge. They said they'd help while I'm involved in this investigation. I'll book the cottage for the weeks of the seventh and the fourteenth. Rosemary and I will arrive at the park Friday after work. I'll settle up with you then."

"Hester and I made progress on the decoding. We might have enough by next week to enable your staff to try again to fill in the blanks."

"Wow. I'm impressed. Can't wait to see what you have. The lawyers are moving forward. I hear Brigitte is contracted to manage Yellow House."

"She starts tomorrow. Another crisis for Trixie. Gotta run. Line 2 just lit up. Busy, busy. Talk later." She punches the flashing button. "Shale Cliffs RV Park...."

"My word is MARRIED, which means the 7 is R and the 29 is D. I will work on your word now. Bye."

"Hester, wait." The phone is dead. In a moment, the dial tone returns.

She hears noises in the kitchen when she rounds the corner. Nick is storing food and stacking dishes. "Where's Trixie? I was gone five minutes."

"Said to thank you for supper and tell you she needed to go back and help Brigitte."

Stella heaves her shoulders. "I told her I'd lend a hand, but she insisted they didn't need my help. Brigitte asked me to go over to Yellow House tomorrow afternoon. I'll offer again. In the meantime," she stands close to his back and wraps her arms around him, "are you interested in spending quality time together?"

He swivels to face her. "Whatever you desire, my lady." His voice is plushy.

"Hester decoded another word. Want to help me try to find more?"

Chapter 10

Curiosity and Concern Compete

She drags a pink plaid shirt over her sleeveless blouse. Nick and Paul plan to meet the septic truck and will be busy this morning. Nick left earlier dressed in what he describes as his poop pants, to prepare for the job of assistant on the pumper. Stella expects he's anxious for Paul to learn the ropes. Eve is scouring bathrooms. The ever-reliable Alice has checked the answering machine and is now returning calls. The poor girl has not been happy since she discovered the need for corrective lenses. Despite her maturity, Alice is convinced old people are the ones who must wear glasses. Duke is certain to turn up later and will expect to find his transportation parked behind the house—self-imposed pressure to start her rounds.

First stop is Mildred Fox. A new season and she never changes. Although not yet ten o'clock, Mildred's fire roars and a cup sits at her elbow. She's wrapped in a raggedy comforter Stella expects hasn't been introduced to a washing machine in years. Her 1956 Cardinal trailer, buffeted by the elements each winter, has become more dilapidated over time. Campers have complained about the appearance of her site in the past, but Stella knows Mildred does the best she can with her meager income. Maybe she'll suggest Nick assign Paul to help repair the old girl's deck this summer, if he has time.

"Hi, Mildred. What's new?" The golf cart purrs to a stop near her rickety stairs.

"Not much. Everyone survived another winter, even my rundown Cardinal." She glances toward her rig. "No leaks. Can you believe the place was dry?"

"Nick told me a celebration was in order when he helped to move you in, because the clean up was minimal."

"Don't know how many more seasons she'll last." She takes a sip of whatever is disguised in the dusty rose Melmac cup. "Don't know how many more I'll last, Stella."

"Are you not well?"

"If old age is a sickness, I'm dyin'. Other than bein' over eighty-five," she points her finger at Stella, "and I don't plan on tellin' you how much over, I'm in perfect health. Crazy, eh?"

"Important to take care of yourself. Anything you need?"

"A good man." The breeze fractures her cackles.

Stella waves while she manoeuvres the cart toward Mildred's neighbours. After a quick exchange with Rob and Sally Black—Rob still gives her the creeps although he has been on his best behaviour since Lorraine died—she moves along to Bob and Louise Stone. It looks as if no one's home, but the truck is parked nearby. As she alights, Louise materializes.

"Here, let me help." Stella rushes to clip the outside door to the wall of the rig. "I don't see a For Sale sign. Did you change your mind? How's Bob?"

Louise appears disheveled, an unusual circumstance for a woman who presents herself to the world as if she just finished filming a television commercial for makeup, hair spray, or a new brand of twenty-four-hour bra. She steps on to the deck and holds a finger to her lips as she motions Stella further away from the door. "Bob is not good, Stella. I'm to the point where I can't manage him alone. I have no choice but to leave for home soon."

Before Louise has an opportunity to elaborate, Stella interrupts. "Leave the unit for sale, Louise, and go if necessary. Trixie's boyfriend is a realtor and he'll manage the listing. We'll keep an eye on the place. You need to do what's best for you."

The older woman leans over and wraps her arms around Stella's shoulders. "You're the sweetest, but we sold this week."

Stella swallows her surprise. "Anyone we know?" She doesn't appreciate the lack of opportunity to screen a replacement seasonal. Perhaps the people who bought Louise and Bob's trailer will move it off the lot and out of Shale Cliffs.

Louise's face breaks into a smile for the first time. "Yes, which is why we never contacted you. Buddy McGarvey is the new owner as of the fifteenth, and we'll be off home to Alberta." She brushes her bangs away from her face. "After six years in a tent trailer, he buys ours because Bell will be more comfortable. Can you believe the guy?"

"Buddy and Bell are next on my list." She lowers her voice. "I'm happy for you, Louise, and sad for us. Everyone will miss you, but Bob's health needs to come first."

"To be honest, Stella, *my* health needs to come first. After the trip home, I plan to place Bob in a care facility. His behaviour issues are too much for me. Life in a confined space has magnified the problem."

Curiosity and concern compete, and Stella waits, but Louise doesn't elaborate.

"I'm okay. We'll be fine. I'll come to the office before I leave. We're paid up for the season and the rent for 1981 was part of Buddy's purchase. Alice won't have any extra paperwork."

As Stella returns to the vehicle, three details puzzle her. What are Bob's behaviour issues? Is Louise safe? What plan does Buddy have for his lot? At least he'll have more room to park his truck when he assumes Louise Stone's spot.

The aging bulldog waddles toward the golf cart. "Hi, Bell. You're a good dog." She ruffles the bulldog's ears. "I hear you and your human are moving to new digs. Aren't you the lucky mutt?"

"For sure, Stella." The tent trailer rocks when he steps out.

"I stopped by Louise and Bob's to check on them, and discovered you bought their rig and will move in next week. Congratulations."

"Do you want to know the scoop on this old bucket?"

"Good to keep the park apprised." Bell has flattened out beside Stella and placed a possessive paw on top of her sandaled foot. She bends to pat her once again. "At least you'll have room to park your truck."

"Yeah, you and me—we'll both be happy." He chuckles. "My brother's two boys want my old pop-up." He points over his shoulder at the rundown unit he's used for years. "I told them to call you. They'll pay me for the rest of the season and stay for the summer. I can't guarantee they'll camp here next year, though." He hitches up his black jeans and places a thumb in a belt loop either side of the zipper.

"No matter, Buddy. Make sure they touch base. Alice needs their information. Congratulations, again." She scratches Bell's ears one more time before she leaves. "You're comin' up in the world, Bell."

"Bell, here, she's a good influence." His guffaw follows her while she points the cart toward a pair of Class C motor homes parked in adjoining sites up the road.

A middle-aged man is perched on the picnic table with his feet on the bench seat. He has a baby on his knee and a toddler beside him. As she approaches, he climbs off with a child in each arm.

"Good morning. I'm Stella Kirk, the park owner. Are you pleased with your stay?"

He surveys the children. "Happy to make your acquaintance. Sorry, I can't shake hands. Jeremy Clyde. Meet two of my kids. The baby here's Millie, and Jessie's the squirmy one. He wants his freedom. Hey Denise, can you take Jessie?"

A young woman, likely in her mid-twenties, emerges from the closer unit. "She blushes when she reaches for the boy.

"Say hi, Denise. This lady is Stella. She owns the park."

"Hello." Denise returns inside with Jessie in tow.

"To answer your question, we love your campground. Both Roberta and Denise are happy on their first visit to Canada. We're from Arizona. Been on the road for a few weeks. Hope to stay through July, travellin' around but back here for a break before we start the trip home."

"The baby is sweet." Stella tries to comment although children, with Mia as the exception, are not her forté.

He glances at his charge. "Millie's the youngest and real easy. Roberta likes to walk the campground with Millie in her stroller."

"Your registration card documents five youngsters between the two RVs?"

"Right."

His expression challenges, compelling her not to ask too many more questions. She maintains her silence despite nosiness threatening to overwhelm her. "Enjoy your visit with us, Mr. Clyde. If you need assistance of any kind, or if you want to extend your stay, don't hesitate to come to the office."

Stella visits with other seasonals like Ted Metcalfe and his new friend, Lily Dunn, as well as two more groups of campers in trailers, a couple in a tent trailer, and then she stops at a tent where the registration card indicates four young women are together. Eve described them two days ago when she came to the house to help Alice. The four wear ankle-length cotton dresses with their arms concealed. They each cover long hair, which is tied in a tight bun, under a little white cap. They cook over an open fire and sleep in a relatively new tent.

She climbs off the cart and approaches. "Hi, I'm Stella Kirk, the park owner. Welcome."

They rise from their lawn chairs in unison and extend their hands. Stella shakes each one in turn. Martha, Sarah, Ann, and Ruth. They are from Didsbury, Alberta. They finished their high school studies in the spring. This is their adventure trip before they each get married. One girl moves to the grass and offers Stella her seat.

Despite the lateness of the hour and the fact she will not complete her rounds before her Yellow House visit, she sits.

Martha acts as the spokesperson. "We are Mennonites. We dress the way we do to set us apart from regular society and to show we're committed to our lifestyle and faith."

Stella has no idea what she means.

The others murmur agreement.

Continuing, Martha adds, "Under normal circumstances, and in our colony, we're advised to avoid conversations with people who don't dress in plain clothes as we do; people outside our culture."

Although Stella feels like she's stepped into a lecture, she responds, "Difficult on a road trip."

Nodding in unison, they resemble the crowd at a tennis match who watch the ball go back and forth across the net. "We have met many wonderful people on our journey. We'll be able to return to our lives in Alberta with a wealth of experience."

Stella spends forty minutes with the Mennonite women. She learns how they were home-schooled together by one of their mothers, how they each have favourite skills—gardening, cooking, or sewing. They giggle when Stella suggests none of them prefers to clean.

They'll be in the park for another week because they're comfortable and safe. High praise indeed.

****

After a midday break with her staff and Nick, she keeps her promise to Trixie and takes a run into town to see how Brigitte has progressed at Yellow House. In her mind, the shadow of Paulina's Buick remains although the car was removed last week. She pulls the Jeep into the now-empty driveway. Brigitte doesn't own a car and Trixie is at work. A sad pleasure engulfs her when she hears giggles flutter through the open windows. Yellow House is hosting a child's laughter, which was one of Paulina's life goals. She steps over familiar and twinkling sea glass at the foot of the first riser. Today will be different in countless ways.

"Aunt Stella! We're thrilled you came to visit."

Mia, now three, holds her mother's hand and stares up at Stella through movie star worthy eyelashes.

"And I am happy to be here." She squats to face Mia. "You look cute today, my 'bestest' great niece."

The little girl bares her teeth in what might be interpreted as a grin.

"She has decided not to talk today, Aunt Stella. Other times, I can't convince her to have a quiet moment. Come in. Come in."

A handwritten sign on the closed door to the reading room on the left indicates it is for employees only. Brigitte leads her through the living room and dining room, still set up as a children's library and a small bookstore, into the kitchen at the back of the house. "I won't be open to the public until Monday." She wiggles Mia's pudgy little hand in hers. "Baby girl and I need a few days to get settled and explore how Paulina managed her business."

Stella makes herself comfortable at the massive kitchen table. Paulina's spirit gathers in the smells, the knick-knacks, and the familiar comfortability. "I've spent many hours in this very spot with Paulina. We were good friends." Brigitte is aware, but Stella is wistful and needs to express her thoughts. "Have you made many changes?"

"No, Aunt Stella. I cleaned her personal possessions out of her bedroom and packed them away in the front library."

"Paulina used that particular space as a reading room for her customers."

Brigitte shrugs her shoulders. "I think I'll experience enough challenges as I try to encourage people to return to Yellow House. I can't imagine a display in the room where Paulina was shot would be good for business. Carter told me to leave the contents intact, in the event a family member turns up to receive the complete estate."

"Who is Carter?"

"Carter Stephens. He loaned me his truck and helped me move in. I signed a contract with them. Is Mom upset?"

"My honest opinion? If her need to resort to me is any indication, she is *very* upset. She told me you said she blubbered too much to be around you."

"Mom is dramatic. I'll have her over every day if she wants to come. She doesn't believe me. When she has boyfriend issues, her emotions fall on me to fix." Brigitte's tone is unusually sharp.

Stella stares at the empty wall. "Your assessment is valid." She can't pull her eyes away from the wall. "Brigitte, did you see a set of cake pans up over the stove when you moved in?"

"Yes. They were her initials. They disturbed me. I took them off and put them in the upper pantry with two others—both fives, but different sizes. If I'm still here in two years, I can make Mia a cake and use one of Paulina's pans."

"Good idea, Brigitte. Paulina told me her cake pans are old and rare. A man she was friends with gave her the initials and she found two number pans but lost interest when she couldn't find any more."

"Funny. Mom has a one, from my first birthday, but she said she never found a two, although she searched long and hard."

Stella's mind clicks into overdrive. *Paulina was fifty-five when she started her journal and spent time with Hester. Could the P or the M be a five?*

Brigitte encourages Mia to sit on her play blanket near the table. "Tea, Aunt Stella? You're as quiet as Mia. I told Mom I was concerned you wouldn't want to come here. Is it hard to visit me because of what happened?"

"Sorry, Brigitte. No, I'm fine—woolgathering. I'd love tea, and will you show me around?"

"Sure. Mia is in the larger of the two spare rooms. Carter helped me set up a new bed for her. He took me to Port Ephron to buy the piece from a lady who sold her children's stuff. We rearranged the furniture. Now, Mia's room can be special for her." She leans over and touches her daughter's wispy hair.

The clock races to three. As much as she loves to visit with her niece and grandniece, she's preoccupied—in a dither to determine if the cake pans might be vital clues into the key to Paulina's code.

****

By the time she arrives back at the park, she's convinced herself the cake pans are a wild goose chase. But—they might be their solution. Her meeting with Hester is tomorrow. Aiden and Rosemary will be in the park tomorrow night. He'll need to know the moment they discover the key. She'll call him from the Painter's farm if they succeed in a breakthrough. She gallops to her office, thoughts of business and supper erased from her brain.

The M is not a five, because AGAIN and ENGAGEMENT don't work. But if the M is a two, as they suspect, then the P becomes a five. When Nick meanders in and plops into a chair across from her, she drags her eyes away from the scraps of paper which now litter her blotter. "Good day?" She forces feigned interest. Her heart thumps. She rubs her sweaty hands. If P equals five, she's discovered the key.

"Not bad. I've put a chicken in the oven—a special dinner for tonight."

She's unable to read his face and finds the circumstance troubling. His words sound playful, but his eyes hold an untranslatable hesitation. Part of her mind remains focused on the key. "What's up? Do we have an issue? The septic truck arrived? I haven't been around much, but I did a tour earlier. Campers are settled in. I heard no complaints."

"The park is fine. All systems are chugging along the way we expect. Duke reports everybody is behaving."

"Did you meet the Clyde family when they checked in?"

"No, but Duke and Alice both made observations. Alice said she couldn't figure out if the kids are his or which woman is Jeremy Clyde's wife. They're each registered with the same last name. Duke said he figured the guy is married to both women."

"Their license plates say Arizona. Is polygamy legal in Arizona?" She shrugs. "Who knows? Do you care?" Her question is rhetorical. "I don't care. Now, since there is no crisis looming on the horizon, and I am poised to blow Paulina's secret code wide open, why the special dinner?"

"My parents called today."

Her heart stops. She knows her heart has stopped. "Will they still arrive in ten days?" Her voice sounds hushed, as if she's whispering to him at a funeral.

"Nope."

Relief spreads through her.

"Sunday. A week early. Dad said Sunday," he repeats. "He didn't give a time."

Sounds echo, like he's in the bottom of a well. She holds her breath long enough to register the words. Her fingers caress her notes while she drags her attention away from Paulina's journal. She'll work with Hester tomorrow and turn their information over to Aiden in the afternoon. She'll prepare to meet Nick's parents and stand by his decision, whatever it happens to be. If he pulls his investment, she'll go to the bank for help. Both commitment and fear clutter her thoughts. She meets his eyes. "We're a team, right? We'll be fine. How long do they plan to stay?"

"Dad said Shale Cliffs is their destination. He doesn't know when they'll leave. I guess their departure date depends on whether I'm cooperative." His expression is defeatist.

She tries to joke. "Well, if that's the case, maybe they'll only be around a short while."

"This isn't funny, Stella." She is duly reprimanded. "I talked with Alice. She rearranged reservations and put them in a site as far away from the house as she could find. Now their stay can be open-ended." His sheepish grin is no doubt designed to appease.

"I gather the chicken dinner is penance in advance?" Her attempt to be upbeat falls on emotionally deaf ears. Her capable, reliable, and determined Nick sits slumped before her resembling a boy in the office of the school principal.

He produces a grim smile. "You, my love, have not met them yet. You may well give me the boot after you have them in your company for an extended visit."

It unnerves her to see him this worked up and insecure over his parents. Yes, Nick's an only child, but surely to God he's able to stand up to them. She isn't overly enamoured by this version of Nick, who quakes at the thought of Tobias and Yona in the dooryard. "No chance the guy who cooks me a chicken dinner receives walking papers." She scoots around the desk long enough to assure him with a hug before he leaves.

If M is two and P is five, how can A be 26?

CHAPTER 11

Don't Even Ask

Hester has positioned herself like a sentry on the steps to the sun porch. Her lined jacket attests to the cool morning.

"Ready to begin, Hester?"

"You said early. I have waited since six-thirty. Eight-thirty is not early." Her tone condemns. Her brows are furrowed.

Stella ignores the mood. "Eight-thirty is early for me. We have until lunchtime." She taps Hester on the arm. "You and I will crack Paulina's journal code wide open today."

Setting aside her original admonishments, Hester tails Stella into the farmhouse and questions the statement. "Why are you sure?"

"I was over to Yellow House yesterday. Brigitte has moved in as a caretaker of sorts. Did you ever notice the cake pans with Paulina's initials on the kitchen wall?"

"Yes. I told her I wished there was an H so she could make me a cake." Hester's face crumples. "She used the P for my cake. She cut and rearranged the pieces to make an H. It was chocolate and not even my birthday."

"Paulina was kind, Hester. We were lucky she considered us her friends." Stella removes her coat as Jewel rounds the corner. "Where's Kenny?" Stella assumed Jewel kept him at her side constantly.

"Oh, he's in his highchair eating Cheerios—his favourite pastime these days. Hester assumed you two would work in the dining room again. I'll fetch a cup of coffee for you."

"Thanks." She notices Hester's frown. "I need a stimulant," she adds as a means of explanation.

They proceed toward the big table. Their previous notes are already spread out on the large surface.

"Did you ever see the cake pans in the top of the pantry—the two fives?"

"Yes. Paulina said she baked a cake for her birthday, because she was fifty-five last December. I told her she didn't act old, and she laughed."

Jewel interrupts for a moment with coffee for Stella, tea for Hester, and four homemade muffins on a green glass plate.

Stella meets Jewel's eyes. "Coffee is what I need, my dear. Thanks."

"Hester was up and ate her breakfast in the kitchen before I came in the door. She's hungry by now."

Hester pats her stomach, a habit she repeats when a favourite food is served. "They are banana with chocolate chips, Stella. If you have one, I will eat three and Jewel will be pleased."

"You don't want to disappoint Jewel—she's your excuse?"

"Try them. You'll understand."

Stella waves to Jewel, who returns to her chores. She reaches for a treat.

"I'm sure the fives are a clue." The muffins are yummy. She takes another bite and, with her mouth full says, "Here's my question. If the M is a two, and the P is a five, the other letters don't make sense. We decided A is twenty-six, but the cipher won't follow in order."

She watches as Hester writes the letters of the alphabet in a list on a long piece of paper. They start to add the values they assume are correct. In addition to the A, D is twenty-nine, E is thirty, G is thirty-two, I is thirty-four, M is two, N is three, P is five, R is seven, and T is nine. "Fill in the rest of the letters." She pants her directions.

"Here's our problem. If we assign numbers beyond the T, then U is ten, V is eleven, and Z becomes fifteen."

"The issue is we have assigned twenty-six to A," Stella agrees.

Hester's long and stringy hair is draped over the list. Stella, seated beside her, reaches out to lift the strands away from the paper.

"20.20 could be fifty-five, Stella, if numbers zero through nine are part of the code."

Anxiety and anticipation catch in her throat. "Okay, okay. List zero to nine and assign sixteen to twenty-five."

Hester scowls and argues. "We're wrong. 20.20 becomes forty-four and Paulina was fifty-five. If I start with one equals sixteen, then zero equals twenty-five and 20.20 becomes fifty-five." She leans back in the chair and stares at her figures. "The exercise has been difficult, but we may have solved the cipher." She sounds underwhelmed.

"You aren't very excited. Let's translate the excerpt and see if the words make sense."

They work for ten minutes.

At 55 years old, I begin this journal as a woman who never believed she could find love again.

He will be my last lover.

Although he is married, I cannot abide the thought of life without him.

Despite the necessary engagement of my escape door, he is my happiness.

Our secret is my light.

Stella and Hester read the introductory paragraph of Paulina's journal in silence. Remnants of banana muffins lay untouched. The sounds of Jewel, as she washes dishes and talks to her little boy, drift into the dining room. The ocean breeze taps the wavy glass in the old windowpanes.

"What do we do now?" Hester's voice is hushed.

"I'll call Aiden." Stella pushes her chair away from the table. "I told him we were on the verge of a breakthrough. He'll come over."

"More coffee? You made a mess of my muffins." Jewel emerges from the kitchen with the pot in one hand and Kenny on her hip.

"We solved the cipher, Jewel, but I figured the code out first."

Stella winks at Jewel. "You can't take all the credit, my friend. We're a team. Yes, I'd appreciate a warm-up, Jewel, and the muffins were—are scrumptious." She pops a morsel into her mouth. "On a more serious note," her voice softens, "the Painter clan is very lucky to have you here."

"Kenny and me—we're the lucky ones. Ken, too. The Painter farm is home now." She pats Hester on the shoulder. "Will you help me with lunch later?"

Hester nods while she examines her muffin. "Stella wants to use the phone. I am of no more use to her."

****

He took forever to answer when the call was transferred. "We solved the cipher."

"Where are you?"

"I'm at the farm. I planned to work with Hester until eleven-thirty, before going back to Shale Cliffs. The park will be busy by afternoon."

"Stay put. I'll drive out and be there in half an hour."

"We'll copy our code sheet while we wait."

"Okay."

The line goes dead before she has a chance to say goodbye.

She leaves the foyer and returns to the dining room. Hester has taken up her perch in the window seat. Her eyes are focused on the new house next door.

"Aiden asked us to write the code for him. His staff will go to work on Paulina's journal as soon as he returns. We may discover the identity of her boyfriend, and even who killed her, Hester."

"I don't want to make a list for strangers. We should be the ones to read her journal, not a bunch of people Paulina never knew." She snuggles further into the corner of the seat.

"You complained earlier in the week. You said Aiden and the police were too slow, and they weren't serious as far as Paulina's murder is concerned. Now, because of our help, the investigation will move forward in leaps and bounds—because of us. Because of you," she persuades. "Can't we create a copy of our list for Aiden?"

Hester returns to her chair and chooses a blank piece of paper. At the top, in capital letters, she titles the page with the precision of a calligrapher: "PAULINA MCADAMS' SECRET CODE." She lists the alphabet from A to Z in a column along the left-hand side of the page and adds the numbers. She begins with twenty-six. Beside the A, she draws a straight line parallel to the bottom of the page and writes twenty-six at the end. She repeats the process for the thirty-six elements which complete the code.

A—26, B—27, C—28, D—29, E—30, F—31, G—32, H—33, I—34, J—35, K—36, L—1, M—2, N—3, O—4, P—5, Q—6, R—7, S—8, T—9, U—10, V—11, W—12, X—13, Y—14, Z—15, 1—16, 2—17, 3—18, 4—19, 5—20, 6—21, 7—22, 8—23, 9—24, 0—25

Stella watches fascinated with the straightness of the lines connecting the letter or number on the left with the corresponding number on the right. "Hester? How do you draw such absolutely straight lines?"

"Can't everyone make a straight line on a piece of paper?" Her puzzled eyes meet Stella's.

"Let me show you." Stella picks up a pencil and writes an A and a twenty-six eight inches apart on the back of their previous worksheet. She connects the two with a line, which is crooked and wiggles in places.

Pointing her nose at the ceiling, Hester barks her response. "What you drew is not a straight line, Stella. Draw a straight line."

"Listen. What you see is the best I can do."

"Focus on the end. Don't watch what your pencil does, watch where you want to go. Here, let me show you." She grabs the pencil and draws a level and straight line from one side of the page to the other. "Okay. You try," she commands as she passes the pencil back to Stella.

Her attempt will no doubt be a lost cause, but she tries one more time. The result is marginally better.

Hester's yelp-like guffaw fills the room. Angel joins her master.

"Angel, hush." Jewel rounds the corner. "Why is she barking? Hester why are you howling?"

"Stella can't draw a straight line." Hester dabs at her teary eyes with the sleeve of her sweater. "She says this is the best she can do."

Jewel peers at the paper. "Her line seems straight to me. I couldn't make one as good as hers, Hester. Show me yours."

Hester points out the cipher translation she created for Aiden.

Making eye contact with Stella, Jewel remarks, "Well, we see who the artist in the room is, don't we?"

"Car." Hester and Angel run for the front door and usher Aiden into the dining room. "Detective North is here. I let him in."

"Good morning, Detective. May I pour you a cup of coffee?"

"Thank you, Jewel." As she hurries back to the kitchen, Aiden removes his coat and turns to Stella and Hester. "Okay, you better show me what you've translated. I called the forensics department in the Port. Two of their staff will stay tonight until the complete journal is transcribed."

Hester holds the deciphered code up for Aiden. She remains silent, deferring to Stella.

"We've succeeded in transcribing the first paragraph. Paulina had a lover. The cipher clarifies the use of her escape door as the way he came and went."

They sit in silence while he reads the translated words. "Your work needs to be delivered to the detachment in Port Ephron. I'm off there now. Will you be at the park later when Rosemary and I move in?"

"Oh, yes. I planned to drive back after we met with you." She takes a moment to pat Hester on the arm again. "You and I have done sufficient damage for one day."

"May I read Paulina's diary after you're finished? I can keep a secret."

"I have no objection, Hester." Aiden drags on his topcoat. "It will be awhile before we have the puzzle pieces assembled, but I guarantee you'll have an opportunity to read her words." He folds the piece of paper, carefully transcribed by Hester, and tucks her work into his inside pocket. He pauses for a mouthful of coffee.

Stella takes her leave after Aiden departs the yard. "I'll keep you posted, Hester. We did exceedingly well. I couldn't have accomplished the job without you."

"Correct."

****

"Have Aiden and Rosemary shown up?" By five o'clock, Alice is ready to go home for the evening and Stella is poised to resume reception duties until eight.

"He waved when they drove past the office, Stella. I was out on the front stoop and wouldn't have recognized them otherwise. He was driving a different vehicle—a black and tan hatchback—perhaps new, but I'm not a car person."

"No kidding."

Alice drives a beat-up ten-year-old Mazda 1200 coupe found by her father in a junkyard. He rebuilt the little run-about for her to chug back and forth to work in the summer. She ignores Stella's tease. "I have the paperwork for the cottage rental right here by the phone. If he wanders up to pay when I'm not here, you won't be forced to dig for forms."

Stella is touched. Alice has anticipated her boss' abject failure when it comes to reception duties. "You're always one step in front of me and your work is very much appreciated." She expects Alice's support is in the faint hope Stella will not make a mess of her system.

After she zips her handbag, Alice fluffs her curly red locks secured with a purple bandanna, grabs her sweater, and walks with Stella through the living room to the back-veranda exit. Paul and Nick are stretched out on rattan loungers.

"Worried you'd never finish, Sis. I have a date and need to get home to clean up."

Nick winks at Stella. "Paul, here, has a new flame."

"What?" Paul turns to Nick. "A flame? What an old-fashioned expression." He lifts his lean frame out of the chair and follows his giggling sister off the porch toward the Mazda.

Alice mumbles over her shoulder. "You'll be home in lots of time."

As they pull out of the parking lot, Stella bends to kiss the top of Nick's head. "Long day?"

"Normal. I expect your adventures were more interesting. We didn't have a chance to talk at lunch—too many staff around."

The evening is warm without a breath of air. "I prepped supper. Not special, but burgers, beer, and a salad. We have ice-cream. Let's find a drink and I'll tell you how Hester and I cracked a cipher."

"Are you serious?" His eyes are soft. "You amaze me."

She chortles and leans against him. "Hester was a huge help. She's the remarkable one, for sure."

Over the next hour, while they putter, sip beer, and barbecue burgers, Stella tells Nick, in minute detail, the story of their work on Paulina's journal. "The cake pans were the biggest clue. I'm not convinced, if Brigitte hadn't removed them from the wall, I would have given them any consideration. Paulina collected two number pans, but I wasn't aware until recently they were both fives. Hester told me code keys often have a significance to the author, unless a corporation or government creates a message where keys are changed on a regular basis."

"Does Aiden know?"

"Oh yes. He came over to the farm and we gave him the deciphered letters and numbers. He said there are staff assigned to translate the journal over the weekend."

"He must be impressed by you. I know I am."

After supper, they sit on the veranda to enjoy the end-of-the-day quiet. No reservations are expected, although an unregistered arrival after supper is not unusual. Business is steady, but space is currently not a problem.

They're surprised when Aiden rounds the corner without Rosemary. His sisters-in-law arrive on Sunday.

"Anybody home? I came to settle my bill."

He's a different person dressed in Bermuda shorts and a golf shirt. His white hair slides across his brow. His skin does not have the ruddy glow of a man who works outside, like Nick, whose tanned complexion follows him well into March.

"Always happy to take your money, my friend. Come on up."

Nick stands and shakes Aiden's hand. "You two do your high finance. I'll clean up the dishes. Will you stay for tea or a drink?"

"Not tonight. I left Rosemary to her own devices for a few minutes. I gave her a faithful promise I'd be back in no time. She's convinced I'll spend hours up here."

Stella leads Aiden through the house and into reception. "I'm given to understand you have new wheels," she teases.

"Oh, yes. Can't justify the use of a ghost car forever. I bought a brand-new Chevy Citation two-tone hatchback. Rosemary chose the model despite my reluctance to let her drive."

"Sounds sporty." They reach the front. "Alice has your reservation ready. I need your signature and your money," she jokes, from the workspace behind the counter. "When Mary Jo and Toni arrive on Sunday, I'll take them on a tour of the cottage and answer questions. You told them to bring their own linens, but not dishes, correct?"

"I made sure they were aware last week."

He pauses for long enough to make Stella uncomfortable. "What's wrong with the reservation, Aiden?"

"Not a thing. I promised Rosie no work on the weekend unless there's an emergency, but I wanted you to hear this information right away. Forensics has done an initial run-through of Paulina's diary. We've learned who her lover was and discovered she has a sister in New York—a sister who has raised her daughter."

Stella's breath catches in her throat. "Can you tell me who her lover was, Aiden?"

"Farley Tompkins. The journal is full of information describing Farley's transformation from a duck to a swan."

"Funny, now that you've said his name, his identity doesn't surprise me. Trixie and Cavelle mentioned Farley appeared as if someone gave him a makeover. They also said Meredith was not appreciative. That was ages ago—maybe even last winter. And she has a sister...and a daughter?"

Aiden nods. "We'll go through the dates to be sure, but I'm convinced the child is Leon's, if one judges by the age and the trip you told me she made to New York the winter after he died. Will you meet me on Monday to sift through the whole journal?"

"I'd start tonight."

"Let's allow forensics to do the work, Stella. I'm as impatient as you, but we'll go over every detail the first of the week. I must run." He points to the front entrance used for reception. "May I leave through this door to walk back?"

"No problem. Is Rosemary okay, Aiden?"

He shrugs his shoulders. "Sometimes I find it hard to tell. I expect she's cut her medication but hasn't stopped taking the pills altogether. Her sisters will keep track while they're here."

"Whatever we can do, my friend. By the way, Nick's parents arrive this Sunday, too." She rebuffs his raised eyebrows. "Don't even ask. I might hide in the pump house for the foreseeable future...or abscond to parts unknown with your new ride."

Chapter 12

You and Aiden are Close

The rumble of a motor announces the approach of a black Mustang convertible. Stella is relaxing on the back veranda with her tea when the driver navigates into the parking space in front of reception. A discussion between the two women occupants sounds heated, although loud discussions are not always arguments.

She wanders into the front office as the two women struggle through the doorway.

The bigger one scratches her brush cut as she blurts, "We have the cottage reserved. Aiden North took care of the bill."

"Mary Jo, give the poor girl a chance to find the reservation. She'll know Aiden's paid. Don't be pushy. You're always so pushy."

As expected, Rosemary's sisters have arrived.

Stella stands motionless in the doorway until the women notice her presence. When they avert their eyes from Alice, she nods. "You must be Mary Jo," she addresses one sister. "And you're Toni. Rosemary and Aiden speak of you often. Welcome to Shale Cliffs. I'm Stella Kirk. This is Alice, my assistant. By the way, great car." She lifts her neck to focus on the Mustang for a moment.

"How do you do? The '65 Mustang belonged to my dear departed Herbie. I prefer not to drive but Mary Jo has no problem behind the wheel. Rosemary has mentioned you. Our reservation is complete?" Toni, her naturally streaked grey hair permed to resemble a helmet, sports a floral-patterned pantsuit with shorts instead of slacks. She studies Stella through wire-rimmed glasses.

Stella and Alice make eye contact for a moment. "Your reservation is in order. I'll walk over to the cottage and you can follow. Once I give you a quick tour, you'll be set."

"You get your exercise, Toni. I'll drive the 'Stang'." Mary Jo lumbers to their vehicle. She drops, with little to no grace, into the driver's seat and lets her arm drape out over the door. "Well?"

"Mary Jo is very impatient. My apologies," Toni whispers to Stella as she hustles to take a position in front of the car.

Stella leads them through the private rear lot, along the narrow driveway, and toward the cottage which was once for the manager's use. Toni huffs and puffs beside her. "I'll show you around and give you the keys. I'm delighted you've come to the park to visit with Rosemary."

"Aiden is hard at work on a murder case. I assume you know. The minute he becomes preoccupied with his job, Rosemary starts to 'reassess' her medications."

The Mustang is right behind them, now. Heat from the motor reaches the backs of Stella's legs and Toni increases her pace.

"You are aware of our sister's challenges. You and Aiden are close," she emphasizes.

"We attended school together. We're old friends and I consult with the police on occasion."

"Rosemary is afraid you are much more."

Stella measures her response. "I have a relationship of my own to handle. Aiden and I work on investigations, and he rents a spot in my trailer park— Rosemary's imagination runs away with her."

Toni turns spectacled eyes up toward Stella. "I doubt if Mary Jo will be convinced. She's divorced, and she always imagines the worst in men." Her curls vibrate when she speaks. "I guess I don't blame Mary Jo, but my poor dear, departed Herbie was the best husband a gal could ever wish for."

Stella feigns interest. "Your husband's death was recent?"

"Oh no, Herbie's been dead for—now let me remember—ten years. He was very young. Had a massive heart attack and never knew what hit him. He wouldn't have wanted to be an invalid." She pats Stella's arm as if in consolation. "He bought the Mustang almost new. I still miss him every day."

Mercifully, the cottage pops into view around the curve of the narrow drive. Stella turns to Mary Jo, scowling behind the wheel. "You can park at the side."

Mary Jo pulls the car to an abrupt stop. The heavy door flies open. "You two walk awful slow. Let me inside first. I need to pee."

"Mary Jo. Please!"

The three women climb the few steps to the tiny porch. The cottage, or "shed" as Nick once called his housing option, consists of a main room with a kitchen to one side, plus a bedroom with a pair of single beds, and an adjoining bath. Stella does a quick survey. Eve did a great job when she cleaned. The unit is well outfitted; even detergent for washing dishes. Basics, except for linens, are provided. Her old appliances, which once graced the efficiency kitchen in the upstairs apartment at the house, appear almost new in their expanded environment.

Toni claps her hands together. "The place is cute—quaint and cozy."

"No TV?"

"No, Mary Jo, but I see a radio on the counter." Toni huffs her displeasure with her sister.

"Where's the fireplace? What do I do if I'm cold at night?"

"The electric baseboard heat works well in the event of a sudden temperature plunge," Stella adds in a less than accommodating tone.

"I'll go fetch the linens after I whiz. I guess we make up our own beds."

"Don't mind her, Stella. She's always been rough around the edges." Toni giggles. "I find myself apologizing for her—often."

"No problem, Toni. Here's your key." Mary Jo finishes in the bathroom and then heads outside.

They chatter about the facilities until Mary Jo reappears. "Do you need directions to Aiden and Rosemary's trailer?"

"I can manage." She grunts as she wedges herself through the open door with an arm load of sheets, towels, and a straw hat the size of a child's plastic wading pool. "Aiden drew us a map. Thanks for your help."

She's dismissed. "Enjoy your stay. Nice to meet you. Feel free to give the office a call, if necessary. The phone is on the wall in the kitchen. If you press zero, Alice will pick up."

Both women have their backs to her as she closes the screen door. On her return trek, she assesses the two sisters upon whom Aiden depends so heavily. Rosemary, Mary Jo, and Toni don't resemble one another in the least. It's plausible they were born to and/or raised by different people. She admires Aiden for his ability to manage the trio, or at least cope with them in a pack.

****

She's standing at the kitchen sink, guzzling yet another glass of water, when he puts his arms around her waist and kisses her neck. "Are you nervous? A shot of rum?"

"Gotta bucket? What time is it? Should they be here soon? What's our plan for supper?"

"No, you're not rattled in the least. We'll figure out what to eat if necessary. I expect they'll want to relax in their rig for the evening. I'm sure we won't see them. I need to go to the pump house and check on Paul. He was flushing the lines. Come find me when they turn up, okay?" He kisses her again.

"I'll be here. The checkouts are finished but we have more rigs besides your parents expected later. Alice is prepared." She grabs his arm. "God, Nick! I'd rather eat dirt than endure this introduction. Stay at the pump house where I can find you in a hurry."

When Duke and Kiki show up for a break, Stella tells him to leave the golf cart. She will bring Nick to the house the moment his parents arrive. "You and your dog are in coordinated outfits today, Duke. Any special occasion for the purple shirts?"

"Nope. We're pretty cute, though." He ruffles Kiki's ears. Since she's rammed into the crook of his arm, she can't complain other to flash her yellowed teeth.

"Make no mistake. Kiki's the cute one." She smirks at her security guy. "Did you hear a diesel engine?" She dashes into her office as a shiny new thirty-foot Class A motor home rolls into the parking spot in front of reception. A very tall, barrel chested, bald, and tanned man makes his way to the door, open to the afternoon sunshine.

"Anybody around? Tobias Cochran here. Where's my son, Nick?"

Dread prevents clarity. She runs on tiptoe back to the kitchen. "Duke, please go out to reception and help Alice talk to Nick's father. I'll retrieve Nick."

"I'll go. You stay."

"Not on your life," she whispers, as loud as she can, before she charges through the living room and out to the veranda.

The trip to reach the pump house and locate Nick consumes a minute or two. She promised to be the stable one. "They're here." She forces the panic out of her voice.

He stops and places a wrench on the bench beside him. "I'm sorry, Stella. I hate to see you this troubled. Have you talked to them?"

"No! I jumped on the cart and came straight to the pump house."

His expression is indulgent; the same as the one he gives Kiki when she falls over her own feet. "You could have called me on the radio; not necessary to roar over here in a panic. Who's with them? Alice?"

"Alice and Duke—and Kiki, too."

"Great. Dad hates dogs, especially little dogs. Let's go. What's the worst that can happen?"

She doesn't dare say.

When they return to the house, the rig and occupants are gone. Kiki, in her purple shirt, perches on Alice's lap. "What happened to my parents?"

"Hi, Nick. Hi, Stella. Your father wondered where you were, but I checked them in—no charge, as you asked—and Duke volunteered to show them to their site. He climbed in the motor home with them like they were old friends."

Stella stands horrified. The Cochrans' first impression of Shale Cliffs RV Park is now Duke Powell, the man who considers himself to be an improved version of John Wayne.

Nick pats her shoulder. "Dad's a big fan of John Wayne. Duke can be our secret weapon."

Nick, under undue stress following the arrival of his parents, has no doubt lost his mind. Her expression manages to convey her thoughts. "Don't worry. We'll take the cart and go over to the site. Duke can drive back. Don't worry," he repeats. "Time to face the music, which today happens to be in the key of Tobias Cochran." He grabs her hand and pulls her out to the veranda and the cart parked nearby.

"You're suddenly under control. I expected to witness you morph into a ten-year-old Nick Cochran again." She rubs her shoulder against his.

He takes his eyes away from the road long enough to provide her with a goofy grin. "The evening isn't over yet. Follow my lead and we'll see what happens."

"Knock, Knock." Nick and Stella stand on the woven rug laid at the foot of the stairs.

Duke emerges in the doorway. "Hi, you guys. I was ready to trudge up to the house."

"No need. Take the cart. Stella and I'll walk back later."

After Duke navigates the steps, they climb up and into one of the most luxurious units Stella has ever had the pleasure to tour. With creamy leather furniture, mahogany cabinetry, stained-glass pocket doors to the master suite, and imitation hardwood on the floor, the effect is engineered to take your breath away.

"Dad, Mom, please meet Stella Kirk, the owner of beautiful Shale Cliffs RV Park. Stella—my parents, Tobias and Yona."

"Pleased to meet you. Welcome to Shale Cliffs. Are you happy with your site?"

Yona stares at her shoes and bounces her chin in what Stella interprets as an enthusiastic nod. Nick's mother is bent a fraction at the waist and Stella ponders whether the poor woman has arthritis. She's dressed in a black cotton sweater and charcoal polyester slacks. Her jet-black hair is secured in a tight bun. Her skin is pasty white with a yellow tinge, in stark contrast to the amateur dye-job.

Tobias shakes Nick's hand.

Stella refuses to acknowledge the slight.

"Well, son, we're happy to see you since you didn't come to Florida for Christmas." He steals a glance at Stella. "I hope you can stick around for supper so we can talk in private."

"After a long day on the road, we wanted to invite you up to the house for a barbecue."

"The drive was less than an hour. We stayed at a real classy park in Port Ephron last night." He glances in Stella's general direction. "The owner loaned me a car, and we ate our evening meal at a fancy place called the Purple Tulip. Your mother will cook a meal for the three of us tonight."

They continue to discuss the trip. Tobias complains about gas prices and litres versus gallons, but Stella heard the slur about fancy Port Ephron RV Park and accepts her dismissal. "I should go back and check on the staff. I'll see you later, Nick. Enjoy your stay." She makes eye contact with Yona, whose sympathy is obvious, and nods in the general direction of Tobias before she exits. Nick does not follow.

He referred to her as the owner. He didn't insist she join them. He didn't touch her. On her way along the sloped roadway to her home, she ponders a possibility. Nick is afraid of his father.

****

"Trixie. Hi. Can you talk for a minute?" The staff are gone. She's seated at her kitchen table with a peanut butter sandwich.

"Sure. You sound upset."

"Nick's parents are here. They rolled into the yard this afternoon with one of the most gorgeous Class A rigs I've ever seen."

"What's the problem?"

"Nick introduced me as the owner of the park, stayed for supper with them, and there was no suggestion I stick around. He treated me as his boss."

"You must be over-reacting. I'd expect Russ to pretend I'm a stranger in front of certain people, but Nick always shows everyone his devotion to you, Stella, even before you were public."

"He didn't touch me; didn't put his arm around my shoulder or lean against me. I expected him to shake my hand when I left to come home."

"What did you do?"

"I said I'd see them later and came back alone. Here I sit in my kitchen, halfway through a peanut butter sandwich."

"You should have called me earlier. Brigitte has seen fit to entertain Carter Stephens tonight—a thank you for his help with her move. I'm *persona non grata*. I assumed she wanted me to babysit Mia but no such luck. The word is, he likes Mia."

"Good for Brigitte. You can't fault her because she wants to meet someone—not you, of all people, Trixie. Especially not you."

"You're right, but Russ has to work—again—and I lean on Brigitte when he's not around."

"Don't take advantage of her," Stella admonishes.

"You're a great one to give advice. Describe Nick's parents."

"Tobias Cochran is a big guy. His voice booms. If I didn't depend on United States citizens for such a huge portion of my business, I'd consider him a typical American—Mr. Clean—he shaves his head. He complained about litres of gas and how he couldn't figure out the mileage when he filled up."

Trixie hoots. "Tell him to average four miles to a gallon and forget the rest. And his mother?"

"Yona is her name. She's tiny and was dressed in black—even with today's temperature. She seems severe, Trixie, and a real mouse around other people—quiet and skittish. She probably just does whatever Tobias tells her to do." Stella pauses. "Nick made no attempt to act as if we're a couple. To be honest, it was unsettling."

"Nick will be fine. He's nervous with them parked in the yard. Hey! Why not plan a family barbecue for next Sunday? I'll help. I can contribute food and bring Russ, Brigitte, and Mia. Nick can go pick up Dad."

Stella appreciates her sister's attempt at comfort. No one is behaving typically today, although the idea of a party has merit and crossed her mind when she first understood the Cochrans would visit. "Aiden and Rosemary are here, along with Rosemary's sisters, Toni and Mary Jo. The two are interesting, to say the least. We can invite them, too."

"Perfect. Let's provide Tobias and Yona with a taste of Shale Cliffs RV Park life."

"Give them a taste of Nick's life."

"I wasn't going to get specific, but yes, Nick's life."

"Time to go, Trixie. He's home. Thanks for the company."

"See you." The phone goes dead—her sister's usual method to end a conversation.

He materializes in the kitchen entry, tall and tanned. As she replaces the receiver in its cradle on the wall, he murmurs, "Glad to be home."

"I was worried." She's afraid to say more. She swallows her anxiety and anger, which allows space for her vulnerabilities to push to the forefront. She meets his eyes.

"Dad never changes. He wants me to contribute the money Aunt Ruth left me into a cockamamie investment scheme. Computers." He remains poised at the entry to the kitchen.

"Let's have tea and you can tell me what you want to do." Stella's voice trembles, despite her attempt at control.

"Oh, the conversation evolved much further." He slumps into a kitchen chair.

"My God, Nick, don't scare me. What the hell?" She leans across the table and places her hand on his arm. Relief consumes her when he doesn't pull away.

"I told him I was invested here and explained you and I are together."

"Good." She hesitates. "And?"

"Let's say they weren't pleased, to the point where I expected they'd leave right away and go back to Florida, but no. Dad said he plans to stay until I change my mind."

"They plan to move to Shale Cliffs?" She attempts a joke.

His response is watery. "Dad's infuriated, Stella. He told me he'd be up to the house to discuss options with you tomorrow. He decided he wanted to see the books and talk to our staff."

"Not appropriate." Stella's anxiety meter spikes, but to learn Tobias Cochran wants to meddle in her business stirs anger, too. "Does he expect to prove you've made a bad investment and force me to buy you out?"

"Perhaps." Nick is thoughtful. "He might want to invest so he can have a reason to keep tabs on me."

"Again, won't happen, Nick." She recalls the conversation she had with herself on the way home earlier. "If I am forced to purchase back your shares, I will." Her voice shakes. "The paperwork is in order."

"Stella, I don't intend to leave. When he can't wangle what he wants, my father rarely gives up. Please understand." He studies her face. "Are you afraid I'll want my money and take off for Florida? Good God, Stella." He pushes back his chair and stumbles around the old wooden table in two steps. "You and I are a team."

"You never said we were romantically involved." She can't help but accuse, despite the closeness of his body. "You introduced me as the owner, Nick. I was afraid you were bailing."

"Every interaction with my father needs to be gradual. He's a bully. I never present him with all the facts at once." His eyes lock with hers. "He has the message we're a couple now, which is why I needed to alert you to his arrival in the office first thing tomorrow." He wraps his arms around her shoulders. His lips touch her neck. "I love you. Dad's a bully. I don't want you hurt."

"Well, he won't have a chance right away, because I'm scheduled to meet with Aiden at the Shale Harbour detachment in the morning." Her immediate escape is narrow at best. "We're ready to analyze Paulina's journal."

"Good. I'll distract him for a few hours. Did you not promise me tea?"

She pats his arm and stands. "I spoke to Trixie tonight. She suggested a family and friends barbecue next Sunday. I can't believe we think alike. If you run out to the manor to fetch Dad, we can introduce your parents to the people who now clutter your life." She successfully masks her underlying concerns. "I'll invite Aiden and the sisters. Rosemary will keep your father busy."

❦

CHAPTER 13

The Paperwork is in Order

Stella makes herself comfortable in the now familiar interview room at the Shale Cove RCMP detachment. The air conditioning, although not excessively powerful, is appreciated even at mid-morning. The weather is expected to be hot this week.

"Good. You're here." Aiden plops an inch-thick typewritten manuscript on the table. "I've skimmed her journal. Forensics provided a summary, but we need to examine her thoughts page by page. After the first entry, she incorporated dates, which makes analysis easier." He scrapes strands of wispy white hair off his brow. "Hi, by the way. Coffee before we start?"

"No, I'm good, but eager for a peek. May I?"

He nods.

She reaches across the table for a stack of pages and begins. Paulina's words are flowery and rich with description. Stella chooses not to read passages aloud. Farley was amorous to say the least. Certain spots resemble a drugstore pocket romance. The various mentions of his change in appearance border on the funny.

As much as my heart flutters the moment he arrives, I worked up enough courage to suggest he bathe before we make love. Farley is a man who pays little or no attention to himself, but I told him I feel the time has come for him to indulge. This, of course, is for my ultimate benefit but he need never be aware. Tonight, we discussed the new clothes he was to purchase, including under garments more suitable for a gentleman his age.

I found it disturbing when he said he expected annoyance from his wife if he spent too much money on attire. I assured him of increased success at work if he were to be more dapper. He will look handsome and sexy with a new wardrobe, and please God, a haircut and trim of his unkempt facial hair.

Aiden is focused on another passage when Stella interrupts. "I've found an entry which reminds me of a conversation with Trixie and Cavelle after Christmas. Cavelle said Meredith was in a lather because Farley gave himself a thorough makeover. She was none too pleased. One of them, perhaps Trixie, suggested Farley was stepping out." She studies Aiden. "I guess she was right."

"The most vital piece of information is the discoveries of the sister in New York City, widowed, and Jane, the child she raised. Have you located the details?"

Stella thumbs through pages. "Here it is, Aiden." The passage is from the month before she died.

Danielle insists I remain "estranged Aunt Paulina" to my daughter, Jane. I linger in this purgatory of parenthood. I paid my dues for birthing a child out of wedlock. My sister, and her husband, Seth Braddon, laid claim to her for twenty-one years. I wrote on her birthday without success. Seth has been dead for two years. Danielle must allow me into Jane's life. She must! I imagine Leon's devotion to her. I often contemplate our future if he had lived, and we had raised Jane together.

I wonder if she resembles me. I wonder if she has her father's height. Are her eyes blue or grey? Leon's eyes were penetrating in their greyness, clouds near the ground. I promised Danielle never to return to New York. She and Seth were to raise Jane as their own, but my child is twenty-one now and Seth is gone. I want to become part of my daughter's life. I want her to meet Farley.

"I've contacted the police in New York. They located Danielle and Jane Braddon with no trouble whatsoever. NYPD completed the notification and asked Mrs. Braddon to contact me in reference to the investigation. I expect the phone call to happen while you're here."

"The existence of a daughter explains her winter in New York after Leon died. She said she stopped travelling to Florida when she met Leon and only spent the one winter stateside afterward. Her excuse was that she couldn't face the first winter here alone. Now we understand she travelled to be with her sister when she gave birth to her baby." Grief for Paulina overwhelms her. "She lost the love of her life and relinquished her child. Poor Paulina. Her aloneness is haunting."

Aiden hands her another few sheets of the manuscript. "She explained the secret door in this section."

Stella holds the printed pages in one hand, and her chin in the other, while she reads her friend's inner-most thoughts once more.

We created a method for our rendezvous. My lovely pantry secret escape door is now Farley's entry. When he finds a way to attend me, he leaves his car at the office or tells Meredith he has gone for a walk and slips into my home unnoticed by nosy neighbours or passersby. We drink sherry, discuss books, trade our deepest secrets, and make beautiful love together. I leave the door unlocked each day. If he isn't by my side at nine o'clock in the evening, he will be unable to come.

I encourage and support dear Farley in his aspiration to write a book. Such a talented man with so many interests. It's imperative he shares his knowledge and imagination with the world.

"The hidden entrance was locked because it was later than nine at night and she no longer expected him, Aiden."

"My interpretation as well. Whoever killed her came through the front and left the same way. Neither Matt nor Mercedes Savioli happened to be near a window where they might see someone. It's possible the visitor, and therefore the murderer, was Farley. He was late, so took his chances at the front when the pantry door was locked."

"Detective North, call for you on line 3."

Aiden jumps to his feet and motions to Stella, who scoops up the manuscript before following him into his office.

"Detective North here."

"How do you do, Mrs. Braddon."

"Correct. We asked the New York City police department to make the notification. I am very sorry for your loss."

"Her body was found in her home on the morning of May 1. We determined she was killed late in the evening of the day before. Were you provided with details?"

"She was murdered. Our investigation has recently revealed you raised Paulina's daughter, Jane Braddon. Is this the case?" He nods while maintaining eye contact with Stella.

"I recommend you make a trip to Shale Harbour, Mrs. Braddon, as soon as possible. Paulina has died intestate. Given the recent information of the discovery of an immediate heir, the law firm of Stephens and Stephens will now proceed with probate and disbursements."

"Very well. Will you notify my office once you confirm plans? The Harbour Hotel will no doubt suit your needs for the duration of your stay. Paulina's home and business are currently leased. I will instruct the law firm to contact you today."

"Thank you, Mrs. Braddon. Yes, your sister's death has been a terrible shock to Shale Harbour, too. Miss McAdams was an invaluable pillar of the Shale Harbour community and we are searching diligently to find the person who killed her."

"Hope to hear from you soon. Goodbye."

Aiden replaces the receiver in its cradle, leans back in his chair with his hands clasped behind his neck, and closes his eyes. "I can't tell if she's shocked but reserved, or indifferent. She plans to make the trip north and Jane will accompany her."

"What does Jane do? She's old enough to work."

"No idea, but I didn't sense any inconvenience for her to travel with her aunt, mother, or whatever."

"Could Mrs. Braddon be implicated? Paulina's diary is clear she wanted to reverse the deception and develop a relationship with her daughter. Danielle panicked and found a way to nip the idea in the bud. I bet she has no clue there's a diary which is detailed and written in code."

"I'm not convinced. She would have needed contacts here. We can check her phone records. If she has connected with people, we're able to find out. I think Farley is our best suspect right now."

Her expression is readable.

"You don't agree."

"No, I don't. You folks pay me the big bucks to provide alternatives," she smirks.

"I'll call Stephens and Stephens. Afterward, I want to hear your 'alternatives', Stella."

Ideas thrash around in her brain for five minutes while Aiden discusses contact information with one of the Stephens' lawyers. *The person who arrived at Paulina's late on the evening of April thirtieth, or very early in the morning of May 1, was known to Paulina. She let the visitor in and returned to her chair in her front room library despite her somewhat revealing attire. We saw no signs of a struggle. After reviewing her journal, it's reasonable to assume she gave up her wait and locked the secret door. When she heard someone at the street entrance, she answered, assuming the visitor was Farley.*

Stella drags her chair nearer Aiden's desk, rests her elbows on the surface, and plunks her chin in her hands. "Meredith might well have been aware of her husband's affair and killed Paulina," she states aloud to the empty office.

****

Stella returns to Shale Cliffs by mid-afternoon. As she navigates the Jeep into a spot near the private entrance to her home, she sees Yona and Tobias Cochran in conversation with Nick in the shade of the veranda. Exhaustion overwhelms her. She has thought of little but Paulina for the last six hours. To change gears and face whatever challenges Nick's parents create for her will be unbearable today.

She trudges up the steps. "Hi, everyone." Nick and his father nurse beers. Yona is without refreshment.

Nick's expression is grim. "We took a tour of the park and met the staff."

"Great." She forces enthusiasm. "I'll check in with Alice and then see if there's any iced tea. Yona, would you enjoy an iced tea since the weather is so muggy?"

"A cool drink sounds perfect, my dear. The boys each wanted a beer, but I said I'd wait for you." Her voice is soft and deep; a low-registered tone for such a small woman.

"Excuse me for a moment." Inside the darkened living room, she exhales. A line of sweat has collected above her eyebrows. She wipes her forehead with the back of her hand. "Alice," she hisses from near reception, "do we have any iced tea or lemonade?"

"Hi. Nice to see you home. Been a busy day. Lots of people without reservations, but I fit them in." Her piled high curls vibrate in her excitement and enthusiasm before she notices Stella's stress. "Yes, I made lemonade before lunch. Do you want me to pour you a glass?"

Touched, she replies, "No. You've done enough. I'll take care of drinks for Nick's mother and me."

With lemonades in hand, she returns to the veranda and sits alone on the rattan sofa. The Cochrans are in wicker chairs which circle the coffee table. She morphs into the rabbit staring down the hounds.

"I showed Dad the work we did, Stella."

She nods. "We've accomplished a great deal over the last couple of years—water and electrical upgrades, a small kitchen update, and a huge upstairs renovation, Tobias. The final project has created a rental cottage which adds to our income." Although his angry expression darkens as she finishes her last sentence, she doesn't flinch, and can guess what's coming.

"In my opinion, not only have you robbed the cradle, but you've availed yourself of my son's inheritance to advance your business." His tone is accusatory, his expression unceremonious and sullen.

Nick opens his mouth to interrupt but she raises an index finger. She will speak her mind. *Deep breath.* "Tobias. Yona. You might already be aware, but my sister and I are the main shareholders in the park. Nick owns ten percent, which represents his contribution to our system upgrades last fall." *Don't let your voice shake.* "His investment in the upstairs renovation, and the total was significant, has been documented as an addendum to the partnership agreement. In the event of my death, my portion of the estate will owe him those funds."

Yona's pose is anticipatory, an attendee at a speaking engagement.

Palms sweating now, Stella adds. "If, at any time, Nick wants to bow out, I will make arrangements to repay him." She takes a breath.

Nick's mother nods.

"The paperwork is in order," she adds, repeating the statement she made to Nick the evening before.

Tobias turns to his son. "I think the little lady is on the offensive, my boy."

"The little lady, as you call her, happens to be the love of my life." Nick's face is red. He reaches for Stella's hand. "Don't continue to bully, Dad. It won't work. I'll ask you both to leave the park if necessary."

With a movement as swift as a cat, Yona jumps from her chair and perches on the sofa. She meets her husband's eyes while she addresses Stella. "I respect and admire you, my dear." Her small hand touches Stella's knee. Her voice rumbles in its depth. "The most important issue is our son's happiness, and I will see that Tobias doesn't interfere. I take full responsibility." She glares at Tobias while she takes a bird-like sip of her lemonade.

Nick beams.

Tobias straightens and gulps his beer. "Yona is the one person on this earth who can tell me what to do," he snarls, by way of humbled explanation.

Yona addresses Stella directly. "We hope to remain at your park until the end of the week, if you are able to tolerate us." She withdraws her hand.

The situation is diffused, for now. Time to be magnanimous. "Any chance you can stay until at least next Monday? My sister and I want to host a family and friends barbecue on Sunday. My father will be here, along with Trixie's family."

Aiden's unmarked car rolls into the lot. "As well as this guy." She indicates Aiden approaching the stairs. "Plus his wife and sisters-in-law, if I can persuade them." She stands. "Come on up. Lemonade or beer?"

Aiden runs his fingers through wind-blown hair and makes his way up the veranda stairs. "Aiden, allow me to introduce Nick's parents, Tobias and Yona Cochran."

Tobias rises and extends his huge paw.

"Please meet Detective Aiden North, Tobias. As you already know, I consult with the local RCMP."

Both men mumble their salutations before Aiden turns his attention to Yona. "Pleasure."

Yona nods but doesn't speak when Aiden shakes her hand. The occasional fierce turtle of a woman has once again retreated into her shell.

"If you will excuse us for a moment," Aiden acknowledges Nick and his parents, "I need a word with Stella, here." He squints at her. "Yes, I've enough time for a quick beer before I go to my trailer."

Stella finds Aiden his drink and leads him to her office. She senses the need for a modicum of privacy. "What's up?"

"An interview with Farley Tompkins on Wednesday morning. He consented to come to the station. Insists he doesn't want a lawyer present. Are you able to join me?"

"To be sure. The park is running smoothly. I shouldn't jinx business, but general operations are under control—no insurmountable problems since we upgraded the systems. How are you faring?"

"Has Rosemary turned up here at the house?"

"No, not to my knowledge. Why?"

"Mary Jo and Toni do their best to keep her busy, and they insist she takes her pills, but Rosemary's in her twilight stage."

"Between properly medicated and—well—not?"

He nods. "She's very unpredictable. You don't need her appearing on your doorstep in a lather; worked up over nonsense."

"We can handle her, Aiden, which begs the question—do you have plans for Sunday? Trixie and I are organizing a barbecue. We want to invite the two of you and bring Mary Jo and Toni."

His eyes widen.

"I know. Trixie and I—not a phrase used often. Life hasn't been normal the last couple of days."

"Thanks. I'll check with the crowd and call you." He points his chin toward the veranda. "And Nick's parents?"

"Bumpy at first. I got nailed right after I got home today, but in the long run, my sister was correct. Nick didn't fail me." She giggles. "Trixie was correct—another phrase I don't use much. The world has tilted, my friend. Come on. We'll go back outside while you finish your drink."

"How about I call you tomorrow morning and we'll review suspects? You still don't think Farley killed her, do you?"

"I can't imagine Farley with a gun."

"It's not impossible to hire her murder out."

She stops in her tracks and turns to stare him squarely in the face. "Hire a hit man in Shale Harbour? You're joking, right?"

"Hit men commute, Stella, as long as you know someone who knows someone. How else do you explain the precision of her murder?"

"Paulina was not involved with any hit men, Aiden. She was well-acquainted with the person she admitted to her home the night she died." She lowers her voice as she nears the screen door, "and familiar enough to invite them inside even though she was wearing a revealing garment."

"It could have been an acquaintance. She flirted with me when I first met her. Remember?"

Stella ignores what she believes could be a fair assessment as she pushes open the screen door.

"We're back. Can I refresh anyone's drink? Aiden and I needed a quick chin-wag to prepare for an upcoming interview."

Tobias lifts his glass toward her. Nick intercepts. "I'll do drinks, Stella. You sit."

"You two on the hunt for a local axe-murderer?" He chuckles at his own joke.

"Mr. Cochran, a friend and businessperson was murdered five weeks ago. Stella found her body."

"Aiden hasn't lived in Shale Harbour since high school. I tag along on occasion to introduce him to the locals."

Tobias' expression is ghoulish. "Tell us what you saw, Stella. I'm fascinated."

She catches a combination of impatience and anxiety on Aiden's face, but she'll provide the standard response. He need not worry. "Paulina McAdams was a close friend. She invited me to her house for lunch and I found her. This is the information I share with the public, Tobias. The murder is an active investigation."

"People are shot every day in Florida. A person needs a gun. How else can you protect your family and property from the bad guys?" He subsequently nods to agree with himself and scraps of sunlight reflect off his dome. "I bet your Paulina-person didn't own a gun. She was an easy target. Even though I worry about travelling unarmed, I decided against concealing my personal weapon in the glove compartment before I started north—law-abiding citizen and all. Figured a cop at the border might confiscate my Beretta. No offense, Detective, but you Canadians are sitting ducks."

✦

Chapter 14

I'm Open to Other Theories

His warm thigh rests across her own. She must have dozed off.

"Stella. Are you awake?" Alice's whisper is forced and nervous. "Can you come to the phone?"

She stumbles out of bed, while Nick impedes her progress by clutching her hand. She can see Alice's red curls in the stairwell. "Phone? I never heard the phone. What time is it?"

"Eight-thirty, Stella, and Detective North is holding on line one. Shall I tell him to call back?"

After second thoughts, she decides against immediately wrapping up in her housecoat and descending to her office. "Give me half an hour."

Her quick glance back toward the bed is rewarded with a lazy smile.

"Sorry, Alice." Stella tries to sound contrite as he watches her, but a flush spreads along her neck. "We overslept."

"I never noticed." Her assistant's chuckle bounces up the stairs. "I'll tell the detective and put on a fresh pot of coffee."

"Thanks." Stella returns to his side. "You, mister, are a bad influence."

Without a word, he lifts a tanned and muscled arm to grab her wrist.

"Not a chance. The staff are here. Up." She motions with her captured hand.

After a quick shower and a hasty choice of linen pants and camp T-shirt, she thunders down the worn stairs and into the kitchen. "Thanks for the coffee, Alice. Good morning, everyone."

Eve, Paul, and Duke munch in unison. "I found cinnamon buns in the freezer. Today seemed like a good day." Alice's expression says volumes.

"Nick will be here in a minute." She attempts to project her gruff boss tone but is well-aware of her failure to fool any of them. "Are we organized?"

"Better a late start than no start," Duke mumbles with a full mouth.

She ignores his remark. "Give me an idea of when you expect to need the cart. I want to do a park tour later."

The phone bleats as Nick materializes. "I'll take the call in my office," she announces as she tears out of the kitchen.

"I turned the upstairs ringer back on," he mutters into her ear when she runs past him.

"What?" His statement registers after she leaves.

"Good morning. Shale Cliffs RV Park. How may I help you?"

"Sleep in?"

"Yes, as a matter of fact." She covers the true nature of her tardiness with a white lie. "My first decent night's sleep in weeks, because Nick's parents aren't insisting he return to Florida." Her concocted, and seemingly recited, reason sounds plausible at least.

"We planned to examine our suspect list today. Do you have time to review every possible person who might be connected, however remotely, with Paulina?"

"Now?" Oversleeping feels like you've run for the bus, and it pulls away as you skid to the stop. She takes a sip of her coffee and silently thanks Alice. "Where do you want to start? The obvious or the not-so-obvious?"

"Okay, Farley and Meredith. Let's put the idea of a hired assassination aside for a moment."

"Consider her sister, Danielle, or even her daughter, Jane."

"There's a chance the murderer is an unknown and spurned lover she didn't reveal in her journal."

"I can't imagine when she found the time for another boyfriend. And Opal?"

"Opal? She's in jail. What is her motive to want Paulina dead? Tell me why Opal comes to mind."

"She said, in her confession, that she wanted to poison Paulina but never had the chance."

"Weak but possible. Farley might be a spurned lover because there was a usurper—or Farley was the usurper." Aiden takes a quick breath. "Meredith is the jealous spouse—an easy motive to imagine. We were never aware of Danielle or Jane, which is not to say they weren't in touch with Paulina—at least Danielle."

"Agreed. Danielle may possess more motivation to be rid of her sister. If the journal is correct, Jane was unaware of her birth mother, whereas Danielle felt threatened."

"In addition to motives, and opportunities, we'll check alibis and start with Farley, tomorrow."

"The circumstances of the evening of the murder still bug me." She organizes her thoughts. "I need to schedule a lunch with Cavelle and Trixie to see what I can clarify."

"What's the issue?"

"On the night of Paulina's death, Russ and Trixie were supposed to join Nick and me for dinner. Russ was not with Grey Cottage Realty yet. He was called to work so Trixie cancelled with me. Then she tried to convince Cavelle to skip the staff meeting at the real estate office and go to supper with her. Cavelle refused because Meredith insisted everyone attend, which means Farley, Meredith, and Cavelle were together for the evening."

"Alibis for Farley and Meredith?" Aiden's tone is questioning. "Points to a hired hit, again. The Tompkins couple were together. They alibi each other."

"Some details are missing—agenda topics, whether both Farley and Meredith were present for the whole time, and if they separated at any point. It's possible one of them sneaked off to Yellow House after the meeting or hired a person who turned up at Paulina's while they were at Grey Cottage Realty. If you don't object, I'll make a lunch date with Cavelle and Trixie for later this week."

"Sounds fine to me, Stella. As for our interview with Farley, can you make a nine o'clock appointment tomorrow or shall we try to accommodate your sleep patterns?"

"Yes, I'll be there." His attempt at a light-hearted slur has not gone unnoticed. "May I pose a few questions since he won't be able to squirm away?"

"I count on them. By the way, the entire clan is keen to attend your barbecue on Sunday. I was told to ask you for a food contribution suggestion, but I already know Mary Jo wants to volunteer potato salad."

"Potato salad is fine. How's Rosemary?"

"Sunday holds promise for one extreme or the other. Toni says Rosie's taking her medication but can't be sure if she follows her prescriptions to the letter. No point in suggesting we count pills because Rosemary's on to me.

She'll flush pills away or hide them. I once found ten capsules inside a pair of socks I rarely wear."

Stella's convinced Rosemary is on the road toward another hospitalization and hopes her sisters will be able to manage her on Sunday.

****

Positioned in her standard five o'clock spot at the oval conference table in the Shale Harbour RCMP detachment, she is lost in her own thoughts before Aiden appears at the door.

"Early, I see."

His teases are always kind and gentle. She's confident and safe in his presence.

"Farley is here," he relents, when she denies him the satisfaction of a response. "I'll go retrieve him when we're ready."

"How does he look?"

"Fretful. Rumpled. Maybe he jumped out of bed a few minutes ago."

She shrugs. "Sounds normal to me; the old Farley is back. All set when you are."

Aiden leaves the interview room for a moment and returns with Farley Tompkins at his side.

"Good morning, Farley."

He raises his eyes from his shoes long enough to scowl before he drops his gaze again. "Why are you here?"

"Stella assists me in interviews, Mr. Tompkins. Stella knows the local population far better than me. Please be seated. Shall we start?"

His nod barely registers as movement. When he sits, his worn and wrinkled sports jacket folds open in the front to reveal a stained shirt. His red hair hangs in his eyes.

"Farley, when did we see each other last—the writers retreat organization get-together?" Stella notices his large auburn handlebar mustache is trimmed higher on one side. His facial hair contributes to his unbalanced demeanour.

"I spend most days in my basement office where I write. I can't bear to walk past her house. I am bereft. Meredith insisted I attend the planning meeting because she wants everyone to understand she's involved for my sake."

"You and Paulina were very close?" Stella changes gears and allows the question to hang in the air between them.

A startled expression prefaces his response. "Are you not aware of our affair? I assumed my involvement with Paulina was the reason I was summoned to the detachment."

"And Meredith's reaction to your appointment with the RCMP?"

"I told Meredith the car required an oil change at the dealership in Port Ephron."

"Do you lie to your wife often, Mr. Tompkins?"

"Yes, Detective. I've lied to her for months. Paulina and I were in love and I cannot imagine the rest of my life without her by my side." His voice wobbles with emotion. "We were careful to make sure Matt and Mercedes never saw me. Did they tell you they did?"

After a subtle check with Aiden, Stella asks, "Farley, was Meredith jealous of your affair with Paulina, or did she not care?"

"Meredith? What?" He sits up straight and places both hands flat on the table. His nails are ragged and chewed; the flesh around them raw and inflamed. "Meredith was unaware. She remains in the dark. You won't tell her, will you?" His tone beseeches; his eyes widen when they dart from Stella to Aiden.

"How did you manage to keep your liaison a secret, Mr. Tompkins?"

"Detective North, I always told Meredith I was going for a walk or to the office. If I took the car, I parked at Grey Cottage. Not once did she ever mention the whereabouts of the car or ask where I was."

"She may well have learned the truth." Stella watches dark clouds form across his already sweaty brow. "Describe your book. What's the story?"

"What? My book?" His struggle to change gears is obvious. "Love—the history of love. Meredith insisted I focus on real estate, but Paulina encouraged me to discuss love."

"Does it have a title?"

"*The History of Love* is the working title, for reference purposes." Farley is enamoured with the topic. "I'll find a snappier title when I'm finished. No one has seen excerpts except Paulina, who read the first few chapters. Meredith has not looked at my manuscript. She showed little interest after I told her I decided to write 'l'histoire d'amour'." His tone is wistful, as if he has taken them into his confidence.

Paulina once described her secret affair as her "affaire du coeur", so Farley's dribbles of French make sense.

Since he seems relaxed, Stella tries another question. "Did Meredith want Paulina dead, or was Paulina involved with a jealous lover prior to you?"

"You're crazy. Paulina engaged in no serious male attachments except for Leon and then me. She has a daughter. I bet you didn't find any information related to Jane." He becomes oddly confrontational. "Paulina told me her secrets." His chin juts. "Her death was a case of mistaken identity—or an angry customer. Yes, an angry customer came to her house late on the Thursday night and killed her." In a much softer and less convincing tenor, he adds, "Meredith was clueless."

"Are you aware if Paulina ever re-established her connection with Danielle and Jane?"

"She loved her daughter and complained Danielle refused to permit her to see Jane even though she's twenty-one." His eyes bulge. "She suspected Jane has problems."

"What sorts of problems, Farley?"

"I don't know. Paulina thought Jane never went to school—same as Hester Painter."

"Did you plan to keep your affair clandestine, or did you expect to leave Meredith?"

"We never discussed my marital status. I would have left if she wanted, but she never asked." His voice shakes and his eyes glaze in realization. "I wish I had done more, but I didn't. Meredith tells me I show no initiative, and I guess she's right." He torments his cuticles; hands, now clasped in his lap.

"May I ask you a few more either - or questions, Farley? Answer with the more appropriate choice, okay?"

"If you insist, Stella, but Meredith had no idea about Paulina and me."

"Who benefits from the death of Paulina more—Meredith or Danielle?"

"How can I choose? I've never met Danielle."

"Which one, Farley?"

"Meredith, I suppose," he mumbles.

"Danielle or Opal?"

"Opal? She's in jail for heaven's sake, therefore the answer must be Danielle."

Stella stays calm, despite Farley's anxiety. "There are no correct answers, Farley. Opal or Meredith?"

Farley remains quiet. "If Meredith was aware—but she wasn't!" His fists are now clenched on the surface of the table. "Are these people your suspects? Meredith, Danielle, or Opal killed Paulina?"

"There are many suspects." Aiden's tone is controlled as he continues to focus on Farley's face. "Including you," he adds with soft insistence.

"Me? Ridiculous!" Farley pops out of his chair.

"Relax and sit, Mr. Tompkins."

"Do I need a lawyer? Do not accuse me. I didn't kill the love of my life."

Stella intervenes. "No one's accused anyone of murder today, Farley. Detective North and I gather information as part of the investigation."

"I want to make two points and afterward, I will take my leave."

Farley has attempted to hijack his interview.

"Fine. Go on."

"In the first place, both Meredith and I were at the office on the night Paulina died. Paulina expected me, but I found no way to break away from our stupid staff meeting before nine o'clock. We made a rule. We decided if I failed to appear at Yellow House by nine, she would lock the side entrance through the pantry. Did you two locate her escape door?"

"We did, Mr. Tompkins. Who else attended your meeting?"

"Cavelle." He turns to Stella. "You check with her. We were stuck with Meredith until almost eleven. I travelled home with my wife. There was no opportunity to sneak over to Paulina's no matter how desperately I wanted to." The muscles of his face begin to collapse. "I was such a coward."

Aiden presses. "Because you failed to confront Meredith with the truth?"

Farley nods.

"And you're sure Meredith didn't leave your home later that night?"

His tone is hushed. "I went to sleep."

"And your other point?" Aiden's approach remains formal.

"Ah, yes." The whine in his voice is disturbing. He stares at Stella. "I want to know who told you about our affair."

"Paulina wrote her deepest and darkest secrets in her journal, Farley. She incorporated a code, but we broke it and deciphered the entries. Paulina admired you, if her comments are any consolation. She appreciated the fact you improved your 'style', shall we say, to accommodate her."

Farley surveys his current personal condition and blubbers into a soiled handkerchief; one Stella notices matches neither his shirt nor his tie. "I have not lived up to the standard she set for me." He leans across the table. His face is flushed scarlet while tears trickle into his uneven mustache. "I loved Paulina. I did not kill her. I'm sure Meredith remains ignorant of our affair. Paulina's assailant must be a stranger, from outside the community. It's the only plausible option."

"Mr. Tompkins, do you or Meredith own, or have access to, a gun?"

His gasp is not contrived. He throws himself against the back of the chair. "A gun? Are you out of your mind?" He sits straighter. "Let me tell you—we attended the annual realtors' convention last winter in Florida and people wanted to talk pistols and rifles, not house deals. Meredith and I were turned off, to be truthful. My God, everyone keeps a revolver in their glove compartment and another one by their bed. I've never been around guns, and to my knowledge, neither has Meredith."

"Perhaps Meredith met someone at the convention who owned a gun; a person who could complete the job for her; a contact who knew a criminal willing to kill for money." Stella watches Farley's reaction to her remark, but she's disappointed.

"Meredith hired a professional killer while we were in Florida, to come to Shale Harbour and shoot Paulina?" He turns to Aiden. "You people have no idea who committed Paulina's murder, and now you want to accuse a woman who was unaware of my affair and was in a meeting when Paulina died. I want to go."

"You may leave, sir, but under no circumstances do you discuss our interaction with anyone. My instructions include Meredith. Clear?"

"Yes, Detective North." His voice becomes eerie and hollow. "I was in Port Ephron at the car dealership, remember?"

He sounds much more confident when he leaves the interview. He's a practiced liar. She's puzzled by his attitude, although not sure why.

****

After Farley departs, they adjourn to Aiden's office. "I'd suggest we go to the café, but we can't chance who might be nearby."

"No problem. What's your assessment?"

"Paulina's death was a professional assassination. I'm convinced. She was killed with a nine-millimetre likely equipped with a suppressor, because the station received no reports of sounds which might have been gunfire, around the time Paulina was shot. A hired assassin fits the crime."

132

"If Meredith or Farley are implicated, they needed to hire help. Farley volunteered information related to possible access in Florida for either one to make a connection through another realtor. Is this the route you want to follow in the investigation?" She's not convinced but avoids a direct challenge to Aiden's train of thought.

"I'm open to other theories."

Her ideas pour out. "These are all possibilities. Danielle was threatened by Paulina. Paulina was in the process of dumping Farley for a new man. Or, she had a previous lover who was jealous of Farley."

"If the latter is the case, Farley becomes a logical target."

"Are the police able to access Paulina's phone records to determine if she made calls to Danielle or Jane?"

"Yes, we can request statements from the phone company. I will also make a request stateside for Danielle's. And you will speak informally with Cavelle?"

"Certainly. If we ask her to come to the office, we broadcast our suspicions to the world. Cavelle is the person able to confirm Meredith's and Farley's alibis for the evening of April 30. I'll make a lunch date."

"Speaking of coming to the office, I expect Danielle and Jane Braddon before the end of the week. As for Farley and Meredith, either one of them could have visited Paulina after the meeting ended at eleven o'clock. One could point the finger at the other."

CHAPTER 15

They Could be a Watercolour

"We'll visit out here at the park on Sunday, but can we try to set up a lunch date for Saturday and include Cavelle?"

"What the hell for?" Trixie is abrasive.

"I want to review what was going on the night Paulina died. You and Russ were supposed to eat here with Nick and me."

"He weaseled out and said a work issue came up. Same old story. Nothing new."

Stella shuts her eyes in a desperate attempt to harness her patience. "You called Cavelle and she was scheduled for a meeting. I understand. The facts aren't the problem. I want to search for nuances. Cavelle's input is important."

"You want to interview her, but not at the RCMP detachment? What's happened? Paulina's sister and daughter are in town. A talk with Cavelle is tangled up with their visit, right?"

"Danielle and Jane Braddon." The act of avoiding a direct answer grates on Stella's sense of integrity, but the situation can't be helped. The ability to share information is limited at best.

"They visited Brigitte today," Trixie replies. "She said both were very nice. Jane is on the weird side. They're not interested in selling Yellow House. They told Brigitte she can stay and run the business for the foreseeable future, if she can manage the expenses. Mrs. Braddon felt the bookstore might be able to provide Jane with a small stipend, although Brigitte thought they don't appear to be people who need extra money."

"Aiden and I interview them tomorrow, which is why I can't meet with you and Cavelle until Saturday. Are you in? Yes or no?"

"I have to work on Friday anyway. Cavelle, too, I imagine. Will you pay the tab? I'm short, with two weeks until payday. Any chance you might write me an advance on my park cheque?"

"How much do your need?"

"Three will work."

"I'll give you the cheque on Saturday. Okay?"

"Thanks. I stocked Brigitte's kitchen and bathroom. I didn't want to confess to her, but my generosity slashed the budget."

"No problem. We'll plan on lunch around eleven o'clock at Cocoa and Café, because I expect the place to be quiet—easier to have a private conversation. If you don't hear back from me, we're set for Saturday."

"And my cheque?"

She tries not to let her exasperation show. "Yes, Trixie...and I'll buy."

After a quick break to refresh her coffee and check with reception, Stella retreats to her office once more, to call Cavelle.

Russ answers the phone. "Grey Cottage Realty. We are here to serve your housing needs. How may I help?"

"Hi! How are you?"

"Good, Stella, good. What can we do for you? Want to increase the size of the park and buy more land?"

His enthusiasm is tiresome and over-reaches. "Not today. Need to chat with Cavelle, if she's around."

"Sure. By the way, I expect Sunday should be quite a shindig, what with Nick's parents visiting."

"Sunday afternoon will be fun, as long as the weather holds. And Cavelle?"

"Yeah, right. Gimme a second."

The line goes dead and for a moment she worries he's cut her off. Cavelle's voice breaks into the silence. "Good morning, Stella. To what do I owe the pleasure?"

"Are you available for lunch at eleven on Saturday? My treat. Trixie will join us."

Silence returns. "What are you up to, Stella?"

"Honest answer? I want to review specific elements of the hours before I found Paulina. We've missed a detail along the way. If Aiden and I ask you to come to the station, tongues will start to wag. We decided a quiet and early lunch at the café with Trixie and me might be the better option." She pauses. "And I didn't spell it out to my sister before talking to you."

"What kind of help can I be?"

"I'm not sure yet, but I want to walk through every minute of the Thursday night when Paulina died. You met with Farley and Meredith, but times and discussion topics may shed more light on the chain of events."

"Do you suspect Meredith or Farley? Because they were with me until eleven o'clock."

"Will you meet Trixie and me on Saturday?" *I'm getting good at this.*

"The discussion isn't official, correct? And no need for a lawyer?"

"No, but confidential, okay?"

"Okay, but don't anticipate much. I am not privy to insider information. You're well involved in your whole murder-investigator job, aren't you?"

"Aiden and the RCMP formalized my role as a consultant. We discuss ideas and interview people related to a case—a small contribution." She hopes the attempt to minimize her work with the police has succeeded.

"Must run, Stella. I'm scheduled to show a house, and Meredith insists Russ tag along."

Cavelle is unimpressed with the idea of Russ as part of her appointment.

As Stella begins her rounds to check on the staff, Nick dances through her thoughts. She has seen a change in how he interacts with Tobias and Yona. In her opinion, they seem closer; more relaxed in each other's company, like the pressure is off. Nick tells her his guard is still up most of the time. Today they took the Jeep to do a tour of Port Ephron and the countryside around the isthmus. She expects them home for dinner. She sees Eve on one mower and hears the smaller version in the distance. Who wins the battle for the bigger machine is never a secret.

****

Stella dresses with care—a rare occurrence in the summer—before she travels into town to Aiden's office where she will meet Paulina's sister and daughter. The reason must make sense to her deepest psyche—the need to present herself in the same light as when she used to go to Yellow House for lunch. Paulina always dressed her best, regardless of the weather, and Stella finds herself compelled to do the same today in her friend's honour. Satisfied with slate trousers, a pink short-sleeved cardigan, and pale rose crystals in her pierced ears, she asks Alice if any errands are required, as she readies to leave.

For a Friday morning in mid-June, Shale Harbour is quiet. With few cars around, she's able to find a spot to park near the detachment. Sergeant Moyer is in position on the front desk and it's always a pleasure to see his familiar face. He heaves himself to his feet and leads her straight down the hall to Aiden's office. "They're waiting for you," he whispers over his shoulder.

"I'm not late," she hisses back, sensitive to her previous experience.

"They were early," he mouths while he taps on the door and pushes inward.

"Miss Kirk's here, Detective North." She's amused by the erectness of his posture when he announces her name.

"Good morning, Stella! Come in. Come in." Aiden stands. "Thank you, Sergeant Moyer. You may close the door. Let me introduce you to Danielle and Jane Braddon. Mrs. Braddon, Jane, meet Stella Kirk. She consults with me on complicated cases and she was a close friend of your sister."

The woman positioned in the wooden chair across from Aiden could be Paulina. She's turned and expectant, while she waits for a response to her outstretched hand. Despite the plumper physique and hair streaked with grey, the resemblance unnerves Stella. "How do you do? Nice to meet you, Mrs. Braddon."

"Please, call me Danielle. This is my daughter, Jane. Dear, say hello to Aunt Paulina's friend, Stella."

The young woman in the second chair lifts her face. Long straight brown hair hangs in curtain fashion along both cheeks. She has a prominent nose and peculiar grey penetrating eyes. She peers at Stella for a moment and says, "Hello," before she turns her attention back to a colourful bridal magazine.

"Mrs. Braddon has told me how she and Jane arrived Wednesday. They met with Brigitte yesterday." He points to an extra chair, absconded from the interview room and positioned beside his desk. They sit simultaneously.

Stella tries not to stare at the two women. They could be a water colour of Paulina and Hester in the distance. The figures before her are the essences of her friends. She wants to hug Danielle; to capture the ether of Paulina. In addition, and to anyone who knows the story, Jane is no doubt Leon's daughter. Stella's heart breaks to meet a reflection of her friend. "Forgive my stare, Danielle. You and Paulina could be twins."

Danielle sits up straighter and picks at imaginary lint on her blue denim skirt. "Paulina resembled me in many ways. I am older by two years. She and I have never lived our lives based on the same values, or even similar preferences."

"My sister, Brigitte's mother, told me you had a productive visit at Yellow House yesterday."

"Correct. We asked Miss Kirk to remain. We have no interest in the property and no need for an influx of cash. I expect the business may provide Jane with a small monthly income based on profit share. Our concern is only that Brigitte maintain the asset and support both herself and her little girl."

"My niece told me she collected Paulina's personal items and stored them away."

"Yes, although I expect to destroy most of the junk she's boxed up with such care. I asked her to ship the lot to New York and I'll face my sister's knick-knacks later." She turns to Aiden. "On our visit to meet Brigitte Kirk, I did not explain Paulina's relationship to Jane. The information is personal. Do you agree?"

"At this point, I see no need to publicize family ties, Mrs. Braddon. Much depends on the progress of the investigation."

In a momentary loss of control, and shocked that Jane knows Paulina was her mother, Stella adds, "Jane has two half-sisters and a half-brother she might want to know."

"And another half-sibling in jail, charged and convicted in the death of her father. Not a wise idea, Stella."

Jane drags her attention away from the magazine. Her eyes are filled with wistfulness and intelligence, but not comprehension. "I want to meet my sisters and brother, but Mother says no. I must listen to Mother's advice." She juts her chin toward Stella. "Because my judgment is poor."

"Mrs. Braddon, Jane appears aware of the circumstances of her birth. If she doesn't need to be excused, will you repeat the details for us now?"

"Detective North, I fear my parents lied to me for twenty-one years. My birthmother was Aunt Paulina. I understand. There are no more secrets."

"Everything is fine, Jane. Detective, my sister was involved with an old farmer named Leon Painter. He had three daughters, a baby son, and a dead wife. His goal was to convince Paulina to become a young mother for his children. One of them, Hester, I am told, faces similar challenges as Jane."

"Can you describe these challenges?"

"Yes, but Jane will tell you." She pats her daughter's knee.

Jane lifts her face again, startled at the intrusion. "I am special. Many doctors suggest I'm unique. I am very smart, but my focus is specific subjects, not people. I can't figure out when topics of conversation are funny or serious. I speak at the wrong time. I am too direct and, as a result, am often frowned upon in society. I am a cake expert."

"You are a cake expert," Stella repeats. She glances toward Aiden and then asks, "Will you explain your specialty, Jane?"

"Don't show too much interest," Danielle warns. "Be brief, Jane. The detective and Stella have a schedule and we must pack.

"My mother has a small catering business for weddings and parties. I do the cakes. I study every nuance of buttercream, fondant, ganache, marzipan, and tempered chocolate. I can decorate in basket weave, cornelli filigree, scallops, or rosettes. I create unusual European tortes and cakes with multiple tiers."

"She will talk your leg off," Danielle interrupts. "Enough, Jane."

Her eyes revert to her magazine until Stella asks, "Do you possess any other special skills, Jane?"

Danielle answers, instead. "Jane is a human diary. She remembers my schedule back two years at least. I never write an appointment on a calendar. I simply tell Jane."

"Describe to us what happened when Paulina contacted you and wanted to come to New York to give birth to her baby." Aiden wants to refocus attention toward the case.

"Leon Painter died in October. She was devastated and shocked to be pregnant. She called me in a panic. Seth and I were married five years and not able to start a family. We never understood the reason. Seth gave her permission to come stay at our home. He and I paid her medical bills, and she turned Jane over to us." She rummages in her bag. "I brought all the papers for the lawyers to see that every detail of the adoption was legal. We spared no expense."

"I don't doubt you for a second, Mrs. Braddon. Why did Paulina end up settled in Shale Harbour in the first place?"

"She fell in love with the community, or the house. I'm not sure. She was very young—with no clue about what she wanted, so our folks lent her money. I can't tell you how much, but they left no savings when they died. The money was for her to travel, but in the end, she bought her yellow house, ran the little business, and wintered in Florida. After Jane was born and she returned to Shale Harbour, she only contacted us at Christmas and Jane's birthday each year, with a card and a cheque. Our agreement included no visitation. She became estranged Aunt Paulina."

A bead of perspiration appears on her upper lip. She swipes at the dampness with one hand and pats Jane's knee with the other. "Jane is fully aware of the information, by the way. We talked, as she mentioned. I told her the truth, but she doesn't care."

"And your parents?"

Danielle sounds impatient. Her shoulders heave before she starts. "Our parents ran a rundown dry-cleaning outlet in Albany, for an irresponsible Lebanese business tycoon in New York City. He didn't pay them much. They worked themselves to death. Both died of cancer. They were young. No surprise."

"What money they managed to scrape together was given to Paulina, correct?" Aiden probes.

"My parents were dreamers who never escaped that outdated solvent-trap hole-in-the-wall they called a business. Paulina was a dreamer, too, and they supported her. They were never fond of practicality."

"You were the practical one?" Stella knows the answer.

"Yes, I attended secretarial school, married Seth, and contributed to our home. We own a small house, but the property has increased in value. We took in Jane. We were a family until Seth died two years ago."

"We are still a family," Jane interrupts. "Aunt Paulina wanted to join us, and you refused." Jane turns her attention from Danielle to Stella. "I was a challenge to raise. My mother needs to be congratulated for a superior job."

"Enough, Jane. Go back to your magazine. When we return to New York, we are scheduled to meet with the Margosians to plan a wedding reception. She wants a cake with flowers and six tiers. Your magazine will give you inspiration."

"Yes, Mother. I am inspired." Jane turns her attention to her lap and the glossy pictures which have, for the moment, not seemed particularly inspirational.

Aiden clears his throat. "Mrs. Braddon. A person or persons unknown entered Paulina's home late on the evening of April 30. We are convinced she admitted them. She was shot. I can imagine a few reasons you might want to guarantee your sister out of your life."

Danielle sits straighter in her chair. She uncrosses her legs and crosses them again. She repeats her habit of patting her daughter's knee. "Detective North, let me be frank. I did not kill my sister. I'm sure you're able to determine our current trip is my first entry into Canada since 1970 when Seth and I took Jane to see the Rocky Mountains in Banff National Park. An extraordinary vacation, correct, Jane?"

Jane nods but doesn't make eye contact. "The United States and Canada do not track specific visitors to each other's countries, Mother."

"She's right, Mrs. Braddon." Aiden watches her face.

"Although the police do not track the travel plans of Americans and Canadians, I am happy to report my mother's schedule for the last month, if the information helps."

Stella recalls Hester's knowledge of every meal eaten in the Painter household; every detail; every choice.

Aiden provides foolscap and a pen. "A list of actions and whereabouts, phone calls, and letters received will prove helpful, Jane. Whatever you can recall."

She reaches for the yellow paper. "I remember, sir. I will start with today and work backwards. You may tell me when to stop."

After Stella secures silent permission from Aiden, she begins. "Danielle, is life better or worse with Paulina no longer in the picture?"

Danielle flushes and sputters.

Before she has an opportunity to craft a response, Jane interrupts her task, to answer. "Life is better for my mother with Aunt Paulina gone because Aunt Paulina wanted to meet me. My mother was afraid of the transfer of my affections from her to my birthmother. I tried to reassure her, but to no avail."

"My daughter has a most annoying habit. She expresses truth no matter how painful."

Stella is not deterred. "Do either of you own a gun?"

Jane guffaws—a bark-like sound which once again reminds Stella of Hester. "Neither of us owns a gun or has ever used a gun of any kind."

Danielle sits in quiet contemplation for a moment. "Seth owned a nine-millimetre pistol. He kept his weapon at a club but never indulged after Jane came. The organization still has possession, I guess." Her shoulders heave. "I lost track."

Stella forges on. "Jane, if I may interrupt, did you ever hear any assassination discussions in your house?"

"Oscar Romero was assassinated on March 24, 1980 and John Lennon on December 8, 1980." Her expression is angelic; secretive. "Your theory is that my mother killed Aunt Paulina or hired an assassin. I will describe each day of her life as far into the past as you care to go. I can write every conversation, client, and call. She has never left me overnight. I expect you are on the wrong track."

"Are you ever alone for the entire day, Jane?"

A frown clouds her face for an instant. "Yes. There are appointments, but you could confirm if she showed up." Satisfaction follows on the heels of her initial expression.

"You see?" Danielle's tone has become more authoritative. "Detective North, we met with Stephens and Stephens. We interviewed Stella's niece and confirmed how we will deal with Paulina's house—soon to be Jane's asset. We answered your questions. May we return to our hotel and pack? We board our plane tomorrow afternoon. I want to be ready to check out by nine in the morning."

"Fine, Mrs. Braddon. We appreciate your time. I expect the body to be released within a few days."

"I am not interested in the repatriation of my sister's remains to New York. She is to be cremated. The people in Shale Harbour can memorialize her whatever way they choose." She stands. "Come along, Jane. We must pack."

"Yes, Mother. I will finish my list and bring your pad back," she says to Aiden. They don't wait for an officer to escort them to the entrance. Danielle's posture is erect, and summons the memory of Paulina one last time. Jane assumes a spot at Danielle's heels. Her shoulders are rounded, and her pace is a shuffle.

The word servitude comes to mind.

Aiden glances at his watch. "Shall we find a minute to debrief over the weekend? I have to be in Port Ephron in thirty minutes." Reacting to Stella's expression, he adds, "We can talk while Rosemary's distracted by her sisters."

$$\clubsuit$$

CHAPTER 16

Consider the Offer

Treasure these mornings. Her mother's mantras always surprise her when they invade her thoughts. Seated in one of the two rattan chairs which grace the small deck off their upstairs suite, she is wrapped in a glorious Saturday. The staff has yet to arrive and, as she scans out over the campground and toward the ocean, there isn't a sound but for birds, and not a breath of wind. *Treasure these mornings.*

Nick steps out on the balcony with two cups of coffee. The woodsy smell of hazelnuts wafts toward her. "Is this a fine day, or what?" He hands her a mug, grazes her hair with his lips, and plunks into the chair nearby.

"You've enjoyed your parents' visit, right?" She needs validation; to be told she hasn't hindered their time together; hasn't unduly influenced the connection he's made with his family.

"We toured the sights, ate in swanky restaurants, including the Purple Tulip again, and now they understand the reasons I live here and why we do what we do." He reaches for her hand where it hangs over the arm of the chair. "Except for your age...."

She drags her gaze away from the view long enough to check his expression; to confirm his words are meant to tease.

Her lover's slow smile lights his face in the same way the sunlight creeps across the veranda. "In all seriousness, they mentioned our age difference often, but I love you and years on the earth don't relate."

"I'm forty-six." She points out the obvious. "I can't change the number, Nick." She looks away. Insecurity's ugly head has reared yet again.

"Just kidding. Come on! You're aware I was kidding! The upside of the story is that Dad advised me to buy Trixie out. He even offered to float me the funds I need if I don't have enough money of my own, but Aunt Ruth's dough is burning a hole in my pocket."

His hand drops when she lets go and sits up straight in her chair. The wicker creaks with the effort. "Your parents said you should buy Trixie's share? Were they serious?"

"Yes. Dad figures Shale Cliffs is a good investment. He said we could use the money you pay Trixie every month now, to negotiate a loan and install a septic system."

"Honest to God, Nick. I'm dumbfounded. I can't *even* predict Trixie's reaction."

"If the money I paid for the upgrade to the water equates to ten percent, we'll calculate the values. You buy five percent and I'll buy forty. We'll be in business together for the long haul. Besides, Trixie might appreciate an infusion of cash." He grabs her hand again and kisses her palm. "I heard Alice and Paul come in a minute ago. Since Eve isn't here today, Paul and I have lots to do. I'll run downstairs and review my list."

"Where's Eve?"

"You gave her the weekend off to attend a family party, remember? She said she was on Grandma Del duty."

"Right." She leans into the back of her chair. "You've stunned me with your idea, Nick. My mind is mush."

"Consider the offer." He studies her face. "No need for any quick decisions. If you want to explore options, we can talk with your sister later."

When she appears, dressed for her lunch date with Cavelle and Trixie, her staff are seated around the kitchen table. Alice has made more coffee. Various jams, peanut butter, a tinfoil pie plate stacked with brown bread toast, a jug of milk, and a bowl of sugar clutter the table.

Alice and Paul, as is often the case, are donned in neon-coloured park T-shirts. Today, one is in orange and the other green. The combo is eye-rattling. Duke arrived before Nick showed up downstairs. Much to Stella's annoyance, he's seated at the head of her table in a muscle shirt designed for a man half his age; his hairy chest and shoulders exposed to the world, or at least to those present in her house. A Hawaiian shirt, patterned with lavender palm fronds, hangs across the back of his chair. "Good morning, everyone. Duke, shirt on in my house, please. Kiki has less hair."

Without a retort, likely because his mouth remains stuffed with toast,

Duke places Kiki on the floor and reaches for his shirt. Kiki, decked out in a lavender T-shirt which matches the palm fronds to perfection, runs to Alice.

"Thanks."

He swallows. "No problem. We're gonna have a hot one."

"True, but when you're at the house or involved in site rounds, I want you to represent the park at least semi-professionally. I'm not sure today's choice fits the bill."

"Gift from an ex-wife. She was a grouch, but I still love it. Right from Hawaii." He straightens the front.

Stella gazes around the table. "I have a lunch date at the café at eleven." She focuses her attention on Alice. "How are reservations?"

"For the middle of June, we're okay, Stella. We have spaces for different sizes, and two parties from the States arrive today, for a week. Lots of checkouts tomorrow. Kids are still in school. I'm under control." Her red curls bob.

"We need to finish the lawns, do water tests, and inspect the filters, but Paul will start with the bathrooms since Eve isn't here."

Paul screws up his nose.

"Janitorial chores are a thankless job, Paul, but Eve cleans every day without a complaint." Stella eyes Nick for confirmation.

"I'll lend a hand. We haven't hosted too many tenters. The bathrooms aren't bad," he consoles while he munches.

"Nick and I have planned a barbecue tomorrow. As is usual, you're welcome to stay." Under normal circumstances, the staff, except for Duke, leave at five in the afternoon. Stella covers the front until eight and manages any stragglers after reception is closed. She always invites the help to attend a family and friends party.

The Morgan siblings refuse in unison. "Mom wants us home for Sunday supper, Stella, but I'll help you prepare if the afternoon's quiet."

She can't comprehend Shale Cliffs without her. What *will* she do without Alice? One more season before she'll be out of university and at work full-time for some lucky employer. "Duke?"

"Not tomorrow. Kiki and me, we're goin' to a big bun-throw over at Port Ephron RV Park. Both the food and the company will be great—no offense."

"None taken. Anybody we know?"

Duke's expression is lustful. "She likes Hawaiian shirts, Stella."

****

Cocoa and Café is warm. There's no air conditioner, but the old carriage factory reborn as a café is bearable with the two ceiling fans and an oscillating version near the till. Stella is the first to arrive and chooses a bistro table in the far corner. Tiffany Blair is behind the counter and nods as Stella crosses the floor.

"Good morning. Nice to see you."

"Hi, Tiffany. Quiet?"

"For another forty-five minutes. Saturday mornings are slow, but we pick up near noon. By yourself?"

"Nope. My sister and Cavelle Painter are due any minute. Will we be able to have lunch this early?"

"No problem. I've made egg salad croissants and coleslaw. Iced tea and strawberry shortcake. Cool choices for a hot day?"

"Sounds perfect. I'll have the iced tea now."

Tiffany sets the tall glass on the tiny table. Condensation soon covers the outside. The bells above the doorway tinkle when Cavelle and Trixie spill into the restaurant. They dance toward her as they gab. Chunky jewellery flashes, suitcase-size purses are dropped to the floor, and short skirts are adjusted as both women settle.

"Good morning, you two."

"Good morning." Trixie is the first to interrupt pleasantries. "What's the special today?"

Stella reaches into her purse and extracts an envelope. "As promised. And lunch is on me—for both of you, Cavelle. I appreciate your time. As for food, I'll let Tiffany tell you. She expects the place to get busy shortly, so I'll ask my questions while the café is still quiet. Okay?"

"As I said, I doubt if I can enlighten you. The meeting was a bore."

With a quick nod toward Tiffany, the owner approaches and confirms they'll each have the special.

Once the iced teas are served, Cavelle adds, "I don't understand what you want."

"I want you to describe both Meredith and Farley's demeanour; how they behaved throughout the evening. Also, what was on the agenda? Were other topics discussed—items not listed?" She turns to Trixie. "I asked you here to tell me your whereabouts before you landed at the park. Consider what you might have inadvertently observed, okay? Cavelle, you first."

Cavelle retrieves a notebook out of her bag. "I copied the agenda before I left the office. I thought the items were stupid at the time. I wanted to list them for you. Meredith bought a VCR after she went to her last realtor conference in Florida. She was impatient to show us a training video."

"How were the items stupid?"

"Three issues were noted: reception rotation, paperwork updates, and new leads."

Stella nods encouragement. "And your concerns?"

Cavelle runs fingers through her shingled haircut while a silent Tiffany places their lunches on the tiny table. "First off, we have a schedule for reception coverage. She made no changes except to say Farley should work more often. As for new forms, we use them now. The updated paperwork was not *brand* new."

"And leads?"

"We chase our own leads. Meredith made a point to ask if I felt overwhelmed. I told her no. I have never been too busy to cope with my workload."

"So, her remarks were odd?"

"Yes. I assumed they related to Farley, who spends more time at home writing his book, now. Whenever he happens to grace the office with his presence, he covers reception duties, but for her, not me. I always manage my own time at the front desk. He's no real asset to me." She pants her frustration. "And the video was for beginners. It was a total bore."

"She hired Russ not quite three weeks later," Trixie contributes. "Meredith might have anticipated business was picking up and she wanted more help. Maybe the need to increase staff was her motivation for the meeting."

"Plausible, but she never said another agent was an option. Then in comes Russ—the new employee. When I reviewed the chain of the events afterward, I wondered if she had already decided to hire him to work at Grey Cottage before we ever met April 30."

"Russ never told me until May 18, when we were at Stella's house," Trixie pouts.

"That's not to say I'm right, Trixie." Cavelle is eager to appease her friend. "Meredith could have been pondering and Russ appeared at an opportune moment."

"Thanks, Cavelle. Can you describe their attitudes around the table?"

"Farley was fidgety. He peered out the window into the gloom a dozen times. He couldn't sit still. He often stood up for no apparent reason and he drank four glasses of water. I recall, at one point, I raised my eyebrows at him. He said his back was sore from sitting at his desk in the basement at home and spending hours writing."

"And Meredith?"

"In retrospect, she acted like she wanted our meeting to last late into the night. She detailed ridiculous issues. Here's an example: I am a licensed professional. I cannot tell you how many real estate deals I've completed, representing the seller, the buyer, and oftentimes in a town this size—both. She insisted we complete a workshop-style instruction on the proper method used to close a deal and obtain signatures." She huffs. "To be honest, an evening listening to Hester present a wildflowers lecture holds more appeal."

"Did you mention to me the meeting ended at eleven?"

"A quarter to eleven. Afterward, I told her I expected to be in late the next morning because I needed to make up for the time I wasted. Funny, she didn't react. She said 'fine' and for me to come in tomorrow whenever I wanted. She'd cover reception. Then we left."

"Do you suspect Meredith made up an agenda to fill time?"

"It sure seemed that way. And Farley didn't want to be at the office, either."

"Thank you. I appreciate this. I can't say more, except your observations may well have moved our investigation forward." She swivels toward Trixie. "Your turn."

"I have no idea what you want from me."

"You were supposed to come out to the park with Russ."

Trixie nods.

"He was called to work. You telephoned Cavelle and when she couldn't skip her commitment, you ended up at my place, anyway."

"Correct. I'm such a loser."

Stella attempts another tactic. "After Lorraine was murdered, do you remember when we both visited Ruby Wilson, and I asked you to observe— to register what you saw?"

"She nods."

"Can you recall your observations when you drove through town before you arrived out at the park?"

"I'm a lovesick fool."

"What? Why?"

"I crept around every street and back alley in Shale Harbour first. I was convinced Russ wasn't called to work. I suspected he had a girlfriend stashed away."

"You must have been wrong. You're still involved with him."

"An overreaction." She shrugs her shoulders. "Me and my emotions." She frowns. "A truck almost like his blue Ford 150 was parked one block over from Main, on Maple Street. I threw a tantrum the next day. He insisted the vehicle wasn't his, although I was certain at the time. There are lots of blue trucks around, and it was parked under a tree in the gloom, but I was furious." Her wrist rattles with bracelets when she fluffs her curls. "He met with a new client in Port Ephron. We're fine now." She doesn't make eye contact with either woman.

"Let's move away from your love life for a minute. Were there any vehicles or people near Paulina's place?"

"Neither man nor beast around Yellow House. Sorry."

****

Back home, the staff have finished their feast of ham sandwiches and fresh strawberries. Duke has returned to his trailer for an afternoon snooze. With Nick and Paul at the pump house and Alice occupied with reservation requests, Stella takes the opportunity to wander around the park and check on her guests. Trixie suggests her habit of visiting with both seasonals and over-nighters invites trouble, but Stella views her visits as an exercise in issue-prevention. People will often talk to the owner when she appears on site but won't venture up to the office to report a problem. Trixie doesn't believe in over-turning rocks.

Buddy McGarvey has moved into Louise and Bob Stone's trailer. His monster truck is wedged in close to his rig. Bell waddles out to the edge of the lot to greet Stella when she approaches. "Hi, old girl. Your dad nearby?" Dogs aren't permitted to wander in the park.

"Right here, Stella. Bell won't leave the site. No need to worry none."

"How's the new place, Buddy?"

"Pretty posh. Me and Bell are comfy. Time for a beer?"

"Thanks, but not today. Makin' my rounds. Your nephews settled in?" She pats Bell once more.

"I'm keepin' an eye on them."

"Okay. See ya."

Mildred Fox, resplendent in a purple and green caftan, is stretched out in a dilapidated orange basket chair on a deck in such disrepair, Stella worries about the old lady's safety.

"Hi, Stella. Checkin' up on me?"

"How've you been?"

"Good. Good." She hoists a plastic glass which Stella is sure does not contain lemonade and cackles in her signature special way. "What do ya think of my outfit?"

"The colour is bright."

"I have two more. Old girl at the seniors' died last month. Her daughters brought them to me after I moved out here. They told me she wasn't dressed in any of 'em when she was circlin' the drain." She scratches her thigh. "Makes no never mind to me if she was wearin' one on her way out. They fit me good."

"May I send Paul and Nick to repair your deck, Mildred? This contraption is ready to fall apart."

"There's no extra money." She takes a sip of lemonade and swallows her embarrassment.

"Nick has spare deck material stashed behind the cottage. I'll ask him, okay?"

"You can share your sexy man with me any time you want." She cackles again.

After more that a dozen stops to chat with guests, she turns toward Aiden and Rosemary's unit. Aiden is using a push mower to tidy the lawn around the trailer. Rosemary and her sisters are nowhere to be seen. "Hi. Busy?" He said they could debrief over the weekend.

"Basking in the sunshine. Rosemary's off with Mary Jo and Toni. They're probably shopping. They might be back at the cottage by now. How did your lunch go with Trixie and Cavelle?"

"Interesting observations." She sits on the edge of the stairs which lead into the trailer and recalls how she yelled for Lorraine to answer her door on that first day before they realized she was missing. The memory is forever burned into her brain. "Cavelle claims the staff meeting felt contrived and lasted until ten-forty-five. Little was accomplished. She said Farley was fidgety. She's convinced Meredith prolonged the agenda. Cavelle told me she even took a chance and complained she needed the morning off to make up for the meeting and Meredith wasn't fizzed."

"Meredith dragged and Farley twitched." He shields his eyes from the sun.

Perhaps he doesn't find Cavelle's observations as fascinating as she does. "Then there's Trixie."

"Trixie? What's her connection to Paulina's death?"

Stella gulps. "I hope not much. Russ cancelled on her. He was supposed to come with her to my place. She tried to entice Cavelle, but Meredith had emphasized the session was mandatory. She drove around town on the hunt for Russ' vehicle and ended up out here for supper after all."

Aiden's attention is sparked. He's lost interest in the mower. "Any sign of a person near Paulina's?"

"I wish. She told me 'neither man nor beast', in her words. She assumed a truck parked on Maple Street belonged to Russ, but he was in the Port to meet with a client."

He squints at her while she sits on the stairs. "I doubt there's any possibility Danielle Braddon hired a professional—a person from her husband's gun club. Jane's list was exhaustive. I still want to investigate further, though, but after we figure out the Tompkins couple. We need to talk to Meredith."

"Agreed. A joint interview with both Meredith and Farley might prove interesting, too."

"We'll invite Meredith in the first of the week. She's still our best suspect."

"Albeit, a suspect with a solid alibi."

Aiden returns to his mower. "A solid alibi until late in the evening, true, but I'm not prepared to give her the benefit of the doubt, yet." The rumble of Toni's Mustang announces the arrival of Rosemary and her sisters. The top is down. Rosemary is standing while she waves a straw bag with a red star flower on the side. When she sees Stella, she flops back into the rear seat, crosses her arms, and scowls.

CHAPTER 17

Diplomacy is a Struggle

The Mustang whizzes past her house mid-afternoon the next day. Toni and Mary Jo must be on their way to Aiden's campsite. Guests will start to arrive any moment. One last survey in the full-length mirror. Wide-legged jeans and a white sleeveless blouse—the best she can do today. She pats her short hair in an act of acceptance and races down the worn stairs into the kitchen.

Nick, in khaki shorts and a navy T-shirt, turns from the sink when she materializes in the doorway. "You look fabulous, my dear."

She blushes, as usual. "You, too." She blushes again. "Are we ready? I expect a big crowd." She surveys the empty kitchen. "Where's my table, by the way?"

"We're finished. I chopped the strawberries while I waited for you." He dries his hands and ignores her question. "Let me show you what Paul and I put together." He clutches her wrist and pulls her through the living room. The dining table is set up in front of the dark fireplace. Plates, cutlery, and napkins are assembled on top of a white linen tablecloth.

"Perfect for the buffet."

"I'm not finished with show and tell yet. Come on."

His hand tightens around hers—a welcome sensation.

Out on the veranda, he's situated the kitchen table against the wall of the house. He found another white cloth somewhere. In addition to glasses, more napkins, and an oval metal tub for ice, there's the huge pitcher of lemonade Alice made after lunch. "I'll fill the old cauldron I discovered in the pantry with ice, soft drinks, and beer from the fridge."

"Aren't you smart?" She catches a whiff of his leathery scent. "I wasn't upstairs very long."

"Paul helped. Alice, too. The food's ready, except for what our guests contribute."

Stella sees Trixie's VW Microbus approach. Russ' new sports car is in hot pursuit. When the two vehicles turn into the back lot, Brigitte is behind the wheel of the van while Trixie rides shotgun with Russ.

"Nice wheels," she hears Nick remark as Russ climbs the stairs to the porch with a case of local brew. "Let me take those off your hands. I have the ice ready. And how have you been?"

Their voices are muffled by the sounds of crushed ice rattling against the sides of the tub. Trixie calls out. Stella races across the lot to help her unload a white pail filled with more ice and lots of cooked lobster from the van. "Great! The salad's made. All we'll need to do is toss in the lobster." Trixie's pained expression screams volumes. "Nick," Stella hollers over her shoulder. "Will you come and hoist this bucket?"

Nick traverses the veranda stairs with two jumps and is by her side in a moment. "Hand over the load, ladies."

"I brought a bean salad, Aunt Stella. Business is crazy at Yellow House. I didn't appreciate how hard poor Paulina worked." She gives the bowl to her mother and reaches back into the van for Mia.

"You need a break from the public at large. I'm happy you closed for the afternoon." Stella leans over to give Mia a quick smooch. "Hi, sweet girl. Come up on the veranda and relax, Brigitte. I have lemonade, wine, beer, pop—whatever you want, and juice in the fridge for our youngest guest." She touches Mia's soft blond curls and leads the way.

On the trek up the stairs, Trixie whispers in her ear. "I think he's going to ask me to move into his cottage with him."

Stella swings around to face her sister. "Really?"

"Don't be shocked. Brigitte's on her own now. He even told me to let her have the VW when she needs it. I'll drive his truck because he prefers the Mercedes. Sounds serious, right?"

As they gather near the stairs, Tobias lumbers his way out to the veranda from reception. Apparently, they walked from their RV site and accessed the house, via the guest area, without her noticing. Stella sees Alice close the screen door before she returns inside. Tobias barks, "Your ride is a Mercedes 280SL. I know my cars."

Russ nods. "Bought her the end of April—brand new and a steal because she's a 1980. My girl, here," he wraps the arm not anchored by a beer around Trixie's waist, "wanted red, but the price on the silver was too good to pass up. Since I'm off the road...."

His voice fades when Tobias turns his attention toward Nick. "What does a man have to do to deserve a real American beer in this place? Didn't I stock your fridge with Budweiser the other day?"

"Comin' right up, Dad. Where's Mom?"

"She took her monster dessert into the kitchen to keep in the freezer until supper."

Before Stella has a chance to check on Yona, the throaty sound of the Mustang invades the yard. Nick whispers in her ear he's on his way to pick up Norbert at Harbour Manor after he fetches beer for Tobias. He'll be back in half an hour.

Aiden and his family approach the stairs. She reads the tense message in his eyes. "Hi, Stella, everyone." He surveys the deck. "I hope Trixie's here. Rosemary wants to visit with your sister," he mutters. His hands balance a vegetable platter and a bowl of potato salad.

Stella nods and accepts his offerings. Yona pops out of nowhere, likely the kitchen, and scuttles off with the food. Introductions will wait. The veranda is chaotic. For two cents, she wishes she had taken off in the Jeep and retrieved Norbert Kirk herself. Mary Jo and Toni escort Rosemary between them as if she's a movie star. "Trixie," Stella shouts through the screen and into the gloom.

"On my way."

"Oh my God, you are a fashion plate, Rosemary. Who did your hair?" The two women embrace.

For a moment, Stella catches Aiden's eye, but he averts his attention to a study of the veranda deck planks. Mary Jo sidles over to Stella. "We shouldn't have come. As much as I hate to admit defeat, she'll be back at the crowbar hotel for a medication adjustment in no time. Toni thought we should have admitted her earlier this week."

"She seems okay." Diplomacy is a struggle, although she understands the situation—the skin-tight and short sheath dress, the stiletto-style sandals, and the exposed cleavage.

"You don't believe we chose those clothes for her, do you?"

The spit from Mary Jo's hissed remark coats her ear. "Hi, Toni. Glad you could come," she adds as Rosemary's other sister approaches.

"I imagine you, me, and Aiden together will be required to corral her today, Mary Jo. She's high as a kite. Afternoon, Stella."

Mary Jo's sigh blends with the wind in the trees. "I'd rather be home with her when she's manic. Sorry, Stella, but Rosemary's worse every day. We have another week. If Aiden doesn't clean up his most recent investigation, we'll extend our stay to help him with her."

"No problem. I'll run into reception and tell Alice to block off the cottage for a third week. We haven't advertised this year. One confirmed reservation in September for the writers retreat and maybe another in August. I can't quite remember." The opportunity to confer with Alice is as good an excuse as any to escape inside.

As she treks through the living room, Stella finds Yona and Trixie seated on a sofa, bookends for Rosemary, snuggled in the middle. Yona is the last person Stella expected to hear in a fashion discussion, but she's an active participant, despite the contrasts. In honour of Rosemary, Trixie dressed in a yellow sun dress and red polka-dot platform shoes. Yona, by contrast, wears her customary black. "Can I fetch anybody a cool drink?" Perhaps the best option is to act like a host, although she can't compete with Nick when social niceties are required.

"I want wine," Rosemary pouts, "but Trixie says I need permission from Big Daddy."

"I believe Big Daddy is her husband," Yona unnecessarily explains.

"Yes. Well, I'll run out and find Aiden. Lemonade for each of you?" She takes a stab at the easy route.

"Wine or zilch." Rosemary crosses her legs and folds her arms.

"I'll have whatever Rosemary has."

Although Stella knows Trixie prefers wine, she appreciates the offer from her sister before she returns to the veranda. Alice will wait.

Russ and Tobias are hovering over the Mercedes while Aiden is seated alone at one end of the wide deck. He nurses a beer and continues his study of the floor. "Hello, my friend. I came to ask you if Rosemary can have a glass of wine."

"Where is she? We shouldn't have come. She's started to unravel."

"Mary Jo and Toni say they'll stay an extra week if you don't wrap the case soon. I'll book the cottage."

"Give her the drink—avoid a scene," he fumes. "We aren't moving fast enough to solve Paulina's murder."

"I know. Here comes Nick back with Dad. One of us always has an eye on Rosemary. Try to have a good time." She pats him on the knee.

"Keep your mitts off my husband. How many times do you need to be told, Stella?"

Rosemary is standing in the living room with her face pressed against the screen. The result is a grotesque monster-like twist to her facial features and breasts.

Stella and Aiden jump up in unison. "Rosemary, Aiden says you may have a glass of wine. I'll pour right now."

She steps away from the screen. Stella hears the word "hurry," before Rosemary turns back into the cool darkness of the house.

Despite the bizarre interaction, she serves wine to an appreciative Trixie and Rosemary, and lemonade to Yona. She talks to Alice for a moment and reserves the cottage for an additional week. She adds the lobster to the salad. Nick finds her enjoying a reprieve while she loads the table in the living room with food. Brigitte helps while Trixie bounces Mia on her knee.

"Need my assistance?"

"No, but I'm happy you're here. How's Dad?"

"Fair to good, as far as I can tell. He knows me, remembers you as my wife, and wants to see Brigitte, Mia, and Trixie."

"And me?"

Nick scans the room. "Trixie, Brigitte. Do you want to take Mia outside to visit with Norbert? He asked for you." Concerned, he adds, "I'll finish up here with Stella."

She sees sympathy in his eyes when he returns his attention to her.

****

After Alice and Paul leave for the day, everyone enjoys a rich summer salad supper. Yona's pineapple and whipped cream dessert is a hit and appears to be Tobias' favourite. He encouraged the choice and took credit multiple times. Stella finds herself seated near Aiden for a moment and watches him size up Russ' new car.

"Cool ride," he remarks.

"Beautiful. He said he could drive the Mercedes more often these days because his travel amounts to real estate showings. No long trips where you need lots of space."

The topic of conversation switches to the writers retreat scheduled for late in September. Trixie is off on a walk with Mia, to admire Auntie Stella's flowers. Brigitte again expresses her concern because she closed Yellow House for the day. She wants to work hard to maintain Paulina's business. "I imagine the retreat will bring in new customers. I plan to order each of the books written by the authors who conduct the workshops. Aunt Stella, you expect the organizers to stay here, correct?"

"Yes. Frances Ellis and her husband, Edward Thomas, along with their adult son, Owen. They live in Port Ephron but didn't want to drive across the isthmus late at night. I can appreciate their decision. Darkness will fall early by the end of September."

"Edward Thomas. Thomas Edward. That man's name can work frontwards or backwards." Norbert wiggles in his chair and slops his tea on the front of his pants.

"You're right, Norbert." No point to say Dad. He argues.

"And Frances Ellis could be Ellis Frances." He crows in self-satisfaction. Stella attempts quiet patience.

"Who else?" He scans the veranda. "Okay, everybody. Give me your name. I'm an old man. I can't remember names."

Each guest states their name, and he repeats the two words in the opposite order. Cochran Tobias. Nope. North Aiden. No good. Carr Toni and Frost Mary Jo. Nope. Nope.

"Andrew Blair from Cocoa and Café, Granddad. He becomes Blair Andrews, right?" Brigitte giggles.

Russ approaches the drinks table. He reaches for another beer out of the oval tub which now contains more water than ice.

"What's you name again, fella?"

Russ hesitates but plays along. "Russ Harrison."

"Harrison, Russ. Nope, but Harry Russell works. Your name works backwards and forewords."

"Good one, Norbert. I never imagined my name that way. Funny, eh?" His cooperative chuckle sounds forced.

Norbert continues to rattle off names of everyone he knows. Kirk Trixie, Kirk Brigitte, Kirk Mia, Cochran Nick...and on and on. He won't be stopped.

As if on cue, Nick suggests the time has come for Norbert to make his goodbyes before he returns to Harbour Manor.

Stella helps him navigate the stairs and supports him as he struggles into the front seat of the Jeep. "I wish you were my daughter, Stella. You're a nice woman and you throw a great party. Thanks for invitin' me."

She gives him a hug. "You are welcome here anytime, Norbert." Her voice is raw, and her throat burns when she talks. "Say hi to Del Trembly when you see her. Tell her your friend Stella says hello."

Mary Jo and Toni approach her in tandem. "I think the time has come to drag our crazy sister out of your hair. We'll be takin' off in a minute or two."

"No need." Yona is cuddled into the settee with Rosemary, and has been, since supper. Trixie and Brigitte are inside cleaning up while Tobias bounces Mia on his shoe and makes horsey sounds. Her shrieks of delight surround the adults. "We're under control."

"Aiden said he needed to return to the office. We'll drive them to the trailer and stay with our sister while he goes into town." Toni curls her lip. "He never quits."

"Not until he discovers who killed Paulina. Let me go inside and find your bowl and platter." She excuses herself and makes her way past her guests.

Yona pats Rosemary's hand as Stella steps around ankles.

"You two seem to be enjoying yourselves," she can't help but say.

"Rosemary is a wonderful although troubled child, Stella." She wraps an arm firmly around Rosemary's shoulders. "You are lucky she is your friend."

"I am indeed."

Rosemary's eyes narrow as she produces a hollow, empty smile and leans in closer to her new ally, Yona.

A prickly sensation scoots along Stella's spine. She nods to Yona and makes her way out to the kitchen where her sister and niece have the dishes almost cleaned up. "Well, you two have been busy." She hugs them both. "Thanks for your help...and the lobster...and the bean salad...and for closing Yellow House for the afternoon. I appreciate every one of your efforts." She touches their arms.

"You're welcome, Aunt Stella."

"A party for Nick's family to meet your relatives was in order. We needed to be here." Trixie is unusually magnanimous. "You have your work cut out for you with his old man," she whispers.

Stella closes her eyes for a moment and nods.

"Has Mia behaved herself?" Brigitte folds the cup towel to hang over the handle on the stove.

"Tobias and Mia are playing horsey. I'll grab Rosemary's dishes. I think the North clan is ready to leave. Toni mentioned Aiden wanted to return to his office."

She hurries outside. The sisters have ushered Rosemary into the Mustang. Aiden lingers on the top step. "Back to Shale Harbour?"

"Thanks for a great afternoon and supper, Stella. Yes, I want to follow up on a detail. I might have a lead; maybe not; who knows?" He rambles and thinks out loud. She knows he has an issue on his mind. "Tell Nick thanks, too. And by the way, your father was helpful today."

"Dad was a help? How?"

"He gave me an idea. I'm curious. Only four o'clock on the west coast."

Stella hesitates. "Okay, I think? Call if you need me. If not, are we still scheduled to interview Meredith Tompkins on Tuesday?"

"After lunch. I'll contact her early tomorrow and request she come in."

****

Nick returns from town a few minutes after Aiden, Rosemary, and her sisters leave.

"Aiden tore up the road as I was on my way in. Does he have a work emergency? Did somebody die? He was movin' awful fast." He drops on to the settee beside his mother.

"He said he wanted to go into town and follow up on a lead." Stella frowns. "He mentioned how Dad was helpful. I can't imagine."

"Your father was in good spirits when I took him home. He insisted we truck along the hall and see if Del was back from her party so he could tell her that her friend, Stella, sent regards." Nick chuckles. "The old guy is a real card."

She's troubled, but without a clear reason. Norbert's dementia presents itself in unpredictable ways. He focuses on absurd topics like backwards names. He remembers distant acquaintances, but any memory of his daughter—the one who gave up a career and moved home to save the park when he could no longer manage—is erased, seemingly for good.

Trixie and Brigitte are seated on loungers. Trixie holds Mia, who faces out to play peek-a-boo with her mother. Tobias nurses another Budweiser. In the meantime, Yona has dashed into the house to find her dessert pan.

With his arm around Stella's shoulder, Nick surveys their family. "Since we're still here and the night is young, Stella and I have a business proposition for you, Trixie."

"What?" Trixie's face pops out from behind Mia. "A proposition for me?"

"Yes. No need for an answer right away, but Stella and I want you to consider the idea of us buying your shares in Shale Cliffs."

"For real?" She turns toward Russ.

He shrugs.

She checks Brigitte's reaction. "The park is your investment, Mom. Do what you think is best. Not for me to say."

"I agree," pipes in Russ, who squints at Stella. "Better be a good deal, though."

"Like I'd flimflam my own sister!" Stella can't keep the exasperation out of her voice.

"How much money and when do you want an answer?"

"She's a woman who knows her mind," Tobias admires from the corner.

"True," Yona contributes from her position in the doorway.

She senses the muscles in Nick's body relax.

"We know what ten percent was worth last year. We can figure out the other forty-five percent. Stella and I hope to be fifty-fifty partners if possible, but only if you want to liquidate."

"That's a lot of cash." She fumbles with the buttons on Mia's sweater. The evening has cooled. "You've surprised me. I'll need some time."

❧

CHAPTER 18

Could a Regular Person Have Killed Her?

She senses more than hears his whisper before she opens her eyes.

"Are you as happy as I am that they're gone?"

Reassurance infuses her insecure spaces. She turns to wrap her arms around his shoulders. "You didn't go with them." Blunt, and not without challenge.

He leans away from her. "Go with them? Stella. Never." He runs a finger along her hairline. "Sooner or later, I'll find a way to convince you I'm here to stay."

She touches his lips with hers before she hides her face in his shoulder. "I'm happy they're gone, too, Nick. The stress started to wear on me. Remember, I couldn't even recall I gave Eve the weekend off?" She meets his gaze. "I was a wreck."

"Yeah, but you hid your nervousness well." He pulls her closer.

Later, before they make their way to the kitchen, she asks, "Did you hear what your mother said to me yesterday before they pulled out?"

"Nope."

"When I bent to hug her, she whispered in my ear that she's blessed to have a daughter, now."

"I wondered." He touches her shoulder. "You made a big impression on both my parents."

"An impression, despite my age?" She giggles. "At least your mother stood up for me."

"Poor Mom," he mutters, almost to himself. "No matter the temperature or the location, she's prepared to attend a funeral at a moment's notice. I wish she would brighten herself up, even a little."

"I don't give a damn how she dresses." She hears confidence in her own voice. "At least with Yona I can be a daughter to someone, if not to my father."

"Norbert is in his own world, my love."

"God only knows what he said to inspire Aiden. I guess the good detective will confide in me when the time's right. We're going to blow this case wide open. I can feel it. The lay of the land has changed somehow. Our interview with Meredith Tompkins after lunch might tell the tale."

"Did she kill Paulina?"

"She or Farley might have hired a hit man—a person they met in Florida last winter. I wonder if you can go to Florida for a real estate convention and find a stranger to kill someone."

"Seems extreme. Any other ideas?"

"Danielle Braddon was threatened by Paulina's desire to get to know Jane."

"Sounds like a reach."

"We're convinced—at least Aiden, given his expertise, is sure—Paulina's death was a professional hit."

"Could a regular person have killed her?"

"Yes. With access to a nine-millimetre weapon and the ability to shoot."

"I wouldn't think there'd be a proliferation of handguns in Shale Harbour. We're no Miami."

"Right. Listen, as much as I would love to, we can't stay up here forever. The staff are downstairs. I want to spend time with everyone before I leave for Shale Harbour, and I need peace and quiet to decide what questions I'll ask Meredith."

As is often the case, Alice, Paul, Eve, and Duke are crowded around her kitchen table. They help themselves to her plentiful supply of brown bread for toast and homemade jam. Kiki snuggles in Alice's arms. With unbridled enthusiasm in the form of soft snorts, she accepts morsels of crust from her indulgent favourite person. Throughout the summer, Kiki becomes more Alice's dog than Duke's.

While she pours Nick and herself their first cup of coffee, the conversation drifts to the workings in the park. Septic services are scheduled today. Nick and Paul will be occupied. Eve has bathrooms and showers to clean. Stella hears her mutter to Alice how men aren't thorough. Nick said he felt they managed when she was gone.

Duke straightens in his chair. "Stella. You need to go talk to those new folks; the young guys in Buddy's tent trailer."

"Problem?" she asks. Duke can be unnecessarily dramatic.

"I saw garbage from Saturday night on the lawn. They let their fire smoke which tormented the neighbours. I yelled at them twice. A bunch of trucks were parked everywhere on Sunday night, even into other lots. Music blared steady."

"Did anyone arrive at the office to complain, Alice?"

"Buddy came in yesterday. He was worried, since Duke had already shown up twice. Said his nephews and their friends were acting wild but he'd take care of any problems."

"I'll talk with them, Duke."

"You need company. Nick's gonna be busy. I'll come along." He reaches across to chuck Kiki under the chin but doesn't make direct eye contact with Alice. "My girl has a first-rate babysitter."

"I don't require an escort, Duke."

"No need to risk a confrontation by yourself, Stella. Let Duke go along." Nick sips his coffee while he peers at her from over the rim.

Concern was pointless. Stella woke up six young men. Buddy stood nearby with Bell and Duke sat on the golf cart. The guys were hungover. Their party lasted into Monday night. Buddy's relatives took responsibility. They were both polite and contrite. She was blunt. If they expected to stay in the park, they must abide by her rules. "Supervise your fires. Learn to build a proper fire without the smoke." She turned to Buddy. "Your uncle will teach you. After eleven o'clock in the evening, you are not to disturb the neighbours. Little ones are in bed." She re-emphasized the regulations related to garbage.

They agreed when she made her point about residency in the park. "I have no problem relocating your tent trailer into the public parking lot. I can rent your spot to another group of campers. The rules are clear. It doesn't matter if you've paid for the season." She shook hands with each one in turn, nodded to Buddy, and hopped on the cart. Duke whisked her away like she was royalty.

"Man, you're good."

She heard the admiration in Duke's voice while they sped back to the house.

****

Office chores occupy the better part of her morning, but routine tasks don't prevent thoughts related to Meredith from sorting themselves in her brain. The biggest question is whether the owner of Grey Cottage Realty was aware of her husband's affair. The woman is smart. Forcing her to reveal her true nature will be their challenge.

The RCMP detachment is quiet for a Tuesday afternoon. She parks the Jeep out front and presents herself at the desk. An unfamiliar face asks her to wait while Detective North is called. She waits. Despite knowing the way by heart, she respects their protocols.

"He says for you to go to the interview room on the right. Do you need me to escort you?"

"No, thanks. I'm a regular." She misses Sergeant Moyer's presence when he's assigned other duties.

The unfamiliar face returns to her paperwork.

"Hi. She's not here, yet, but I expect her any minute." Aiden scowls. "She was not the least bit pleased when I suggested she come to the detachment. She asked if she was under arrest and needed a lawyer. I said my request didn't involve an arrest, although we want to discuss Paulina and what she knows." He stops for a breath. "She gave me to understand she knows very little. We may not discover any new information from her."

"I have an idea. Let's operate under the assumption she suspected Farley's dalliance and see what happens."

"Okay. I hope she doesn't drag legal counsel along." Aiden continues to fume.

"She's a controller, Aiden. She wants to manage you." Meredith arrives fifteen minutes late. By the time she's ushered in by the constable Stella saw at the front, Aiden has calmed.

"Good afternoon, Detective North...and Stella Kirk. Why are you here in the police station?"

Aiden, now composed, answers. "Stella is a consultant on investigations, Mrs. Tompkins."

Meredith makes herself comfortable. She adjusts her white silk blouse visible under the grey pinstripe of her suit jacket, tailored to perfection.

Stella wonders how a woman works in such a tight skirt. *Stop judging.*

After she takes a moment to brush a stray lock of long hair off her face, Meredith places her arms on the table, and clasps her hands. "Now what can I do for you today?"

"Paulina McAdams' murder is an ongoing investigation. Please tell us your whereabouts on Thursday evening, April 30."

Although very poised and collected, Stella notices Meredith's thickly mascaraed eyes narrow before she answers.

"You don't consider me a suspect, do you?"

Aiden provides the standard response. "While we investigate, we gather information from everyone."

"I was in a staff meeting at my real estate office, from seven o'clock until almost eleven. The need for a discussion was critical. Cavelle Painter and my husband, Farley, were with me. You can check with them."

"What made the get-together critical on April 30?"

"Detective North, I run a busy real estate company. Roles and responsibilities are crucial. Everyone must work as a team."

"The subject was teamwork?"

"Yes."

"And the timing of your conversation was important because...?"

Meredith withdraws. She entwines her fingers in her lap and no longer makes direct eye contact with Aiden. "The topic was a priority at the time," she murmurs.

"I have a question, Meredith." Stella begins.

"I'm happy to assist any way I can." She sounds rehearsed. "What?"

"In January, Farley gave himself a significant makeover. Everybody noticed. Were you pleased with his new style statement, or annoyed he spent resources on himself?"

"Very pleased." She plays with her bracelet. She doesn't meet Stella's gaze.

"Meredith, were you jealous or angry with regard to Farley's affair?" The opportunity is seized.

Her eyes shoot up. "Affair?"

"You are a very smart woman. Your husband was involved with Paulina McAdams." She capitalizes on her bold statement. "You knew this."

The white silk collar, exposed above the edge of her suit, shudders in response to the weight of her expulsion of air.

Stella does not back off. "Farley was mesmerized by Paulina. He was serious. Were you jealous or angry, Meredith?"

"All right. If you insist. You obviously have the sordid details. I was more angry than jealous. Farley has become less of a partner and more of a liability over the last years. You'd be angry, too. I followed him one night. I watched the idiot park his car in the lot at Grey Cottage before he skulked along the street and disappeared behind the overgrown bushes in Paulina's driveway. My annoyance and curiosity don't mean I killed her. I have an alibi."

"Understood," Aiden remarks.

"Okay. Are we done here?"

"Meredith, I'm still interested in your staff chat the night Paulina was murdered. Farley has pulled back from his responsibilities. Was this the issue?"

"Correct." Meredith's posture relaxes. "He thinks he's writing a book." Her condescension is palatable. "He spends most of his time locked in his basement office with his scribbles."

"Can you describe the topic of his manuscript?"

She examines her nails. "I wanted him to explore real estate, but *she* convinced him to write about love." Her eyes snap and she glares, first at Aiden and then at Stella. "Farley—a writer of love." Her derisive snort is unexpected. "What does he understand about love? When has he stood beside a person who contributes nothing; provided for a person who never noticed you were even in the room? Farley is an ignorant fool." She's emptied of a measure of her venom; breathless.

Stella knows, now, how jealous Meredith felt. Jealousy is a stronger motivation for murder than anger. "What did you do after you discovered the affair, Meredith?"

"First, I started to organize the writers retreat. I wanted circumstances to appear as if I cared enough to pitch in and create an event geared for him. He didn't want to work much anymore, so I explored the option of hiring another agent."

"Russ?"

"No, not until later. At one point, I approached Pepper Ferguson to see if she might be interested in learning the business. Pepper's goal is to be the manager at the Harbour Hotel." Her eyes narrow. "Can you imagine managing that rundown old hotel as your life's goal?" She sounds disgusted.

"How long have you and Farley been married?"

"For twenty years, Detective."

"How did you meet?"

"We were both twenty-five. We learned real estate with a big firm in the city. Farley and I teamed up and did well. We made decent money." She meets their eyes from under narrow, plucked brows. "He used to have an aunt on his mother's side, who lived nearby. He loved to visit, and the village was without an agency. Once I became a broker, we moved. The rest, as they say, is history." She squeaks when she clears her throat. "Are we through here? I have no pertinent information." She picks up her handbag and makes a move to stand.

"Not yet, Mrs. Tompkins." Aiden turns to Stella.

"If you are to be completely honest with us, Meredith, you were wildly jealous of Paulina. How did you act on your jealousy?" Stella holds her breath.

"I visited her once."

"When did you meet with Paulina?" Stella forces the muscles of her face to remain still. She has discovered the topic of unpleasantness her friend wanted to discuss with her on May 1.

"The week before she was killed."

"Please tell us what happened, Meredith—every detail."

"I went to see her. I saw the visit as a gracious attempt at reason. I accepted a cup of tea. We sat at her kitchen table as if we were old friends. She could have been my mother. Why Farley was attracted to a woman ten years his senior is beyond me."

Stella does not turn although she desperately wants to gauge Aiden's expression.

Meredith covers her mouth with her hand for a moment. The motion comes across as contrived. "My remarks are not a comment on the age difference between you and your handyman, Stella." She pats her hair. "Although, if the shoe fits...."

"Nick's the park manager. Continue," Aiden prods, his tone impatient.

"We had a frank conversation. I told her, in no uncertain terms, Farley would never leave me. I am his meal ticket. I even buy his underwear. Her response was unhelpful."

"And what was her response?" Stella knows the answer.

"She insisted Farley was capable of purchasing his own clothes, as evidenced by his recent new wardrobe. She also emphasized she didn't care if he left or not. She was content with their current arrangement and would never apply pressure on him to leave his marriage for any reason."

"Did the conversation go further?" Stella can tell Aiden is ready to push.

"Yes. She suggested if I wasn't happy, I should buy Farley out. She yapped on saying how I don't respect Farley and how I diminish him at every opportunity." Her voice cracks and she swallows. "She told me he loved her."

"Mrs. Tompkins, did you kill Paulina McAdams or hire a person to kill her for you?"

Meredith's eyes darken with rage while she tries to control her shaking hands. "I hoped not to insinuate, but Farley probably murdered her or, more likely, hired a person because he's such a coward."

"And your rationale for this particular theory, Meredith?"

"He couldn't rid himself of her. She really expected him to leave me and he refused. Once the affair soured, he killed her." She drops her focus to her lap once again. "After the staff meeting."

Aiden closes his notebook. "Mrs. Tompkins, we completed a lengthy interview with your husband, and he has a different perspective."

"When did my husband talk with you, Detective?"

"Last Wednesday."

"He was getting the car serviced last Wednesday."

Aiden clips his pen to his inside pocket. "He continues to lie to you, Mrs. Tompkins."

****

"Well, what's your opinion, my consultant friend?"

"She has a great motive but not much opportunity on her own. Farley was agitated the evening of April 30 because he wanted to be with Paulina, and Paulina waited for him in her prettiest peignoir. I'm convinced the murderer wasn't him." She's quiet for a moment to organize her thoughts. "Paulina told me she wanted to discuss an issue with me. It was no doubt Meredith's visit. She might have wanted to tell me she was afraid."

"Look at the situation from the opposite perspective. What a perfect set-up. Farley has an excuse because of the meeting and he's confident she'll sit and wait. After their pre-arranged door-locking time, he has his hit man approach the front door. He's the only person who knows the routine, besides

Paulina. She may have wanted to tell you Farley was upset with her and she was afraid."

"I can't see a way to tease out the truth." She hears the frustration in her tone.

"I expect an air mail package from Vancouver tomorrow. I have a lead on the hired gun, but you must brace yourself. If my hunch is right, the consequences won't be pretty."

"Can you give me the details?"

"Not yet. I don't want to cause you to worry if I happen to be wrong, and I may well be. The minute I receive the information in the mail, I'll share the contents with you, good or bad. I could be out in left field."

Does Aiden not trust me? "What makes the material sensitive? You said Dad provided you with the idea."

"He did." His tone is apprehensive. "If I'm right, the solution to Paulina's murder will have ramifications throughout the community, which includes you. I won't tip my hand until I have concrete evidence, and your help to resolve the matter will be critical."

Aiden will not be deterred. He's as stubborn now as he was in high school. On her drive home, in a bolt of paranoia, she wonders if Aiden suspects Nick is a gunman for hire. *I may be eating, working, and sleeping with Paulina's murderer. Possible? Never. Maybe. Where was he on April 30? Could he have left the house while I was sleeping? Don't let your imagination take control.* Her sweaty hands slip on the wheel. The light glitters off the water. She can't find her sunglasses. Tears soak hot cheeks. She slows the vehicle and pulls into a picnic stop on the side of the road. *I can't go home. I have no idea what to say to him.*

She turns the Jeep back toward town and the police detachment.

"Detective North, please."

"Stella, what's the matter? Come to my office."

He leads the way. She remains silent. She doesn't want to be overheard. Once he closes the door and motions her to a seat, she confronts him with her fear. "Do you suspect Nick is a hired gun?"

"For the love of God, no!" He touches her shoulder for the briefest of moments. "Your father's backward names foolishness got me thinking."

She tries not to blubber her relief. Investigating this case has made everyone she knows seem like a suspect.

"Russ Harrison. Harry Russell. I once attempted to nail a hired assassin named Harry Russell. I need a picture. They've airmailed me one from the west coast. I'm sorry. I'm not convinced so I wanted to wait. I'm sorry," he repeats. "I should have shared with you and trusted you. I hope I'm wrong."

CHAPTER 19

Not Enough Evidence

"I can't tell if the man in the photo is Russ. Is this the best picture they sent?"

Stella and Aiden lean over her desk, eyes fixed on a blurry photograph which shows a bearded figure exiting a rundown apartment building. The setting could be anywhere. He could be anyone.

"This surveillance photo dates from fifteen years ago. I called yesterday, when the letter arrived, and asked staff to see if a better one might be found. I'm sure, back when we worked the case, we took more pictures. We followed him for weeks."

She picks the image up and peers through squinted eyes. "There's no point in talking to Russ based on this photo, Aiden. Even if you were able to show he lived in the apartment block, whatever the location, we can't establish the man is Russ."

"Correct. I need a better excuse to invite him into the station." He sits. "Once I'm back at the office, I'll contact Meredith and Farley to come see us for an interview. Watching the two of them together might prove to be an enlightening experience." His expression is hopeful. "You'll assist?"

"When?"

"Day after tomorrow—Friday."

"I'm trying to imagine Russ as a hired gun. Did he kill Paulina for one or both Tompkins and afterward decided he wanted to sell real estate? Sounds far-fetched when I say it out loud. The more we brainstorm scenarios, the weirder the options become. Besides," she continues, "under what circumstances did a person or persons unknown learn Russ kills people for a living—if this is, in fact, the case?" She shrugs her shoulders and plunks into her chair. "I'm confused." She chews her bottom lip. "And worried as hell, if the truth be told."

"What date did Russ start selling real estate for Grey Cottage Realty?"

"He told us his official retirement date was May 18. Arrangements were confirmed for him to go to work for Meredith, and he started right away."

"We need to assemble a schedule of the times he's been out of town and try to match them up with homicides in other locations."

She frowns, imagining the fall-out if they're right.

As Aiden stands and reaches for the picture, Nick pops in the door. "Good morning, Aiden." He surveys the room. His gaze settles on the photograph in Aiden's hand. "Are you two okay? Stella, Alice needs to discuss a bunch of reservations with you." His eyes fall back to the photo. "Is that an old picture of Russ with facial hair? Is he twenty-five?" He raises his hand in an apologetic salute. "Sorry I interrupted. Talk later." He disappears as quickly as he showed up.

Stella and Aiden stare at one another. "Nick assumed the person in the photo is Russ." She moans her frustration. "Aiden, if Russ is involved in Paulina's murder, how in God's name will we ever handle Trixie? And do the police need to protect her?"

"He kills for money. Trixie's safe unless we corner him too early. Don't give her our hypothesis yet. I want a better photo. It's important to complete the Tompkins interview on Friday, too. One step at a time." He turns at the door. "Talk to Nick. Tell him our suspicions. No need for Trixie to learn the details and alert Russ. He'll end up on the move, and then she could be at risk."

"Why didn't you catch him years ago?"

"Not enough evidence. I was certain Harry Russell was a hired killer—at least three hits I investigated—but we never found a way to assemble enough evidence to nail him. He's very skilled at his job. We might not be able to attach him to this crime either."

"Call me with the time of our interview on Friday."

Aiden leaves for Shale Harbour. Stella meets with Alice. The park is busy. School isn't even closed yet, and the reservation desk is swamped. Stella spends the remainder of her morning sorting through confirmed reservations while Alice mans the phone and the checkouts.

Her mind swirls. She wants to talk with Nick at noon, so arranges for them to eat upstairs in the privacy of their own quarters. Once she takes a break from reception, she organizes lunch for the staff and themselves.

"When Nick comes in, tell him I've taken our lunch upstairs, Alice. I laid out fixings for sandwiches. Build your own. There are also chocolate chip cookies, strawberries, and lemonade."

"Thanks, Stella. Sorry I never found time to help." She grins.

"No problem. Don't forget Nick, okay?" She hopes she doesn't sound too twitchy or rattled.

She uses a wooden tray to transport ham sandwiches, carrot sticks and dip, cookies, and drinks upstairs. She'll return to the kitchen for tea after he comes in from the yard.

When he arrives, she's out on their small deck.

"Hi. Alice told me I'd find you up here. Problem?"

Turning away from the distant ocean view, she stands, knowing her eyes have puddled.

His arms are wrapped around her in a moment. "My God, Stella. What's the matter? Alice said I was invited to a private lunch."

"We need to talk." She pulls back to meet his gaze.

"The picture?"

"If you were right, and the surveillance photo sent to Aiden from Vancouver is Russ, a.k.a. Harry Russell, I can only imagine the consequences."

"Let's sit down. Start from the beginning. Tell me the story."

Nick never interferes in the work she does with Aiden. He accepts information shared but doesn't ask. He maintains her confidence. He curbs any curiosity he might harbour and provides support when needed—the perfect combination.

"Okay. Aiden and I concluded Paulina's murder was a professional hit. Someone wanted her dead and hired a person to kill her. One suspect is Meredith, because of Paulina's affair with Farley. Another is Farley, if his relationship with Paulina somehow went wrong. Perhaps Danielle Braddon was involved because Paulina asked for access to Jane. There seems to be no connection to Russ, though. We've gone over and over availability of weapons and ability to hire a contract killer. Danielle's deceased husband belonged to a gun club. He owned a gun and Danielle assumes the weapon has remained at the club since his death."

"Is the photograph of Nick?"

Her shrug speaks volumes. "Dad became obsessed with backwards names on Sunday. Russ Harrison is Harry Russell backwards. Aiden tried to arrest a hit man named Harry Russell out on the west coast fifteen years ago."

Nick asks the question another way, and slower this time. "Was Harry Russell the man in the photo you two were studying?"

"It was a surveillance picture of Harry Russell, and neither of us felt sure the figure was Russ. Then you came in and asked what was up with the picture of Russ." She exhales and reaches for a sandwich. "Aiden has requested they search for more photos. The guy was watched for weeks back when he was under suspicion. We'll see."

"What's the connection with Meredith and Farley Tompkins?"

"We aren't sure. Granted, he works for them, but she offered the new position to Pepper Ferguson first. She didn't plan to hire Russ."

"Is Trixie aware of the investigative details to this point?"

"No, and we can't let her find out. Aiden wanted me to talk to you and make sure you don't mention the picture or our suspicions." She shuts her eyes in a faint attempt to block the almost certain pending chaos. "She will be devastated. I'm not sure what will happen if our theory proves true."

"If Russ changed his name to hide his past, how would anyone in this town know his background?" Nick sips his lemonade.

"Someone figured it out."

****

Stella arrives at the RCMP detachment in Shale Harbour at one o'clock in the afternoon on Friday, June 19. She's nervous and troubled but can't determine why. Meredith and Farley Tompkins mean little to her. They are fellow business owners in town and have engaged in various collaborations over the years. They are not friends.

As is most often the case when in the company of women who present themselves as put together and attractive, she is intimidated by Meredith. Stella, in her wrinkled linen pants, baggy shirt, and purse which doesn't match, always assumes the persona of an unmade bed around such company. She takes a breath, squares her shoulders, nods recognition to Sergeant Moyer, and makes her way to the interview room.

Much to her surprise, Meredith and Farley are early. She observes them through the glass partition. Neither one of them has noticed her yet, although she's clearly visible.

It seems they've adopted a role reversal where attire is concerned. Farley looks very dapper. His hair is combed, his clothes fit well, and he has a purple square in the pocket of his tweed sport coat. Meredith, in contrast, slouches in old blue jeans and a sweater which belongs in the rag bag. Her hair is tied with a kerchief, as if she was in the middle of housework when she remembered their meeting. *Meredith Tompkins' hair is tied with a kerchief!*

Aiden approaches the window and stands beside her. Farley glances up and sees them in the hallway. As a result, they exchange no words and enter the interview room together.

"Good afternoon, Mr. and Mrs. Tompkins. May I call you Meredith and Farley?"

"Stella does. I suppose formality doesn't matter." Meredith's response is sullen, and she resembles a moody child. Farley nods and remains focused on his hands.

"We are here today to explore Paulina McAdams' death and the relationships cultivated by both of you with her, as well as others."

"Our lawyer is on his way, Detective." Meredith is defiant. "I will not participate in any more discussions without him present."

"I'm sorry, Detective, Stella. I told Meredith she didn't need to involve Carter Stephens." Farley squirms.

Aiden makes a valiant attempt to cover both his surprise and his annoyance, but Stella reads his emotions.

"If you'll excuse me, I'll notify the front desk to expect Mr. Stephens." Aiden pushes back his chair with what Stella considers excessive force, and leaves.

Meredith glares at Stella. "I see no reason for you to be here. You should be in the park. Don't you need to mow a lawn or empty a sewer tank? Your job description, right?" The woman struggles to take control of the room.

Understanding this, Stella's confidence is boosted, and she answers the question. "Yes, Meredith, we mow lots of lawns and empty lots of sewers. Let's wait for Aiden and your lawyer, shall we?"

The air drips with anxiety and anger. The door finally opens as the atmosphere becomes unbearable. Aiden re-enters, followed by Carter Stephens, Brigitte's new beau. Carter, attaché case in hand, takes up a post beside Meredith. His boyish looks conflict with his profession.

"Detective North, I will help in whatever way I can. Unlike my wife, I see no reason for legal representation."

"Thank you, Farley. I appreciate your clarity."

Meredith stares at Aiden and Stella. She refuses to utter a word.

"I will answer on behalf of Mrs. Tompkins, after any necessary collaboration with my client. I hope our protocol proves satisfactory." Carter whips out a yellow legal pad and a fountain pen.

Aiden begins. "Today, I want to learn from each of you, how you came to be acquainted with Russ Harrison."

Farley fidgets in his chair but reacts first. "Russ Harrison? What an odd question. He joined the business the middle of May. The man is too enthusiastic. He's annoying and sets my nerves on edge, if I am to be blunt." He's distracted for a moment. "I thought we were to talk about Paulina."

"Annoy you, you idiot? You're never in the office."

Carter reaches out and touches Meredith's hand with his index finger.

She smothers a gag-like cough.

"Tell us how Russ bothers you, Farley."

"He's very gung-ho—as if he has to please Meredith in one way or another every single day. I asked him once if my wife was blackmailing him. Maybe he gambles, and she helps him hide his habit or fronts him cash. He refused to answer. I've never found out."

Aiden turns to Meredith. "Do you possess incriminating information on Russ, as your husband suggests?"

Meredith makes eye contact with Carter, who nods and directs his response to Aiden. "Mrs. Tompkins has no idea what your question means, sir."

Farley interrupts. "Russ is Meredith's trained monkey when she's in the office. He'll do whatever she says."

"You don't know what you're talking about," Meredith sputters, despite a glare from Carter.

"As yet, my question posed initially hasn't been answered, Meredith. How did you meet Russ Harrison?"

"He bought a cottage outside town and renovated every inch." She addresses Stella. "You're aware of the details. Your sister is tangled up with him, for God's sake."

"Why did he come to Shale Harbour and buy a cottage through you? There are many communities with cottages for sale, correct?" Stella suddenly realizes no one has the vaguest idea why Russ ended up here.

Meredith wriggles in her chair. Carter blinks in her direction. "Ask Russ. We live in a nice enough part of the world."

Farley sits up straighter and frowns. "I remember when he first came in the office on the hunt for a cottage. I was covering the front desk, Meredith. You managed the complete sale. Cavelle never even showed him any properties. You handled the details."

"Correct?" Aiden jots notes.

"Allow me to confer with my client." Carter leans over and Meredith whispers in his ear. "Mrs. Tompkins has no recollection of the specific events. She was in the office, a new client came in, and she opened a file—normal procedure."

"Bull crap," Farley mumbles.

****

"What's your opinion?" They have retired to Aiden's office after the silent departure of Meredith, Farley, and the lawyer.

"I can't imagine Russ is part of Paulina's murder, Aiden. I don't want it to be true, but the question of why he came here remains a mystery, at least to me. I suspect, if an arrangement of any kind exists between Russ and Meredith, she will report our conversation back to him before the day's over."

"Agreed. The dots aren't connected, yet, but Meredith and Russ are in some sort of symbiotic relationship, using the skills of the other to further their own ends. I can sense there's a connection, Stella, but I want a better photograph before I ask Russ to come in."

"Do you need an excuse?"

"No, but I don't want him to run. Meredith might talk to him, but he'll not risk his new life unless he's convinced we've figured him out."

"On another topic, I wonder how many blue Ford trucks are in the region."

"Blue Ford trucks?"

"Yes. On the night Paulina was killed, Trixie drove through town, on the prowl for Russ' truck. She was afraid there was another girlfriend stashed away. She saw a similar one parked on Maple Street, but he swears he was in Port Ephron to meet with a client."

"What year is the truck?"

"I'm not sure, but around 1976 or 1977. Not old."

"I'll find out, although we'll have to track down any others to determine whereabouts that night."

"I'm curious to see the dates Russ has been out of town the last little while, too. There are more than a few, based on my sister's complaints."

"Can you ask Trixie and not be obvious?"

"She'll no doubt be out to the park within the next few days." Stella retrieves her purse from the floor but has second thoughts and places the bag back. "How's Rosemary?"

"Not well. Thank God Toni and Mary Jo will stick around for another week. After they leave, Rosemary either goes back to Port Ephron with me or straight to the psychiatric ward. The process will be easier if Paulina's murder is wrapped up."

"Her sisters say she needs a medication review again."

"Correct, but to be honest, I'm not sure I appreciate the Rosemary who turns into a zombie after those admissions. She's on tons of medications. She sometimes even has difficulty dressing." His expression is sheepish. "I prefer the Annette-Funicello-Rosemary. I might be enabling her."

Stella nods agreement. "The whole point is to manage her on her pills. Right now, she's either one extreme or the other. In my estimation, she isn't managed. Have you given any thought to obtaining a consultation with a second psychiatrist?"

His expression is shocked. Stella hopes she hasn't insulted him. He's the person who must live with Rosemary.

"You might be right. As a family, we've gotten into a rut. We take her to the hospital, they fill her full of drugs, she's discharged home, she deteriorates over time, and back she goes."

"I understand—a vicious circle." She retrieves her purse from the floor for the second time. "I hope we can enjoy a quiet weekend at the park. Nick and I are around if you or your sisters-in-law need us. Pop up for a beer or lemonade."

"We'll let Meredith fret for a few days. I'll check out the truck and wait for an updated photo. You chat with your sister."

"If Meredith talks to Russ, Trixie will sense any upset on his part. I'll see what she has to say."

CHAPTER 20

I Want to Talk to Stella

Sunday morning is a perfect collaboration of docile ocean breezes, warm sunshine, and the familiar salted scents of mowed grass mingled with freshly turned earth. They linger on their private balcony to savour a few more moments before work begins.

Nick conquered the coffeepot ahead of staff arrivals. Now, an early morning hubbub reverberates below. Alice checks the answering machine. Eve and Paul bang around in the kitchen. Duke arrives. His enthusiasm percolates through the floorboards when he tells Kiki to go find Alice. The day has begun.

"Do you plan to talk to Trixie?"

She wishes a call to her sister involved nothing more than an invitation to a barbecue. "Yes, I'll invite her out to the park for the afternoon. A lot depends on whether Meredith has been in touch with Russ. If he suspects a problem, Trixie will get a whiff in an instant."

In the pause which punctuates her response to Nick's question, silence invades their space. The din has ceased.

"Is downstairs quiet all of a sudden?"

Stella smirks. "When kids play together and the place goes quiet, they must be up to no good. Time we made an entrance. Let's go see what's happened."

When they arrive at the kitchen, Stella recalls those freeze-frame games people play at parties—when one person says the magic word, everyone maintains their position. Alice is standing at one end of the table with Kiki under her arm. The only motion is the trembling of her red curls. Eve and Paul are seated facing each another. Paul has a butter knife in his hand while Eve holds a glass of juice. Duke seems to have not noticed their reactions.

He continues to chew. At the foot of the table, with her back to the door, sits Rosemary North. She does not turn around.

Alice is the first to find her voice. "Well, Nick and Stella are here." Her eyes communicate much better than her mouth. "We have a guest who stopped by to say hello."

"I did not 'stop by to say hello'." Rosemary mocks Alice's words. "I want to talk to Stella." She remains rigid in her position.

"Wonderful to see you, Rosemary. Nick and I take extra time on Sunday morning." She sidles around the table toward the coffee pot. Her explanation is not intended to be an apology.

Nick follows her and sits closest to Rosemary. "Busy summer with both your sisters here, eh Rosemary?"

She keeps her head and neck stiff. When she replies, her gaze focuses on the moulding near the ceiling. "As I said, I am here to have a discussion with Stella—in private, if you don't mind. Your interference is unnecessary, Nick Cochran."

"Kiki and me, we'll take the golf cart and do a run. You comin', my girl?" Duke struggles to jump out of his chair, reaches to take her from Alice, and chucks the Pomeranian under her chin. The dog's ears flatten. Kiki's thoughts are never a mystery. They both disappear in a flash.

Alice mobilizes her manners. "May I pour you a cup of coffee?"

"Or tea?" Caffeine might be a mistake. The woman resembles a tethered and panicked dog.

Rosemary stands. "I wish to go to the privacy of your office. You allow too many people in your kitchen." She marches out of the room.

Stella gives Nick and her staff a wide-eyed gaze before she follows their troubled guest. She hopes Nick remains within earshot.

"Okay, Rosemary. What can I do for you?" Stella cannot prevent an element of annoyance from influencing her tone. She chooses one of the two chairs positioned in front of her desk to be in a safer spot near the door. She indicates Rosemary should take the other seat.

Unlike Rosemary's normal appearance when in this stage of her mental illness, she isn't dressed as a 1960s soda fountain girl. She's disheveled. Her slacks are a size too small and not suitable for what promises to be a warm day. Her cardigan has a stain. She wears no makeup.

"You still engage with my husband behind my back. I want your affair to stop now."

Stella bends toward Rosemary, but quickly straightens when she sees the hatred seething in the woman's eyes. "Aiden and I consult—on occasion. We are old friends. You know this." Constant reassurance will not be enough at this juncture.

"No, I don't. I followed him Friday morning. He was here before he ever went to work. I often wonder if he actually goes to the detachment."

"Where were you on Friday morning? You should have knocked on the door. You're always welcome here."

"I was in the bushes at the edge of the field."

"Aiden and I are in the middle of a high-priority investigation. My friend Paulina is dead, and we want to find her murderer. The need to solve her case is almost an emergency. I'm sure Aiden has explained."

"My husband's in love with you." Rosemary's expression has softened, but by a mere fraction.

Stella takes shallow breaths. "Aiden and I dated thirty years ago. We are friends. Do not, and I repeat, do not feel threatened because of me. Aiden adores you and I am in love with Nick."

Rosemary's shoulders heave. The air in her lungs expels in a shudder. "I don't know why I act this way."

"It's okay. Nick and I want to be friends with you and Aiden. Shall I walk you to your trailer? Okay? The day is beautiful." Her pounding heart slows.

****

The Mustang skids into the back lot.

"Where is she? Rosemary, for God's sake, give Stella a break." Mary Jo thumps through the living room on the way to the kitchen. Toni shuffles behind her, as Stella emerges from the office with Rosemary.

"We were about to walk to her trailer, weren't we?" She addresses Rosemary, who stares at the floor like a disciplined child.

"Thanks for your help, Stella. Sorry for the trouble. We'll take her." Mary Jo reaches for Rosemary's arm.

Nick makes his presence visible in the doorway, although the staff remain tucked away in the kitchen.

Rosemary leans into her sister as if she can't support her own weight. Toni buzzes near them both.

"How did you two know to come to the house, Toni?"

"We ran into your security man when we were on our way to Rosemary's trailer for coffee. He continued on to find Aiden, but we turned around."

"Where's my hubbie?"

"Don't fret. He's coming." Mary Jo pats her arm. "We'll go home and get you breakfast, okay? Toast and a nice soft-boiled egg. You'll be right as rain."

"She always ends up realizing we need to find help for our sister, eventually," Toni whispers in Stella's ear. "Mary Jo will come to her senses. I hope you two solve your case soon. Aiden should spend more time with his wife."

Stella manages a watery smile.

"Rosemary!"

Aiden stumbles in the door followed by a nervous Duke.

"I brought him as fast as I could. I'm out on the veranda if you need me."

Rosemary's eyes narrow when she glares at Aiden. She remains mute.

Mary Jo pats her sister's hand. "We'll drive her back, Aiden. She's fine; wanted to have a chin-wag with Stella."

"We're okay, Aiden—under control."

Toni hustles her sisters toward the door. Aiden stares at Stella. "Rosemary needed to get an issue off her chest. We resolved the problem." Her remark is not true, but she needs to reassure him.

Aiden, Mary Jo, Toni, and Rosemary approach the car. Stella hears Rosemary mutter "bitch", before she climbs in the back seat of the Mustang beside Aiden, and assumes the reference is directed toward her. Nick stands close. She senses the touch of his arm against her shoulder. He heard Rosemary, too.

"Are you okay?"

"Fine, Nick. Don't worry. She's harmless." Her attempt at rational calmness is less than adequate.

"Everyone is busy with their assignments. I'll stay here."

The concern projected from his troubled face does little to appease her mood. "I'm fine, Nick," she repeats. "Go to work. I'll call Trixie before I arrange the reservations for the writers retreat with Alice. Ham and cheese bunwiches for lunch."

He shrugs his shoulders. "If you say so. Tell Alice, if Rosemary shows up again—and I'm convinced she will, probably not today, but she will—to come and find me. The woman's unpredictable when she starts to fixate, Stella."

"I know." She takes a deep breath. "I imagine she'll be back to the psych ward in no time. The whole situation is simply sad."

"Paul and I want to edge flower beds. I won't be far away."

****

She attempts a contrived and more positive expression before she picks up the telephone receiver. No one answers at Trixie's. The plant hasn't been open on Sundays for a while. She'll be at Yellow House with Brigitte.

It takes four rings before Brigitte picks up. "Yellow House. How may I help you?"

"Hi, sweetie. How are you?"

"Good, Aunt Stella, but I have customers inside right now. Did you want to talk to Mom?"

"Yes, if she's nearby."

"Upstairs with Mia. I'll tell her to grab the extension."

Stella detects muffled murmurs while Brigitte apologizes to her clientele and runs to the foot of the stairs. There's a click when Trixie answers and another as Brigitte replaces the downstairs receiver.

"Hi, Stella. What's up?"

She sounds upbeat enough. "I hoped to invite you out to the park for a visit, but you've got your hands full." Mia babbles in the background.

"I do today. Tomorrow instead?"

"No work?"

"Oh, I can have as many hours as I want, but I cut back to help out here. I'm amazed at how busy Yellow House is. I told the factory I want to slow down, and they gave one of the other girls more time." She stops for a second and talks to Mia. "Brigitte wants me to give up my rental place and move in here. Plans are still up in the air." Trixie is unsuccessful in smothering the anxiety mixed with frustration fluttering in her tone.

"You must miss Brigitte and Mia living with you."

"A big change, for sure. I'm happy to say Brigitte is concerned she can't do the complete job on her own," she whispers. "Even if Russ ever makes up his mind to want me to move in, I'll still help my daughter."

"Does Russ want you to be around Brigitte less since she's moved out?"

"Frankly, I have no idea what Russ wants. We've plans to have dinner out at his cottage tonight and I may confront him. If I sound frustrated, I am," she huffs. "I'm invested in the guy. I'll tell you about our chat when I see you—get your opinion."

Stella bites her tongue. Trixie's annoyance with Russ' lack of commitment is good. If their working theory related to Paulina's murder is true, Trixie is better served to be dissatisfied now. Her annoyance might make her circumstances easier to bear later.

****

After the call to Trixie, it's time to focus on work. She shouts toward reception. "Alice, do we have the list of guests from the writers retreat? I want to book them in adjacent sites if we can manage. They can mingle when they're away from the conference."

"I'm in the kitchen, Stella. Will you go through them with me after lunch?"

"No problem. Let me help. I didn't realize the time when I hung up from Trixie. I'll pour juice."

They perform familiar tasks in companionable silence for a few minutes. The last of the sandwiches are made and stacked high on a platter when the crew turns up.

Eve and Paul struggle to wriggle through the door first. They wash their hands at the sink and sit with thuds on the wooden chairs. Stella turns when Nick arrives. He meets her gaze for a moment before announcing he'll go to their quarters to clean up.

Duke, with Kiki under his arm, brings up the rear. The dog squirms to be released and manages to twist one paw out of her "Daddy Loves Me" T-shirt in the process. She struggles, resembling a spinner toy Trixie owned as a child. Once you pushed the wooden plunger a few times, the metal sphere, shaped like a Christmas tree ornament, spun around the room in random patterns until spent.

Alice bends to pick Kiki up and adjust her shirt. "Poor little girl. Won't he help you?"

Not in the mood to wait for the rest of them, Duke reaches for a bunwich. "I helped her," he says between munches. "I stopped for her to do a whiz, didn't I?"

"You take excellent care of her, Duke. I know you do. I was teasing." Alice attempts to pacify a cranky Duke. "What's the matter?"

"I'm sorry for poor Mrs. North. She's a nice lady. Her bein' on the loony side ain't her fault."

"You're right, but she needs more help. The family can't manage on their own all the time." Stella places a container of cookies on the table.

When the phone rings, Alice manoeuvres around the kitchen to answer. "Yes, he's here. One moment please." With Kiki still under her arm, she struggles to cover the mouthpiece with her hand. "Duke, the call's for you." She holds the receiver at arm's length.

"Duke Powell. Can I help you?"

"Yes, I'm John Powell."

"Is she okay?"

His eyes dart around the kitchen as anxiety takes over. Nick, having returned from their suite on the second floor, slides Duke's chair closer to him.

"When did it happen?" Duke sits with a thump.

"I see. I'll leave as soon as possible. Thank you for your help."

Alice removes the phone from his clutches and replaces the receiver on the wall-mounted base.

He scans the room, but his eyes appear not to register what's in front of him. "My mother died a few minutes ago. I guess an aide checked on her and she was dead. She choked on her own vomit."

Paul lays his sandwich on his plate. Eve holds hers poised halfway to her mouth. Alice, still with Kiki wedged under her arm, sits.

Stella gathers her thoughts first. "Duke, I am terribly sorry for your loss. Poor Loretta."

"Was she sick?" Eve's voice sounds frail in the quiet kitchen.

"Nope. My mother always had a very close relationship with the bottle. A visitor smuggled booze in for her—didn't take much." He studies his plate and scrapes at a single tear dribbling through the stubble on his cheek.

"Oh, Duke. I'm sorry. What can we do to help?" Alice rises to move closer and pat him on the shoulder.

"Thanks, old girl. Ain't a lot to do except watch Kiki for me. I guess I'll be takin' a few days off to organize a funeral and settle her affairs."

Stella nods.

"She didn't have any money. Never did. She drank every extra dollar she scrounged."

"No need to worry. Alice and I can manage Kiki. Paul and Nick will take over your duties and keep an eye on your trailer. You go to the care home and be with your family."

Duke surveys the room. "You folks are my family. I don't have kin except my mother, and now not even her." His voice catches and he coughs. "Means a lot you're able to help a guy out."

"Do you want to leave today, or wait until the morning?"

"Today. I can make the four hours easy enough." He hauls his round and compact frame out of the chair. "I'll go and get Kiki's stuff and give you a key to my trailer in case I'm gone for a while."

"See you back up here later, Duke." Nick starts to clear dishes and stack them on the counter.

After the staff return to their activities, and Kiki is with Alice in the office, Stella expresses her thoughts. "Poor Duke. You know, even after three wives, he's alone in the world. I hope the woman he mentioned over at the Port Ephron RV Park is interested in him. He has the potential to become a very morose specimen in short order, otherwise."

Nick wraps one arm around her shoulders while she continues to wash dishes. "Over the winter, we'll invite him for dinner now and again; keep an eye on him. Hey, I know!" He bops her on the bicep. "What about offering to dog-sit? That way he can take a vacation to Florida—and visit Mom and Dad." He chortles at his joke.

"Good idea. He could go instead of us. Aren't you the smart one?" She chuckles. Any faint hope to be excused from a trip to Nick's parents is okay with her.

"Speaking of family, how did your call turn out with Trixie?"

"Fine, I guess. I didn't get the impression she's observed any out-of-the-ordinary behaviour on Russ' part. She said she wants to run a few ideas past me because Brigitte is encouraging her to move into Yellow House. If Aiden's hunch proves to be correct, living with Brigitte might be the best option." She leans into him as they finish the dishes. "I can't imagine life around here if Aiden is right. God, what a day!"

Chapter 21

No Need to Rub Salt

"Must I take my boots off?" She stops to stare at her footwear for a moment. "Although a pain in the ass, they're my proof Russ Harrison used to want to buy me presents." Trixie struts across the living room, past Stella, without waiting for an answer.

"Sure. No problem." Trixie's shiny yellow leather boots reflect the light pouring through the window over the sink. "I made coffee."

She throws her hobo-style bag on the table and herself into a chair. "You pour. I'm so mad I could spit."

"Not in my kitchen, thank you very much." Stella tries to keep her tone upbeat. Guilt seeps between her words. This conversation will not be authentic. Yes, she has concerns for Trixie and her relationship with Russ, but her sisterly affection is not the driving force behind any questions and comments today. "Here's your coffee. Did the two of you have dinner? Did you talk to him?"

Trixie scrapes a blond curl away from her cheek. "We met, but not at his place."

"Where?"

"At the hotel. He's irrational, Stella."

Her heart thumps. Her palms are sweaty. "Russ is never irrational. What do you mean?"

"I confronted him. Once we were alone, I asked him outright if we have a future. I told him I need to make up my mind whether to move in with my daughter or does he want us to start our life as a couple under one roof." She stops for a gulp of coffee. "After the time we've spent together, I was shocked."

Stella waits motionless.

"He told me I should take advantage of the space at Yellow House. He said he might ask Cavelle to sell his place because he's moving to Europe. To Europe, for God's sake."

"Why Europe?" Stella suspects he stands a better chance of becoming lost outside North America.

She huffs. Her curls vibrate. "He mentioned the Eiffel Tower and the Swiss Alps. He's off his rocker."

"More coffee?" The goal is to encourage Trixie to talk, recall, and analyze. "You and Russ have dated for what—seven or eight months, right?"

Trixie accepts her refill. "I first went out with him last August, although he's been in town longer." She winces. "Obviously, we haven't been involved for *years*, but from the start I felt Russ was the one." She uncrosses her long legs and plunks bare elbows on the table. Her T-shirt says "Glammie," in glitter.

"Did he suggest you go with him?"

Her eyes meet Stella's. "No need to rub salt. Do I look like a woman moving to Paris? He said I wouldn't be happy. Who isn't happy in Paris?"

"Maybe Russ is considering your emotions if you're away from Brigitte and Mia."

"Okay. Fair enough." She shrugs. "If that were the case, we could've had a discussion."

Stella takes a breath and dives in. She might as well try to tap into Trixie's unconscious awareness. "Where did Russ live before he moved to Shale Harbour?"

"Out west. He's never shared the details."

"I wonder why Shale Harbour. He could live anywhere."

"You're right. At first, I assumed he must have a long-lost relative here, but in truth, he saw a brochure featuring Shale Harbour when he was on a job. He told me he came to visit and fell in love with the place—perfect retirement."

"Kind of random."

"We were born here, Stella. We don't appreciate seaside ambiance. He wanted to retire but kept accepting contracts. Once he gave up the Human Resources Management Consultant business, I hoped we were on the right track." Her eyes fill with tears. "I'm sure we're over."

Pangs of conscience threaten Stella's purpose, but she forges on. "He travelled often before he started to work for Grey Cottage Realty. I remember last October when he couldn't come to the end-of-the-season party. And he said no to Christmas with the family. Then, there was the night Paulina died."

Trixie rummages in the cupboard until she locates a bag of cookies. "Those were the dates he cancelled where you were included. He stood me up on others."

"How many more?" Stella tries to sound supportive—the sister who cares. Her heart continues to pound. If Russ turns out to be involved in Paulina's murder, hell will break loose when Trixie discovers she's been manipulated.

"He took off sometimes twice a month. Once he flew to Vancouver because I saw the plane ticket. Once he accepted a contract in Edmonton. I know because I answered the phone and the person on the other end said his flight was confirmed. The trip was a surprise. He drove straight to the airport after he dropped me at home."

"Can human resource consultation, or whatever, be that demanding? Sounds far-fetched." She lets her words sink in, and hopes Trixie will realize, on her own, his work was nefarious in some as-yet-to-be-determined way.

"Russ always said his boss was exacting and every client he met was a ball-buster in one way or another. The phone often rang in the middle of the night and he'd leave the next morning. He drove to Montreal last winter when the weather was horrible. I worried."

"I suspect you did. He hasn't gone away since he started to work for Meredith and Farley?"

"No. Now, my issue is that he spends more time with Meredith than this girlfriend," she points a thumb at her chest, "feels is necessary, but I don't dare say much." She chuckles. The sound is forced, laced with sadness. "Cavelle told me Russ and Meredith first bonded over mutual friends stateside."

"What do you mean, mutual friends?"

"They know the same people in Florida. Russ had to meet with some guy when we took our holiday, and then he said the guy knew Meredith and Farley."

Stella focuses on remaining calm. *Is this the link?* "Do you remember his name?"

"Russ never gives me information about people he meets—clients or friends."

"Was this person a friend?"

"For sure. Russ had known him for a long time. He said he thought about selling real estate there. It's where he got the brochure about Shale Harbour—you know the one I mean. Meredith sponsors them and then sends them all over the country. She takes a bunch to Florida every winter for the convention. It's how Russ found out about this place. I told you he discovered Shale Harbour in a brochure."

She sounds annoyed, but Stella knows she's upset. "Maybe Russ will go back to Florida where he has this friend."

"I'm doubtful, but no point for me to worry any more. He dumped me last night." She sniffs. "If he plans to move on his own, I might as well pick up my stuff at his cottage."

"Maybe I should tag along. Do you have a key?" An ideal opportunity to have a snoop around.

"No key. He never gave me one, but I'll tell him I want to move my extra makeup and clothes to Brigitte's. If he lets me in while he's at work, we'll go together. Besides," she stands to leave, "he might rethink his decision when I ask." She puts her cup in the sink. "Ever the optimist." Pearly pink lipstick-saturated lips stretch into a line, unable to force a smile.

Stella's heart breaks, but she's relieved at the same time. Trixie is hurt now. If Aiden's conclusions are true, and she suspects he's right, her sister is better off out of the picture.

"Not to change the subject, but are Brigitte and Carter Stephens a couple?"

Trixie drags her purse off the table. "Such appears to be the case. I want her to be happy. He likes Mia, which is a plus. Despite her romance, she still wants me to move in and I imagine I will." She turns to face Stella. They stand a foot apart. "I have mulled over your buyout option. You and Nick have a good partnership. Tell him I'll take you up on your offer."

In a spontaneous, albeit guilty, show of affection, Stella wraps her arms around Trixie. "You do whatever is right for you. One step at a time. Call me and we can drive over to Russ' cottage." She leans back and meets her sister's eyes. "You'll be fine."

"I always am. Lots of experience." She clicks across the hardwood. "My only wish is for a man to love me the way Nick loves you." She points a long and manicured index finger toward Stella. "Be careful not to squander his affection. Men don't appreciate women who are distant. You can be distant."

The provision of relationship advice is not Trixie's best move under the circumstances, but Stella accepts her opinions with grace—atonement for today's deception.

****

"Hi, Aiden. Glad you're in the office. Trixie left the park five minutes ago."

"Any luck?"

"I'm not sure, but I have vague dates."

"Let me find my pen."

"I hate myself right now. The one positive note is they've broken up, at least in Trixie's opinion. He told her at dinner last night he was considering listing his cottage for sale and moving to Europe. He insisted Trixie wouldn't be happy abroad—but I doubt if he would take her if he intends to disappear. He doesn't need a fretting mother and grandmother tagging along. I don't have every date he was out of town, but I have incidents."

She rhymes off the times when he cancelled family parties and adds the trips to Vancouver, Edmonton, and Montreal mentioned in the conversation with her sister.

"Your information will help one of my investigators match up potential murders. Did she say where he came from and why he moved here? The guy bothered me from the first time I met him, but I couldn't figure out why."

"Yes, I remember dinner here at my place when you asked pointed questions, and he avoided direct answers. You seemed suspicious, but never explained." She takes a breath. "As for history, Trixie remembers he said he moved here from the west. Apparently, he saw a brochure depicting Shale Harbour, while on a job in Florida, and considered the community both a suitable and charming spot to retire. He invested piles of cash in the cottage. Originally, he planned to stay."

"I appreciate your assumption but guys who kill people for a living never stay and never change. Twenty years and the absence of the beard clouded the obvious." He pauses. "I don't expect he'll take off right away. He isn't certain we're on to him, so he'll try to tie up loose ends. Guys like him—it's their nature to be methodical. I should have a second photo by Wednesday, and we'll confirm."

Better come clean. "Aiden, I said I would go with Trixie if she drives out to Russ' place to pick up her stuff while he's at work."

Silence. "How amicable is their split expected to be?"

"Her plan is to tell Russ she wants to take makeup and clothes over to Brigitte's. He'll either leave the house open or give her a key. She isn't even sure they've officially called it quits. She hopes the suggestion she's moving her belongings might wake him up."

"I'm doubtful. Russ is concerned for Russ."

"You don't object if I peruse the place?"

"No but be careful. Hands off. Observations only. Without a warrant, all you can do is enter the house because of your sister. Get a feel for the place. You have a legal right to be there because of her conversation with Russ. Tell me your observations afterward."

"Okay. I'll call."

****

Tuesday is bright and sunny. The wind whips off the water. Mildred's tattered striped awning flaps in the morning sparkle. As Stella purrs nearer in the golf cart, she sees the old woman perched in her orange basket chair on the rotten deck. Stella vainly hopes the coffee, in a Melmac cup at her elbow, isn't doctored.

Mildred waves her flabby arm, visible beneath the threadbare caftan, and stubs her cigarette in a saucer. "Is today the day?"

"Indeed. I have a date with my sister, but Paul and Nick are on their way with the lumber."

"I'll put my chair out on the grass and enjoy the view of those tight butts." Her signature cackle dances on the wind. "More good times spent in paradise."

"Miss Fox! Behave yourself, my girl. By the way, Rob Black plans to help, too. Sally will keep you company." The Blacks spend their summers in a trailer one row back from Mildred. They're often with the old lady, enjoying her lemonade.

"Tell me what your boys are gonna do again."

"Nick said they'll rip your deck off, put new posts in the ground, frame out and build a new deck, and screw in a set of stairs. He has an old set from another site and mentioned they'll work for you. He can modify them if they aren't the right height."

"I'll see the furniture's moved."

"No need. The guys will lug and lift. Find a comfy spot on the lawn to hold court while they're here."

"How long?"

"Plan on the day, but they'll break for lunch and you'll be able to access inside."

"I might have an excuse to use Sally's bathroom. It's bigger. More room for this ass." She slaps her rump with unbridled enthusiasm.

"Have fun, Mildred. Better run. Trixie should be here any minute." Stella jumps back on the golf cart and returns to the house. Eve is assigned to make Duke's rounds, which means she doesn't need to take the time to tour the park herself.

****

Trixie parks her VW Microbus on the grass as usual. She sits. Stella can see her in the driver's seat, head bowed, shoulders curved. *She's crying. He must have been pleased she wants to retrieve her possessions.* Stella plants a benign expression on her face and bounces down the veranda steps toward the vehicle.

As she opens the passenger door, Trixie swipes at a tear, checks her mascara in the rear-view mirror, and turns toward Stella. "Hi. Tryin' not to fall apart."

Moved by her sister's obvious pain, she asks, "Are you gonna be okay?"

"I've given up. When I called last night and told him I wanted to come over and pick up my stuff to take to Brigitte's, I expected he might ask me to drive out right away. Instead, can you imagine what he said?"

Stella can imagine, but mumbles "no" as she closes the door of the van.

"He said he'll be busy but will leave a key under the plant pot on the veranda. He said he'd be out on a showing. I am to lock up and put the key back. He'll swing by and retrieve it later." Her voice catches and a gurgle punctuates her breath. "I guess he doesn't want me to hold his key, even for an hour." She turns in her seat. "Let's go."

Stella clutches the door handle and watches her flower beds as the VW careens around the edge of the parking lot.

"He doesn't have the balls to break up with me. Russ is spineless, Stella."

"Better you found out now."

"I gave notice to the landlord, too. I'll move in with Brigitte the end of next month. With no rent to pay, and a buyout from you, I may not go back to work."

"Don't jump the gun, Trixie. You're upset, but what if Jane Braddon wants to sell Yellow House? You and Brigitte might be without a place to live. You'll need your job."

"Brigitte has first refusal. Here we are." She pulls the van up to the front veranda. Her bottom lip trembles.

Stella admires the 1920s Craftsman, restored with meticulous care to its former glory by Russ. The fog grey with green undertones on the cedar shingles, the ivory pillars, and the antique wrought-iron pendant lights impressed her the last time she and Nick visited. She stands for a moment to drink in the beauty of the architecture.

Trixie, encumbered by a scarred suitcase, scrambles up the steps to retrieve the key. She unlocks the glass entry door and motions for Stella to follow her inside.

"I'll run upstairs and pack. Do you want to come? You've never seen the upper floor."

"Sure." Stella's eyes scan the space, the corners, the furniture. The oak stairs, square newel posts, and heavy railing make for a dramatic rise. Blue irises reflect the light through the stained-glass window at the level of the corner landing.

The house has three bedrooms and two baths. Russ refinished the solid wood doors and the baseboards. An oriental carpet covers half the upstairs foyer floor. His master bedroom has French doors. The king size bed is situated opposite a panoramic window. The view of the lawns and ocean beyond is stunning.

"See what I mean? Do you understand why I wanted to live here?" Crumpled emotion pinches her cheeks. She shakes her curls and hustles into the bathroom. "I was under the impression we made a deep connection. Chalk it up to lousy judgment, I guess," she hollers from inside.

Stella wanders through the room. With as much stealth as she can muster, she slides open the drawer of an end table. Empty. She meanders around to the opposite side, ears pricked for the sound of Trixie when she finishes in the bathroom. The second drawer is heavier. She shoves her hand, covered with a tissue, inside and touches a panel which makes the drawer seem only half as deep. She silently slides the drawer closed.

"Come have a swoon. Isn't this the swankiest master bath you've ever seen?"

She pretends to enjoy the view for another moment before she joins her sister. Stella and Nick renovated last winter. She loves their finished space. In her unexpressed opinion, Russ' bathroom is over-designed with reproduction penny tile on the floor, a glassed-in shower, and a claw-foot tub. The taps appear old, but she saw similar versions when she and Nick shopped. They're meant to imitate the originals. "He did an expert job. If I judge cost by our renovation, he dropped lots of cash in this place. I doubt he'll ever see a return."

"Russ doesn't need money. He works because he likes to, he says, although I sneaked a peek in his cheque book once and the balance was two hundred and twenty dollars."

"He must have funds invested. You finish up. I'll go downstairs and wait." Stella returns to familiar territory. Russ has an office off the kitchen. She tiptoes in and scans. His desk is locked. She lets her eyes settle on the surroundings. *Don't look. See.* The desk is positioned in front of a three-pane bow window equipped with a built-in box seat. When she sits in his chair, her back is to the window and the side yard.

She swivels around and examines the wooden top of the window seat. Seams in the wood run perpendicular to the grain, creating a door-like panel.

"Need help, Trixie?"

"Nope. Give me five minutes. Almost done." Her sister's voice trickles from the floor above.

"Okay."

She pulls the tissue out of her pocket to push on the panel. No response. She slides the tissue around the seam, while she exerts pressure every inch. With a snap, a hidden door opens to reveal a safe. Paulina's secret access to Yellow House has given Stella experience. While she listens for the tap of Trixie's heels on the stairs, Stella takes extra care when she closes the door. The mechanism clicks back into place.

When she returns to the living room, she pats her hair and rubs sweaty palms on her jeans. Trixie's on her way.

"I want to make one cruise around the kitchen. I took my dishes home whenever I brought food, but I'll have a snoop since we're here."

Trixie stands motionless for a full minute, although her shoulders shake.

"I told myself no tears. What do you call this? Abject failure?" Her mascara has run.

Stella places her arm around Trixie's shoulder. "Come on. Open the cupboards and have a peek."

After their successful excursion—Trixie located a floral platter and a glass dessert bowl—she locks the Craftsman, replaces the key under the plant pot, and they begin the five-minute trek back to the park.

As they trundle along in the van, Russ' truck passes them travelling in the other direction. He lifts one finger off the wheel in recognition. Stella imagines he was tormented by second thoughts and decided not to leave Trixie unsupervised. He's too late. Despite her guilt, relief overwhelms her.

✿

CHAPTER 22

Sand in My Suitcase

"Good morning. Shale Cliffs RV Park. How can I...?"

"Stella, I was right. Russ Harrison is Harry Russell." He's breathless. "We tried to catch him twenty years ago. I have copies of my old case files from Vancouver."

"Enough for a search warrant?"

"I hope. The picture is our best bet. Russ is a suspect, for sure. What did you see when you were at the house yesterday?"

"A combination safe hidden in a window seat behind his desk. Our experience with Paulina's secret emergency exit helped me notice. Oh, and one of the bedside table drawers in the master might be built with a fake back."

"Great work. I'm off to Port Ephron to scare up a warrant."

"Before you go, I've thought about it all night and I might have found a link to Meredith and Farley."

"How?"

"Russ met with a real estate person when he and Trixie were in Florida last March on vacation. I guess he told his friend he bought a house through Grey Cottage in Shale Harbour. His contact knows the Tompkins from the annual real estate convention and recommended them to Russ in the first place."

"Did she tell you his name?"

"No, but she thought Russ was old friends with the guy."

"One more piece in the puzzle. If I can pull the arrest off, we'll search his residence, work, and both vehicles, all at the same time. You need to explain to Trixie and keep her away. Patrol will man the causeway." He sounds like he's panting. "Talk to you in an hour."

Stella turns to Nick. The staff will arrive any moment. "Aiden is closing in on Russ. He'll call back at some point and ask us to find Trixie."

"Okay. I'll stay put in the pump house. If we need to go to the fish plant or into town to Yellow House, come and fetch me."

Thoughts trip over one another. What should she say? Trixie needs to be aware. When Alice strolls into the kitchen, ready to begin her workday, Stella sees the girl senses a problem.

"Are you okay, Stella? Paul's here. Eve, too. They're out in the yard. Paul stopped to help her fix the strap on her helmet." Eve commutes to the park on a scooter.

"I'm fine, Alice. I pulled messages off the answering machine and left them in reception. Have you eaten breakfast?"

Alice continues to watch her but asks no more questions. "I ate at home. Paul, as you might suspect, will happily eat again."

"I'll be in my office. Call me if you need me." She picks up her coffee cup and escapes Alice's perceptive expression and well-honed intuition.

The phone is eerily quiet all morning. When the contraption finally bleats, she glances at her watch—after one o'clock. She's called Brigitte and knows Trixie's at the plant today. "Shale Cliffs...."

"We're ready here. Find your sister and keep her away from the cottage or the realty office. It's important. She could tip him off, inadvertently or otherwise."

"Brigitte told me her mother is working." She can hear the tremor in her voice. "Nick and I will go talk to her. How much should I say?"

"Tell her the truth. We think he's Harry Russell, a hired killer from the west coast. We consider him to be a suspect in Paulina's murder. Who engaged his services remains a mystery."

"I'm pleased they're sort of broken up. If there was a proposal on the table, or if they were living together, circumstances would be way more traumatic."

"A permanent relationship is too risky for Harry, or Russ. Call the station when you find her and leave a message with the desk." The phone clicks in her ear.

She manoeuvres the Jeep along the single lane to the pump house. He's in the doorway before she has the vehicle in park. His presence calms her. She takes a breath and opens the door. "Aiden called. Will you come with me to the fish plant?"

"Ready, willing, and able, my love. Aiden approves?"

"I want you with me."

Trixie's long-time place of employment is beyond the wharf, outside town by a half kilometre. The parking lot, as has been the case for some time, requires a few loads of gravel and the attention of a grader. They careen into the yard and stop behind Trixie's van. The office, attached to the front of a warehouse-style building, is dusty. Salt spray stains on the tinted windows are reflected by the afternoon sun.

Nick follows her inside via the wind-break porch. Trixie, who works reception, glances up when the door opens.

"What's wrong, Stella? Did somebody die? Is Brigitte okay? Has Mia been hurt?" She's across the floor in her bright red stilettos in a second.

Stella is quick to shake her head while Nick raises his hand to calm her sister.

"Nobody's hurt. Your family is fine. I need to use your phone and then we can talk in the conference room."

"Sergeant Moyer? Please inform Detective North that I'm with my sister." She does not meet Trixie's eyes. The glare from the other woman in the office is both annoyed and impatient.

"Come on." Trixie puts her lips close to Stella's ear. "What the hell is going on?"

Stella knows the layout. She and Aiden interviewed Ken and Jewel Winslow here last summer when Lorraine Young disappeared.

The meeting room has an oval table and a glass partition with a view out to the plant. Once inside, Stella indicates for Trixie to sit and pulls up a chair close to her. "Aiden asked me to come find you because of developments in Paulina McAdams' murder case."

Trixie wiggles to get comfortable. "Great, but how does this relate to me?"

"While we're here, the RCMP are executing search warrants at Russ' home and work, his vehicles as well. They're picking him up for questioning right now."

Stella waits and watches as Trixie absorbs the information. No need to pile too much into the first paragraph. See if she has any questions.

She continues to maintain eye contact with Stella. "How is Russ involved with Paulina?" A sudden realization flashes in Trixie's eyes. "Russ was not Paulina's secret lover." Her voice wobbles, and an element of hysteria invades her tone. "God, Stella, tell me he wasn't."

"We don't believe he was romantically involved with Paulina. Russ' name is Harry Russell."

"Who? You make no sense." The hysteria elevates.

"Harry Russell is a professional assassin from Vancouver."

"Hired to kill Paulina McAdams?"

"We suspect."

Trixie flounces. Her eyes flash. "The cops have screwed up. Who would hire a person to kill Paulina...and why? The idea is nonsense." Now her hysteria has been replaced with outright hostility.

Stella meets Nick's gaze and appreciates his nod of support. She tries again. "Let me explain, okay?"

"Sure. Give explaining a try." Trixie crosses her arms and her legs at the same time.

"Do you remember when Dad got all focused on backwards names at our party?"

"He was acting as typical crazy-ass Dad."

"Obsessed, right?"

She nods.

Stella watches recollection flood Trixie's face and perseveres. "Russ Harrison. Harry Russell. Aiden remembered a hit man from out west called Harry Russell. He thinks this person is implicated in three other murders and maybe more. They couldn't charge him at the time."

Trixie sniffs. "The RCMP make mistakes on occasion."

"On occasion, but Aiden sent for a picture. Although the photo was old and out of date, Nick recognized Russ right away. He received another photo yesterday and for sure, Trixie, Russ and Harry are the same man."

"Okay, let me see if I understand." Her voice has a snide tinge. "Aiden North sent you here today to tell me how my boyfriend...."

"Ex-boyfriend."

Her response is defeated. "You're right. He's my ex-boyfriend. Aiden asked you to tell me Russ is under investigation for Paulina's murder, his real name is Harry Russell, and they are searching his vehicles, cottage, and the real estate office?"

"Correct."

"Who the hell hired him?"

"Not sure. We have suspects. If they find his gun and can identify it as the weapon used to kill Paulina, Aiden expects he'll confess and give the police his employer's name. Aiden wants him to confess to those cold case murders in Vancouver, too."

"I bet he goes to jail and never says a word. Russ, or Harry, I guess, is a determined and disciplined man. He's always in control. Even when he seemed irrational and talked about moving to Europe, he was calm." A small frown creases her otherwise perfect makeup. "He never showed real emotion, which always bothered me."

"Russ moved here to quit work. Maybe he'll talk to Aiden on the chance he might be out of jail in a few years and enjoy his retirement." Stella turns her attention to Nick. "Are we ready?"

He nods his assent.

"Trixie, I think you need to go home, or at least back to Yellow House, for the rest of the day. You don't want to sit here with what's-her-name, all curious and judgmental."

"I'll be fine. One person can't man the office alone, but I promise I won't call Cavelle or drive to his house or be stupid. You can depend on me, Stella. All this has to sink in." She stands and straightens her skirt. "I can't believe I was involved with a guy who kills people. I put Brigitte and Mia in danger."

"No, you didn't. He only murders for money."

"The one positive," Trixie adds, as tears puddle her eyes and risk her mascara, "is at least I'm not the problem. He didn't want to make a commitment, but his reason wasn't me."

****

"What's happened. Have you heard?"

"No, Trixie. Aiden told me they picked Russ up at a house showing yesterday while we were with you at the fish plant. They held him overnight while ballistics tested his weapons. I expect a call from him anytime."

"I called Russ' house and when he didn't answer, I reached out to Cavelle."

"You were instructed not to interfere."

Trixie ignores admonishments. "Cavelle told me they were at a joint showing. Two police officers turned up and Russ left with them."

"I'm glad we could give you first-hand information regarding Russ, Harry, whoever he is, before the arrest happened."

"Will you call me with an update? Only Mondays and Wednesdays at work for a while, so I'll be home or with Brigitte. See you."

As is her usual habit, Trixie doesn't wait for a response before she hangs up. Stella continues to pace the floor. She vacates her office in favour of the kitchen and a mid-morning coffee. Alice has made a fresh pot, and she reaches for a cup as the coffeemaker completes its gurgling crescendo. Kiki isn't underfoot. She must be in reception with Alice.

The staff turn up for a muffin and a drink. The phone refuses to ring. Nick and Paul return from yard work. Eve stuffs her cleaning supplies in the pantry cupboard reserved for such products and Stella hears her tell Nick that one of the toilets in the men's bathroom won't stop running. He'll try to repair the fixture after their break. The phone still refuses to ring.

By late morning, concentration is elusive. She and Alice work on a layout plan for the writers conference. Alice presents a brilliant proposal. She suggests the park should host a reading one evening—perhaps two or three amateur authors could benefit from exposure and experience in front of a like-minded audience.

Her idea is solid. Since she doesn't want to contact Meredith, and Frances Ellis has agreed to manage the artistic arm of the conference anyway, she calls Port Ephron to suggest the idea to Frances herself. They assemble a plan where attendees, whether they reside at the park for the convention, or stay at another location, will congregate at Stella's house to participate in the event.

When the phone finally jangles, Stella is preoccupied with Kiki and Alice answers. "Stella," she shouts from the screen door.

"Come on, Kiki. Enough sniffing. Okay, Alice. You take the pooch and I'll take the call."

"Detective North," she whispers to Stella as she reaches for the leash.

"Hi. Out with the dog." Her greeting is breathless. "Did you get the ballistics report?"

"Yes. You have Kiki? Duke still away?"

"Yeah. He called. He'll be a week or two more, at least. I gather he discovered issues—money irregularities. Enough of Duke." Impatience wins. "What's up?"

"Ballistics matched the bullet that killed Paulina with Russ' nine-millimetre Beretta. And I was right, by the way. He used a suppressor. That bedside table drawer you mentioned had a false back. The gun was in there."

Stella's voice catches in her throat. "My God, he murdered her."

"Lots of money in his secret safe, too. Harry Russell is a dangerous man. I have him in holding and he'll be charged before the day's over. Will you accompany me when I talk to him?"

"With pleasure, although I didn't want to ask."

"You have a consultation contract." He chuckles. "You're not assisting because we're friends, remember?"

****

Aiden meets her at the door to the detachment. "We'll talk in the interview room." He addresses the desk sergeant. "Moyer, he can be brought up now."

Moyer nods to Stella before he picks up the phone. Stella hears him tell the person on the other end how the detective is ready. She and Aiden walk along the hall side by side and settle before Russ arrives.

He saunters in, with a constable at his elbow. "Please wait outside the door, Constable. We'll call you when we're finished." Aiden turns his attention to Russ. There's a sarcastic edge to his voice. "Have a seat, Russ, or is your preference we rid ourselves of the formality and address you as Harry."

"No matter. I haven't used my real name, which is neither of those, in twenty-five years."

"What's your birth name?"

He shrugs.

"Listen, Russ. You killed Paulina. We executed warrants at your cottage, your place of work, and on both vehicles. We tested your Beretta. You're done."

Stella watches his eyes narrow in silent hate and fury. "Couldn't stop digging, eh Stella? Your sister will lose her chance at happiness."

Don't let him crawl under your skin.

"I thought you might be the one charged for the job but no such luck," he continues. "Not when you're cozy with the detective here." He crosses his legs and leans against the back of his chair.

"We need the name of the person who hired you, Russ. The Crown will negotiate if you tell us who wanted the hit."

Russ smirks. "Oh, you haven't finished the puzzle yet. I wondered."

"You're going to jail regardless."

"I remember you from back in the day, out on the west coast. You people followed me and tormented me for months. Amateurs—the whole bunch. I admit, I was worried when we first met at Shale Cliffs, but you didn't recognize me."

"No, I didn't—not until Norbert Kirk enlightened me with backwards names."

"The old coot."

"We suspected you in three murders in Vancouver. I was a junior detective back then." Aiden leans forward and places both elbows on the table. "Listen, Russ. We want names of victims, who hired you, and your full cooperation regarding details, including Paulina McAdams. The Crown will arrange for you to do your penance in a nice minimum-security prison. You can take classes, write a book, watch movies."

"You paint a pretty picture."

"If you don't provide information, we'll charge you for Paulina's murder anyway. We've nailed you, Russ. You'll be gone a long time. I know about three murders out west plus this one. How many more?"

He glances toward Stella. "You could have been my sister-in-law," he drawls, before returning his attention to Aiden. "I'll provide evidence on five hits back in the day, not three. And there are three more, besides Paulina, since I've been in this neck of the woods. I'll even tell you where to find the body of a guy in Montreal your people are still lookin' for."

Stella waits a moment before she speaks. "Did Meredith or Farley engage your services?"

"What makes you think one of them put out the contract?"

"We are aware Farley was involved with your victim and we understand Meredith was incensed."

Russ pauses before he replies. He focuses on Aiden. "A deal?"

Aiden opens the file folder in front of him. "I have your offer in writing. You will be formally charged and, as you've been informed, can have a lawyer present whenever you want, but here's the agreement." He hands the single sheet of paper to Russ.

Russ extends his right hand to Aiden, who offers a pen. Neither man speaks. Russ signs the document and turns his attention to Stella. "To answer your question, Meredith hired me."

How can a man in his position be so smug? He's been in her home, eaten at her table, slept with her sister, for God's sake!

"And the other hits?" Aiden has serious unfinished business.

His blank expression is designed to shock. "You have two guys in jail who said they were innocent at the time you investigated the Vancouver hits. They are. Give me lots of paper. I'll provide all the gory details." He sneers.

"Okay. Let's go back to Paulina. Can you tell me how Meredith hired you?"

"Sure, but Meredith has her secrets and I still can't fit some of those puzzle pieces together, myself. I moved here because I found a brochure in the office of a real estate buddy in Florida. He told me he knew the couple who own Grey Cottage Realty—sees them every year at a conference in Miami—and if I decided to move into the area, contact them to help me find a place."

"You met Meredith and bought your cottage."

"Right. We discussed our mutual acquaintance in the real estate business in Florida. We laughed and agreed we lived in a small world. I even saw my friend when Trixie and I took our vacation."

"How did Meredith obtain information that you were a hired assassin?"

Russ guffaws. "You mean a Human Resources Management Consultant? I don't have any idea. After she came back from the last conference, she telephoned me. When I met her at the office, thinking she was listing an investment property I might be interested in, she called me Harry Russell. She wanted me to get rid of her husband's lover and if I didn't, she would talk to you."

"You took the job because you were blackmailed?"

"Exactly. Trixie always says she has sand in her suitcase. She wanted to take another trip south. The sand in my suitcase ended up being one last job. Paulina was to be my final hit. I told Meredith I'd handle her problem in exchange for a position at Grey Cottage Realty, and I'd be out of the human resource management business for good." He snickers. "A guy always needs a way to keep an eye on his blackmailer. I had Meredith on a short leash." His expression turns thoughtful. "I should have done the hit on Meredith instead."

Over the next two hours, Russ laid out every detail of the night he killed Paulina McAdams. "One of the easiest hits, ever," he said. It was late. He just walked up and knocked on the door. When she opened the door, he figured she thought it was Farley. He pushed his way in, shoved her into the nearest chair, and shot her before she even recognized him from around town. In and out in less than two minutes.

Stella sat stunned as Paulina became little more than Russ' paperwork—his final contract. He related the story as if he was proud of his accomplishment.

"What was your intention, Russ?"

"I wanted to marry your sister; retire and give her a taste of the good life. Another hit wasn't in the plan, but there would have been no way to pin Paulina's murder on me if you hadn't started to snoop."

"What about Meredith?"

He leaned across the table, his voice low and menacing. "Becoming a realtor kept my enemy close. I had her so scared of me, she was willing to do whatever I asked. I expected to become a very successful agent."

Russ agreed to provide them with details regarding who hired him and to testify in court, if he could be placed in a protective environment, for nine murders including Paulina. Stella was certain there were more. Aiden called the Crown prosecutor, who delivered the relevant paperwork before the day was over. Russ was moved to cells in the Port Ephron detachment.

By four o'clock in the afternoon, Stella is physically and emotionally exhausted. Russ has been charged, and another of the partners at Stephens and Stephens engaged to represent him. "I guess Meredith is next."

"I've sent a car with an arrest warrant for her. We can conduct the interview tomorrow—provided you're recovered from today." He gives her arm a quick nudge. She's surprised how his touch jolts through her, and she steps back.

"Lots more questions, my friend." She struggles for composure. "You will be up to your elbows in paperwork for weeks."

"Do you have time to take part?"

"I'll make time. Your sisters-in-law are returning home on Sunday, which means we have two days to wrap the case up and turn our evidence over to the Crown. Rosemary needs to have her husband back."

Aiden tilts his head—his bird-listening-for-a-worm position—and his eyes warm under her gaze. "You think I should spend more time with my wife?"

Chapter 23

Death Always Makes Me Sad

The interview with Meredith Tompkins is scheduled for one o'clock Friday afternoon, less than twenty-four hours from when she was arrested. She spent the night in a holding cell after she was formally charged with conspiracy and murder in the death of Paulina McAdams.

Carter Stephens is shown into the room first. He met with Meredith this morning. He sits across from Aiden and Stella, says not a word, and polishes his glasses.

Aiden and Stella remain silent, although she can guess what's on her friend's mind. Meredith enters, escorted by a constable. Stella can't conceal her surprise as Meredith is accompanied to a chair before the handcuffs are removed. Meredith was arrested at work yesterday and is still wearing a stylish pale pink suit with a rosy silk blouse underneath. Her hair shows the residual signs of a perfect coif. She has the attributes of a woman who has experienced the recent misfortune of sleeping in her clothes. She's rumpled.

"I will speak for Mrs. Tompkins." Carter Stephens assumes his best legal posture.

"Fine." Aiden is noncommittal.

"On the night in question, Mrs. Tompkins met with her real estate team. The people in attendance can account for her whereabouts. You have the information from a previous interview with corroboration by Mr. Tompkins. My client has been arrested, charged, and held in jail over night." He points out the obvious.

"We intend to sue." She leans sideways toward her lawyer, but her eyes remain fixed on Stella. "Tell them. Go ahead and tell them we'll sue their asses off."

Aiden's expression remains blank. He watches Carter and ignores Meredith. Stella admires his demeanour.

"What evidence causes you to think charges of both conspiracy and murder will stick? You're reaching, Detective."

"Well, Mr. Stephens, Mrs. Tompkins, we have a signed confession from the contract killer hired to assassinate Paulina McAdams. We have documented conversations with a Florida contact who introduced Mrs. Tompkins to a third party. The third party provided information which identified Russ Harrison as Harry Russell, an assassin for hire. The confession of the man who has posed as Russ Harrison is extensive. It involves unsolved cases from across the country and two examples of miscarriages of justice. We can prove the link between your client and a hired killer."

"Permit me to confer with my client."

It appears to Stella that Trixie didn't reveal Russ' suspected identity to Brigitte, who might have shared the information with Carter, who was certainly taken off-guard.

"By all means." Aiden nods to Stella. They both leave the interview room and stand in the hall away from the glassed opening.

"Russ gave you the name of his real estate friend in Florida?"

"Yes. He isn't involved. The fact that Russ' buddy, Henry Cameron, introduced Meredith to Jackson Deveau was random bad luck. Deveau knows the 'gun world' as Cameron stated. We assume she discovered Russ' identity through Deveau."

"Why Russ?"

"My guess is Jackson Deveau and Meredith discussed their mutual acquaintance, Henry Cameron, and how another friend of Henry's—in this case, Russ—moved to Shale Harbour.

"The Gods conspired against Russ. Meredith discovered who he was, and if he didn't do what she asked, his cover would be blown."

Carter opens the door to the interview room. "Please come back in, Detective North, Miss Kirk."

They resume their seats. Stella notices a distinct change in Meredith's expression. She's haughty; annoyed.

"What's your decision, Mrs. Tompkins? Have you decided to cooperate?"

"Not on your life. My lawyer expects I'll be granted bail later today. I intend to go home."

"We'll see what the judge has to say. The charges stand." He glares across the table at Carter. "We have a strong case, a credible witness, and a third-party connection, Mr. Stephens. Wisdom dictates a further discussion of the consequences with your client may be in order."

"Russ Harrison has the credibility of a common thief."

"Do not expect bail. The Crown has already stated they will petition the court for bail not to be granted."

Before Aiden and Stella leave, the constable returns, places Meredith in handcuffs, and leads her away toward the cells. She'll be transported to Port Ephron later in the day. Carter Stephens exits without a word.

"There was no need for me to be here today, Aiden. I didn't contribute."

"I prefer you to be nearby, Stella, in case I drop the ball or miss a detail. I also value your opinion. What did you think?"

"Realization has set in. She can't find a way out. Her dreams and her perfect life are circling the drain. Sad to watch, although she deserves whatever punishment is doled out."

****

Addressing the burden head-on, Stella begins to organize a memorial for Paulina. Her first contact on Monday is to the funeral home. Paulina's body has been cremated and Danielle Braddon has been contacted. No date for pickup was established.

"I should call Danielle and Jane to see if they will come to a celebration in memory of Paulina. What do you think?" She is plunked in a kitchen chair as Nick wanders in for mid-morning coffee. The crew won't be far behind. Kiki, the princess she is, sits on a baby blanket near Stella's feet.

"You might want to set a date, first; book the community hall. I assume the gathering will take place in town and not here?"

She scrapes her fingers through her short hair. "You're right. I was ahead of myself." Before Nick has his coffee poured, she's on the phone to the caretaker of the hall.

"Good morning, Andris. Stella Kirk here. I want to schedule a memorial service for Paulina McAdams."

"When?" She motions to Nick, who grabs the calendar off the fridge. "Do you have an event scheduled on Saturday, July 11?"

"Fabulous. How do I confirm?"

"I'll meet you later today. We'll plan our event for two o'clock until four on Saturday afternoon. We won't interfere with the concert." She pops into her office to jot down the details.

Her kitchen is crowded when she returns. "Wise to book first," she whispers to Nick. "I'll call everyone before I go into town." She turns to the staff. "The place is almost full for the start of the week. Everybody busy?"

Eve and Paul chatter at once. "The bathrooms were a mess today. Did the tenters have a big party last night?"

"No idea, but no checkouts are scheduled, which is unusual for a Monday. School is finished, which might account for less movement. Lots of children around."

"Paul and I will change the filters at the pump house." He lifts his brows. "Not the job I hated before the upgrade."

"I need to mow near the cliffs." Eve is happy to be out of the bathrooms. "The edges are shabby."

"Well, I'm organizing a memorial for Paulina. I'll be busy on the phones and then off to town after lunch to sign the forms at the community hall."

Ever conscious of workload, Alice pipes up. "What's the date, Stella?"

"Saturday afternoon, July 11. You guys can manage a Saturday afternoon?"

"Certainly. Let me review registrations." She returns in a moment. Kiki's nails click in rhythm behind her. "We are fully booked on the eleventh— nobody in, nobody out."

"Perfect. I'll be in my office if you need me."

The staff disperse to their various tasks. Stella settles in her chair. For a moment, she indulges herself and permits grief to wash over her before she gulps emotions back down where they belong.

Her first call is to her niece. "Brigitte, good morning."

"Yes, we're fine out here. Your mother moved in yet?"

"No, I didn't need to talk to her. I've scheduled a memorial for Paulina on July 11. I want to invite Danielle and Jane Braddon. Do you have their telephone number?"

"Great." She writes the number on the sheet of paper in front of her.

"Thanks. We're booked from two to four. Tell Trixie, okay?"

"I expect she'll avoid attendance because of Russ, too, but you can represent Yellow House. Attendees will be local business owners, for the most part."

"You enjoy your day, Brigitte. Hugs to Mia."

"Hello, Danielle. Stella Kirk from Shale Harbour. I hope I didn't catch you in the middle of baking."

"We are an hour later here. The reason I've called is to invite you to a service we have planned for Paulina."

"Not right away—July 11 at the Shale Harbour Community Hall and Playhouse. Are you able to come?"

"The funeral home told me they contacted you after the cremation. I'm glad you and Jane want to take her ashes back to New York with you."

"Yes, we'll sprinkle a small vial here near Shale Harbour as well. If you need any assistance with reservations at the hotel, or transportation, call me. See you soon."

Her next contact is Farley Tompkins. She finds him at Grey Cottage Realty, which is not a great surprise since he and Cavelle are the only staff now. He answers the phone breathless, as if he's at the end of a marathon run.

"Hi, Farley. Stella here. Listen, I'm unsure if you want to be involved, but Nick and I have scheduled a small service for Paulina."

"You're welcome to attend. You can say a few words, too."

"July 11 at two o'clock at the community hall. Danielle and Jane Braddon will come. I'll invite most of the businesses in town."

"No need for guilt, Farley. Her death wasn't your fault."

"Should you have owned up to Meredith? Hard to say. She was aware you and Paulina were involved. If you openly confessed to her, would she have been influenced? We'll never be certain."

"I don't have the impression people hold you accountable. You'll attend?"

"Okay. Cavelle is welcome, too, but she wasn't well-acquainted with Paulina, from what I understand."

"Hi, Jewel. Is Hester there?"

"Hester, how do you feel about a memorial on July 11 for Paulina? Jacob can accompany you, or I'll send Nick out to the farm to pick you up."

"Flowers are always wonderful. What a super idea. Your garden must be in full bloom right now. Here's a thought. I'll collect you Saturday morning. We'll take the flowers into town and decorate the hall. Afterward, we'll return to the park for lunch before the get-together."

"Jacob can meet you at the hall and drive you home. No problem."

"Pick you up at ten-thirty? Sure. See you then."

By noon, Stella has also contacted Mercedes Savioli of Parlour Antiques, Tiffany Blair of Cocoa and Café, Mrs. Carlyle, the weaver, Mark Bell at the Shale Harbour Savings and Loan, Pepper Ferguson from the Harbour Hotel, Theodore Gorman, the printer, and various other merchants around the little town.

"Good morning, Sergeant Moyer. Is Detective North in his Shale Harbour office today?"

"Thanks."

"Good morning, Aiden. I've planned a service for Paulina." She gives him the details and adds Paulina's sister and birth daughter will arrive from New York. "Do you want to attend?"

"I hope you and Rosemary can spend more time at the park since the case is buttoned up. Lots of court work for you, but justice for our victim will be served."

"Glad to hear. Once Mary Jo and Toni left, you and Rosemary kind of vacated the premises."

"A few days of vacation? Rosemary will be pleased."

****

The weather is muggy and hot. Mid-July feels warmer every year. Even the trees, with their broad summer leaves, appear thirsty. The hall isn't air conditioned. Hester bustles around, preparing her flower arrangements for the memorial. She included a spray bottle with her paraphernalia. She plans to spritz her creations throughout the afternoon.

Stella watches her friend arrange and rearrange various vases. She hasn't shared her feelings regarding the service today and Stella decides not to push. She's wearing a dress—a long, cotton shift affair with drop sleeves and little ties from the waist which cinch in the back. She could be twenty-five, not forty.

Hester's eyes dart around the hall until she finds Stella in the gloom. "Will you please spray each bouquet after the stems are properly arranged? My flowers are in shock because they've been cut, set in water, and now must rest in this gloomy and dusty spot. A mist is the least of what they deserve for their sacrifice."

"Let me remind you how you volunteered the flowers." Stella points out the obvious.

"Yes, but they will die, and death always makes me sad."

"Hester."

"Yes?"

"Aiden told me we could read Paulina's journal now. The police have made a copy, but it's just for you and me. Do you want to spend an afternoon with me sometime next week?"

"I would like to read her journal from the beginning to the end. You know, Paulina might have made an excellent mother."

"I also have a gift for you." Stella rummages in her bag and pulls out a journal with a picture of wildflowers on the cover. "This is for you, so you don't have to use a scribbler anymore."

Hester reaches for the spiral-bound book with the lined pages. Her eyes fill with tears, her only response.

They return to the park and eat lunch with the staff. Stella can tell Hester studies each person in turn. She munches on a chicken salad sandwich and drinks her lemonade.

"I imagine your dress is very cool on a warm day." Eve is the first to try to engage their guest.

"Correct. Jewel and I are learning to sew. The pattern is simple." She takes another bite. "The ties are handy because," she pats her stomach, "if this bulges too much, I can loosen them." She purses her lips and gazes around the table. "Versatility is important if you want your garments to last."

Nick suppresses a giggle when he makes eye contact with Stella. A tiny part of her ego desperately hopes he hasn't noticed the elasticized waistbands on her newest linen pants.

****

Stella squeezes Nick's hand before she climbs the steps to the stage in the theatre of the Shale Harbour Community Hall and Playhouse. A hush falls over the small group gathered to remember Paulina McAdams and celebrate her life. She positions herself in front of the podium. "Good afternoon, everyone. Thank you for coming. Paulina McAdams was my friend. It's important to me that we honour her today. Hester Painter, another long-time friend, has provided the flowers." She scans the group. "They are lovely, Hester. Thank you. There are those who want to say a few words. We'll begin with Paulina's sister, Danielle Braddon." As Danielle rises to approach the podium, Stella adds, "and we are delighted her niece, Jane, made the trek from New York with her." She hugs Danielle and resumes her place beside Nick.

"Hello. Good afternoon. I am Paulina's older sister. Although we had little contact over the last number of years, I want you to hear about her from me. First off, she loved Shale Harbour. She adored Yellow House and her little business. Jane and I are thrilled Brigitte Kirk has agreed to maintain the enterprise." She scans the audience, catches Brigitte's eye, and nods. "As you might expect, after knowing Paulina and meeting me, you understand we weren't very much alike." The assembled group titters. "I always said my sister was my parents' favourite." People react with a slight gasp, but she raises her hand. "No need to worry. I came to terms with Paulina's free spirit many years ago. I see her in my daughter every day."

In response to a disruption behind her, Stella turns and observes Jane rise from her seat and move two aisles over to sit beside Hester, while her mother continues. Their shoulders touch. Words are not exchanged.

Danielle leaves the stage. Farley Tompkins fumbles with a scrap of paper pulled from his suit jacket while he climbs the three steps and shuffles toward the podium.

"My presence here is awkward and most of you assembled today understand the reason, but current events are not the topic of conversation. We are here to celebrate a beautiful woman, a generous soul, and a kind heart." He continues to describe Paulina's ability to engage with children, her charitable efforts, and her influence on him as a person. He refers to her as his love. "Once in a lifetime, you have the good fortune to meet a human being of impact. Paulina was a woman of impact. I am irrevocably changed because of our 'liaison amoureuse'."

After Farley makes his way back into the audience, Stella remains seated for a moment, stunned by his overt and public admission. She returns to the stage. "I want to express my gratitude. Paulina was a force in our little town, and she will be missed. I will forever bear her loss." Her index finger touches a tear which threatens to roll down her cheek. "We will reconvene at Cocoa and Café. Tiffany and Andrew Blair have generously provided a small reception for us."

The Blairs closed their business for the afternoon. When the group arrives at the door, they are greeted by Tiffany who left early to assemble coffee, tea, lemonade, and trays of sweets. At first, Stella sticks close to Nick. Her part is over. Relief is a welcome emotion.

"Can I have a quick word?" Aiden approaches her.

She nods at Nick. "Yes, by all means."

"Wanted to tell you this before I leave. We may avoid a trial. Florida police picked up Jackson Deveau, a two-bit hood who manages apartment complexes and who knows what else. He's agreed to cooperate, which permits us to tie our last loose end. I think the Crown will try to leverage Meredith before the week is over."

Stella hopes her mouth isn't hanging open. "Poor Paulina. Her life ended because one person had a contact who happened to know Russ was a killer. The circumstances seem entirely random. Russ' past caught up to him, even though I think he honestly wanted to start fresh."

"I agree with the random part, but Harry Russell would never change. I'll call if we need to conduct another interview, but I expect Meredith's lawyer will encourage her to take a deal." He pats her arm. "Gotta run. Promised Rosemary I wouldn't linger."

Before she returns to Nick, Stella approaches Hester and Jane who are thick into conversation. Stella has never seen Hester this animated.

"Jacob will deliver you to the farm and you can teach me how to decorate a cake."

"I want you to teach me the names of each of the flowers you put in the hall."

She doesn't interrupt and, instead, turns her attention to Danielle, positioned off to the side.

"The two of them are getting along like a house on fire."

"No doubt. It's easy to tell they're related. We'll make plans to stay a day or two longer and they can spend time in each other's company—for Paulina's sake."

"And for Jane. Forgive me, but she has a right to know her half-sisters."

Danielle responds with a grimace. "Yes, I could have managed Jane and Paulina's predicament much better."

After a cup of tea and various benign conversations focused on the tourist season and local gossip, Stella finds Nick chatting with Mark Bell.

He sees her approach. "Ready to go?"

They make their goodbyes and return to the Jeep, parked near the hall. She sits in the passenger seat with her eyes closed for a moment, happy to have the event behind her, content to have given Paulina an appropriate send-off, and especially pleased Hester and Jane have connected.

220

CHAPTER 24

Partnerships Require Compromise

Finally! Stella collapses on the sofa beside Nick and Kiki who are stretched out in front of the fan. She plunks her bare feet on the coffee table. The air remains warm and muggy, even as sunset approaches. Campers have started their fires. The faint smell of smoke wafts through the open windows. Unlike Stella, who craves more space, Kiki wants to cuddle. She pats the little dog who closes her eyes in a gesture of pure bliss. "Duke will be back in three or four days, and not a minute too soon." Her attempt to be gruff ends with a giggle.

"Duke has managed to settle up with the care home and close his mother's estate?"

"I gather. He called earlier today and spoke with Alice. She said he's impatient to get back. Are those lights? Did you hear a car?"

"Geez, Stella. It's after nine. You aren't expecting a late arrival, are you?"

"No. Besides, we're full."

Nick peers through the screen. "Trixie." He throws on the backyard switch and flips the latch which secures the door.

Stella scrambles to her feet. She watches her sister, chin lowered as if she's carrying the heavy air on the back of her neck, turn toward the house.

"Hi. The air's so sticky, I thought you two might still be up."

"We were sitting in front of the fan relaxing after a tough, albeit rewarding, day. What's brought you here this late, Trixie?"

"I came to discuss money."

"Of course, you did." Stella doesn't mean to sound snide but can't prevent the comment from falling out of her face.

Trixie, in flip flops, a tank top which has seen better days, and cut-off blue jean shorts, struts up the stairs and into the living room. She ignores Stella's sarcasm. "Don't forget to turn out your porch light. The June bugs will make us crazy in another half hour." She fluffs her curls. "I have nightmares where the damned creatures are tangled in my hair."

"Iced tea?" Stella opts for a more gracious approach.

"Sure. I wanted a quiet time for the three of us to discuss the buyout idea." She throws herself into one of the leather chairs near the dark fireplace while she simultaneously tries to pull a folded piece of foolscap from her over-sized red purse. "I put figures together with Brigitte's help." She reaches across the space toward Nick. "Here. Have a gander, since you're the person who'll owe me the lion's share of the money."

"I'll fetch drinks?" Her remark becomes a question.

"Good idea." Nick scans the paper Trixie offers. "Let's see what you have and then we can discuss." Nick positions the note under the light of an end table lamp.

As Stella trundles into the kitchen, she tries to hear the conversation.

"I want the same evaluation as when you bought five percent from each of us."

Did Nick say okay? I need to check her figures. She fumbles with the pitcher. *Why are my hands shaking? Answer: because I have no money to pay her for the five percent she needs to receive from me. Fifteen thousand dollars. Be honest, Stella. You don't want Nick to own fifty-five percent. You need to find some money.* She assembles a tray and returns to the living room, now heavily shadowed.

Trixie morphs into a businessperson Stella finds both unfamiliar and unsettling. She sits up straight in her chair and folds her arms. She doesn't completely succeed in her attempt at professionalism, if one considers her attire. "We decided the value of the property and Nick paid us three thousand dollars a share. If you give me the same, I'll take the buyout."

Stella stares at her glass. She's aware of Trixie's eyes on her.

"Listen. I know you can't buy your five percent but check the figures. If you continue to pay me my thousand a month, your debt will be cleared by next October—1982."

"A viable option, but we'd better listen to what Nick has to say. He's the one who needs to come up with the big bucks." She purses her lips while she focuses on his tanned face.

"The idea is great, Trixie. I'm happy to offer you three thousand a share for forty shares. The whole deal doesn't need to be dragged out until October 1982, though. If Stella pays you your monthly cheque for five months, then we can complete the sale the end of the year."

Pressure smothers her. "Raising an extra ten by December might be a stretch, you two." She pats Kiki, who swelters on her knee. The Pomeranian's fur is prickly against her warm and bare legs. She attempts a joke. "Can't sell the dog. She's not mine."

"Stella, we'll make the buyout work. Don't worry. What we need right now is a letter of intent."

"Oh, easy-peasy. Carter Stephens told me they have a real estate lawyer in their firm who can do the paperwork for us. I'll call tomorrow to schedule an appointment." Trixie wiggles in her chair.

"Right. Once you have your money on December 31, Stella and I will each own fifty percent of Shale Cliffs RV Park." He reaches out to hold Stella's hand.

Trixie gulps her tea. "Must rush. Can't be back too late. Brigitte worries."

Stella remains seated. "I thought you might be interested in an update on Russ. Aiden gave me permission to share a detail or two with you."

"I don't give a rat's ass about Russ but go ahead." She stands by the chair.

"Russ will testify against Meredith. He's confessed to several murders. He expected Paulina to be the last job, and he wanted to retire with you."

"And what a great life to fall into—married to an assassin." Her pain is unmistakable. "I guess I owe you a debt of gratitude, but not today—not ready to say thanks today. I'm done with Russ, done with the rental unit, done with work and the lazy cow I was forced to sit beside, and maybe I'm even done with men. Gotta go." She stops at the door long enough to turn around. "I'm glad we've settled on a price. Good for me; good for you two."

Once she hears the crunch of Trixie's van tires in the parking lot, Stella takes a final sip of her tea in momentary silence. "My sister has changed. I miss the gushy person she used to be, and there's no way I can raise ten thousand by the end of December, Nick."

"Trixie is grieving. She'll be back to herself, eventually. As for the money, we're okay. My gift to you."

"You know I can't let you pay for part of those shares."

Mercifully, as is Nick's predictable manner, he doesn't push the idea.

****

Tuesday, September 1, 1981

A week from today, Eve, Paul, and Alice will be gone, returned to university. Duke and Kiki will remain until official closure after Thanksgiving weekend. Today, Stella's grateful she can still attend her meeting in town and leave reception in Alice's capable hands. The final get-together of the committee, struck to plan the writers retreat, is scheduled for ten this morning.

"Alice," she shouts from her office, "do you need me to do any errands in town?"

"I put a grocery list on the kitchen table. I expect you'll want to add other stuff. The printer has our new reservation cards ready to be picked up, too." Alice materializes at the door as she continues to talk. "I can't believe our summer is over next Monday." She lifts her brows. "Paul said, on the way home last night, he wished you were open year-round so he could stay and work."

"There's no future here for a young, smart guy like Paul."

"Oh, he knows, but I think he loves the park even more than I do. I have one more season, Stella, but if I find a job before I graduate, I'll be gone."

"My God, you'll make me cry if you don't stop." Stella jumps from behind her desk and gives her assistant a hug. "Let's leave the worry until next year." She leans back and focuses her attention on Alice's face. "I'm not sure how the park will manage without you."

"Eve is good. She can run the front when I leave. She and Paul still have three years here. You'll be fine." Her last sentence ends in a gulp. "Anyway," her red curls vibrate when she swallows again, "right now, we need a few groceries and those reservation cards. You're due at the hall in an hour." She taps Stella's arm. "Time you left." She disappears around the corner of the office, back to reception.

Stella races off to the kitchen and retrieves her list before she drives to the work shed and says goodbye to Nick.

Crisp and clear describes her morning. The trees and the ocean project the sensation of fall. The water appears cooler—rich turquoise tinged with grey. Leaves seem spent. Reds and yellows will explode into view any time. Stella revels in the changes and anticipates a cozy winter.

But what of Nick's suggestion? He said the ten thousand she will owe Trixie at the end of the year can be his gift to her. She was thunderstruck—dumbfounded—wordless. She's remained in the same state for the past six weeks. Although she's avoided the subject and he's applied no pressure, the undiscussed offer fills her with overwhelming anxiety. She understands he wants to be supportive. Warmth trickles through her—a quiet glow to be cherished by another person. She doesn't want to take Nick for granted. She also needs to maintain a separation between the business and their personal life.

Errands can wait until after her committee meeting. She parks the Jeep in a spot near the community hall. As she slides out of the driver's seat, she hears a voice behind her.

"Stella. Great to see you."

When she turns, Mercedes Savioli sashays along the street to join her on the walk into the facility.

"I haven't seen you since Paulina's memorial. How have you been?"

"Well, thanks. Busy, the same as you, I imagine. The season has been hectic."

Mercedes pushes a strand of rich dark hair away from her face. The gesture reveals a brilliant pair of chandelier earrings, her signature style statement. These ones are made with red crystals and reflect the shade of her wraparound dress. "Matt stayed home. We heard a bus tour will arrive in town before noon. Tourist don't buy bureaus, but they always manage to find a spot for a candy dish or a cup and saucer."

Voices drift up the hall from the conference room as they walk along the dim corridor in the basement. Stella enters to see most of the group assembled. She notices at least two people who weren't at the first session and, obviously, Meredith and Russ are in jail. Despite what one might expect to be challenges, Farley is positioned at the end of the table, prepared to chair. He glances at Mercedes and Stella.

"We're ready to begin. Let's start with updates from each of those present. Frances," he acknowledges the author from Port Ephron seated closest to him, "and I will button up the details when we finish. Please introduce yourselves. Pepper?"

"Hi, Farley." She glances around the table. "Everyone, I'm Pepper Ferguson. I represent the Harbour Hotel. Every room is booked for the event.

Participant guests begin to check in on September 23. The bus tour group will leave on Sunday, but others plan to stay until Monday. Copies of our menus, which include 'writer specials', are ready for the gift bags, thanks to Mr. Gorman." She graces the middle-aged and corduroy attired printer with a smile designed to dazzle.

"Thank you, Pepper." Farley gazes around the table.

"I'm Mercedes Savioli. My husband, Matt, and I are responsible for coordinating the volunteers. The people in our community represent an embarrassment of riches. I will pass out the list of tasks and assignments for your information. Matt apologizes for his absence today, but the shop is busy. He was overwhelmed by the cooperation of the committee when he touched base with each of you in July."

"Hello. My name is Hope Carlyle. The locals refer to me as the weaver. One of the five additional authors conducting seminars for the retreat will stay with me. Frances reached out because my guest goes everywhere with her little dog." Hope suppresses a tiny laugh. "I am told she prefers a human companion as well, so did not want to stay at the hotel or in a cottage. I have agreed to host her." She gazes around the table. "Frances tells me she is from Vietnam and I am hopeful of an opportunity to broaden my cultural horizons."

"Good morning, everyone. I am Theodore Gorman and I will continue to contribute any printing required. My shop has designed the signage for the door of the hall, and small posters for local businesses. Surrounding attractions may want to include their brochures in the packages for participants. I am given to understand, from the tourism association, that after people attend an event such as our retreat, they often return to the area for a second visit. Shale Harbour must take advantage." He stops for a breath. "No need to focus on the subject, but I want to acknowledge you, Farley. You have risen above the horrible events of May 1, and their consequences, to carry on with your responsibilities here today." He surveys the group. "You are to be commended."

Edward Thomas leads scattered applause.

"Thank you, Theodore. Your comments are very much appreciated." Farley avoids eye contact. "As I move along, please make note of a change in the schedule. Stella has agreed to host an evening of amateur readings at Shale Cliffs RV Park on the Friday night. Details are in your packet. The gathering is sponsored by Stella—no need for the committee to contribute, except in the way of supportive attendance."

Frances Ellis wiggles straighter in her chair. "We, as authors, will encourage a few gifted attendees to share their work. If budding writers are shy, Edward and I will step in and show them how readings are done, right Edward?"

Her quiet husband nods with unbridled enthusiasm.

Stella jumps in, requiring no introduction. "Nick and I are excited to host the evening event. As you know, we are without staff after Labour Day, but will do our best." She chuckles. "Since Grey Cottage has assembled the gift bags, I'll see my brochures are delivered Monday. Thanks for the reminder, Mr. Gorman."

Farley's meeting does not drone on. When Stella glances at her watch, she knows she'll have time to do the grocery shopping, pick up the registration cards, and make it back to the park for lunch.

****

Wednesday, September 23, 1981

The first trailer owned by writers retreat participants rolls into Shale Cliffs at three o'clock on Wednesday, as expected. Stella registers them. Duke, on the golf cart, escorts the couple to their site. Kiki sits by his side, bejeweled in a new collar and neon yellow T-shirt. Her little fluffy face has become a cotton ball poked out of the neck.

Right after they leave the front lot, a blue Chevrolet sedan pulls in. Frances Ellis, Edward Thomas, and their adult son, Owen, alight and file into reception.

"Welcome to Shale Cliffs. Your cottage is ready." She places a registration card on the counter in front of her. "If you folks fill out the form, I'll find Nick. He'll show you around. Here's your key."

She runs through the living room and sees Nick at work behind her desk in the office. The warmth of his expression always makes her weak at the knees. "Hi. The authors who rented the cottage are here. Will you give them the tour? I don't want to leave the front."

"No problem. I was on the hunt for commercial plumbing contractors listed in the phone book. I thought we could talk to different businesses, get bids, and schedule installation of a septic system this fall."

Despite her anxiety, she makes a faint attempt at enthusiasm, "Good plan. Can you take a break?"

He unfolds his lanky frame as he stands. "To be sure, my love. I'll wait for them on the veranda."

Frances points the Chev in the direction of the back lot, and they circle the house to find Nick. He pops into reception twenty minutes later.

"Busy day for you." He wraps an arm around her shoulder.

She leans into him and absorbs his unmistakable physical and emotional support. "I miss the staff."

"No doubt, my dear, we depend on the crew, but we're a good team. The lawns are mowed, and the bathrooms are clean. There are no problems with the water and power. I expect we'll have the best year the business has seen in some time. Tea?"

About the Author

L. P. Suzanne Atkinson was born in New Brunswick, Canada and lived in both Alberta and Quebec before settling in Nova Scotia in 1991. She has degrees from Mount Allison, Acadia, and McGill universities. Suzanne spent her professional career in the fields of mental health and home care. She also owned and operated, with her husband, both an antique business and a construction business for more than twenty-five years.

Suzanne writes about the unavoidable consequences of relationships. She uses her life and work experiences to weave stories that cross many boundaries.

She and her husband, David Weintraub, make Bedford, Nova Scotia their home.

Email – lpsa.books@eastlink.ca
Website – http://lpsabooks.wix.com/lpsabooks#
Facebook – L. P. Suzanne Atkinson – Author